BRING HER HOME

C. E. NELSON

Cover by Dusan Arsenic

Chapter 1

It was a nasty night, rain sheeting down the windshield so heavy he felt like he was under water. The wind was leaning on the trees until some couldn't handle it anymore, a tall dead birch landing in the lot just behind him. Smaller branches banged on the hood and roof. There had been a minute of small hail earlier, white BB's that fell from the sky and put him on alert, unsure of what was happening. The sharp reverberations of the hail were a contrast to the steady dull pounding of the rain on the roof of his truck, and in the scant light he watched the hail bounce off his hood and then disappear into the darkness. A flickering silvery curtain of rain undulated under the yard light in front of the bar, dancing in a rhythm dictated by the wind. The thunder had subsided now, but it had been a steady rumbling interspersed with an occasional flash, and then a resounding boom like a fireworks show.

He didn't mind. He'd always liked storms, ever since he could remember. It was almost as if his body knew when a storm was coming, waking him in the middle of the night so he could go to the window in his bedroom to watch the lightening and listen to the thunder. He liked the storms during the day best, because he could see the storm coming, feel the atmosphere change, and then watch its fury. There was a thrill about being out in the storm, the rain stinging as it hit him, watching for the closest lightening strike, the thunder booming around him, the trees bending and breaking. Almost like he was standing up to God.

The driver sat in the cab of his beat-up black pickup, drinking Dr. Pepper and eating Fritos. Dr. Pepper was his favorite drink, as could be attested to by the large number of empty cans on the floor behind him. He loved the sweet taste of it and the carbonation as the fizzy liquid moved over his tongue and down his throat. It was especially good when he combined it with the salty Fritos. Sometimes he'd trap a Frito between his tongue and the roof of his mouth and suck out the salt, washing it down with the soda. With the storm going, it was turning into just about a perfect night.

He watched the side door to the bar, just like he had done for the last three nights. The outside lights in front and the lights in the window had gone out when the bar closed at one, but they might just as well have shut things down an hour earlier when the last customer had left. He'd watched the man walk to his car and was pretty sure he was drunk, although it was a little hard to tell because of the storm. But the man stumbled and nearly fell twice as he leaned into the wind, holding his hand in front of his face, and so the driver thought it was likely he had had a few too many. He'd noticed the car there on two other nights so he assumed the man was a regular at the bar, probably lived close by, not too much chance of hitting anything way out here but a deer or maybe a tree. Might be a little tougher driving drunk tonight. Might hit that tree.

She had closed up the bar a little after one-thirty each night. Someone helped her close each night, another woman the first two nights and a man the night before. The man had been there again tonight but had left before one, leaving the woman alone. The driver guessed that they had been closing things down early, and the woman had told the man she would finish up, telling him to go. He didn't know this for sure, but he thought about these things as he sat and watched the bar, and of all of the reasons he could think of why the man had left the woman alone at the bar, that seemed the most likely. Whatever the reason, he doubted the man would return. This would make things much easier.

The driver tilted his head back, the last of his Dr. Pepper dripping onto his tongue, and dropped the can on the floor behind the passenger seat. He thought about having a few more Fritos from the open bag on the seat next to him, but then he'd have to open a new can of pop, and he decided the timing wasn't right. He needed to be ready. Through his observations he had found that people were predictable, liking routine and doing what provided the least resistance. He also found that one conclusion would often lead to another. Because of his assumption that the man and woman running the bar had begun to clean up early, and that the woman had sent the man home because they were almost done, he also guessed that she might leave a little earlier tonight. He thought she would come out soon.

The bar was like any of a thousand small-town taverns across the Midwest. Booths with uncomfortable worn wooden high-backed benches lined one wall while a scattering of Formica-topped tables surrounded by metal-framed chairs with cracked vinyl seats on wood-planked floors speckled with popcorn from the help-yourself machine at the end of the bar. The bar had four beers on tap: Michelob, Michelob Light, Budweiser, and Sam Adams for those who wanted something a little more daring. A grill and oven in the back produced burgers and fries and pizza from the freezer. The bar was on the main road; the first building as you entered town from the east, a small engine repair shop next to it, an open lot that had been cleared at one time but never developed was across the road.

Employees parked on the side of the building facing the repair shop, entering and exiting by a single door there. A sliver of light appeared on the side of the building about ten after one, as the door opened just an inch or two. The driver sat up, his hand on the door handle, his door now ajar. The door on the bar stayed cracked open for a full minute, and he was wondering what was happening, when she burst out, pulling the door shut behind her and then running for her car.

He had opened his door and stepped out as soon as he saw the bar door open but he hadn't counted on her running. He had disabled the light in his cab so he couldn't be seen, and he could see better, but the rain hit him full in the face, and at first he wasn't quite sure it was her, the woman not much more than a shadow in the light of the single bulb above the door. She wore a navy blue rain jacket; the hood pulled up, and held it closed just below her chin as she ran. He paused a moment and then inwardly cursed his stupidity, knowing she was the only one working. He ran towards her, the wind pushing his door shut behind him.

She fumbled for her keys as she stood next to her locked car, searching her purse before remembering she had put them in her front jean pocket so they would be easy to retrieve. As she squeezed her right hand into the pocket she thought she heard a sound behind her, like the shutting of a car door, but in the storm it was hard to hear anything and she ignored it, intent to get out of the rain. She knew her jeans were getting too tight, she had put on a few pounds lately, and now they were wet and she was having a hard time getting her fist with the keys out of the pocket. She cursed out loud just as she felt a tap on her shoulder.

Jackie Neese thought maybe it was the wind, but she turned back to her right to look anyway, letting go of the hold she had on her hood as she did. Immediately there was an incredible flash, a blinding light, and then a buzzing sound. In the next instant she felt something slide inside the top of her jacket, grabbing her just below the collarbone, and shaking her whole body rapidly. Neese gasped for air, thinking she might pass out, before she dropped face-down to the ground feeling completely fatigued, unable to stop shaking.

Someone grabbed her by the top of the head. She felt pressure on the back of her head that moved around the side and then covered her eyes and around the other side of her head, all of this accompanied by the sound of something being torn. This did not terrify her nearly as much as the pressure she felt immediately after. It started on the back of her head, just above her neck, and moved around her skull. She thought she should scream, but she couldn't seem to generate any sound, or move her mouth. She tried to suck in a big breath through her mouth but her chin was suddenly pushed up, banging her bottom teeth into her top, and the pressure moved over her mouth.

The tremors slowed, but her body still shook, screaming for air like she had just run a marathon. She nearly choked trying to suck in a breath as her head was dropped back to the ground, her face landing in a puddle. As she jerked her head back she felt her arms being pulled behind her. She began to lose consciousness.

Chapter 2

The rain kept coming. It had been two days without a break, the wind from the northwest pushing it so newly discovered cracks around windows and doors appeared hourly. A cold rain that left you chilled and feeling damp even if you hadn't been out. The clouds were heavy and low, dark churning masses moving fast, convincing you they would soon move on and skies would clear, but any hint of brightness was squashed before it could seep through.

July is the only month of the year where there is no recorded measurable snowfall in the state of Minnesota. Don Trask, lead investigator for the Minnesota Bureau of Criminal Apprehension (BCA), looked out the window of the Lone Pine Café in Chase, Minnesota sipping his morning coffee, thinking that historical record could be broken today.

The Lone Pine Café sat just off the highway on the northwest corner of the intersection with First Street. It was in the parking lot of the motel behind it, the source of a good amount of its business. The Lone Pine tried to infuse an up-north, old-time atmosphere with pine-planked walls lined with framed black and white photographs of loggers and miners and trappers and men holding stringers of huge fish, despite having been built less than twenty years earlier. Half a dozen raised booths were along the window facing the highway, and an equal number of round heavily shellacked tables with tubular stainless steel framed chairs on the floor. An empty salad bar was to the left of the cash register, just in front of the kitchen. The smell of bacon and eggs and fresh-baked cinnamon rolls filled the air. The only visible pine tree was across the highway in a small park.

"Well junior, should we go to the bar now or wait an hour?" asked Don.

Junior was his identical twin brother Dave, sheriff of Lake County in northeast Minnesota. Dave sat opposite Don, looking at the weather radar on his phone.

"We got an hour left of this, maybe two," he said holding up his phone so Don could see the green blotches moving across the screen. "WeatherNow says the winds will die after the clouds move on. It's going to be nice by noon."

"Like I believe that. Last year I was fishing and WeatherNow said it wasn't going to rain for 110 minutes. Ten minutes later I was soaked."

Dave tucked his phone back in his pocket, sipped his coffee, and stared out the window at the gray day. The brothers had met here two days earlier, part of a planned five-day fishing trip for bluegills and bass. So far Dave's boat had not moved from the trailer in the driveway of their cabin. The cold rain would have made fishing miserable, the winds made it impossible. They had consumed all the alcohol they brought for the trip and played more cards and cribbage than they had in the last five years combined. Don, who hated to read, especially anything about crime, was halfway through a John Sanders novel he found in the cabin.

Dave continued to stare out the window, coffee cup in hand, watching young poplars bending in the wind, when his eyes moved to a half sheet of paper taped to the corner of the window. He slipped his finger behind the sheet, lifting it until the tape began to pull away from the glass, moving his finger behind the piece of tape to pull it free. He folded the tape behind the paper and laid it on the table between them.

"They're still looking for her. I remember reading about this. BCA ever look into it?"

Don turned the paper so it faced him. A picture of a blonde-haired woman took up the top third of the page. Below the picture was printed:

> *Carol Algaard*
> *Birth Date: 8/12/1986*
> *Height: 5' 6"*
> *Weight: 120*
> *Missing Since: 7/14/2014.*
> *Last seen wearing tan slacks, short-sleeved light blue blouse. If you have any information please call the Chase police department at...*

Above the picture was the headline, all in caps, BRING HER HOME.

Don picked up the sheet and then set it back down. "I don't think so. Cute girl."

Dave laid a twenty on the table, picked up the sheet, and slid out of the booth. "Let's go talk to the Chief."

Don, reaching for his rain jacket to his right, turned to his brother. "You know, I always knew you were dumb, but now it's clear you're just plain stupid. What the hell do we want to do that for?"

Dave slid his arms into his jacket and zipped it up. "Why not? We're both bored and I, for one, am sick of looking at your ugly face."

The brothers were in their mid-forties and six feet tall. Their weights hovered around two hundred pounds, their bodies solid, both men continuing to exercise regularly. Don sported army-length brown hair, his brother choosing to let his grow so that its natural waviness showed, parting it on the right. Don also had a goatee, mostly gray, that gave him a mean, tough-guy look that he liked, while Dave was clean-shaven. Their faces were round and pudgy with full cheeks, noses broad and flat.

Dave looked back down at the picture of Algaard. She was a pretty girl. "Come on. It'll kill an hour and then we can go fishing."

Don mumbled an obscenity under his breath and slid out, his jacket in hand, and followed behind.

Highway 71 cuts through the middle of town. When the highway was built it was on the west side of the city, but businesses had gravitated to the highway on both sides and apartment buildings, two hotels, a restaurant, and newer homes built west of 71, so now the population was pretty evenly split between east and west. Residents referred to the area west of the highway as 'new Chase' and the area east with the original downtown as 'old Chase'.

The restaurant where the Trasks had eaten breakfast was in new Chase. Don waited in his Lexus for a semi to pass in front of him at the stop sign on 71 and then cut across, past a big black bear statue in the city park bordering the highway, and then turning left. Half a block down he pulled to a stop in front of a newer looking single-story beige brick building with the words 'Chase Police Department' in six-inch silver metal letters across the front of the building.

The rain hurried Dave to the door, Don close behind. There was a solid wall of what looked to be the same brick on the exterior of the building lining the interior wall to their right as they entered. To the left, behind a three-foot wall of honey-stained oak panels, was an open area with desks separated by tan fabric panels, a few walled offices against the far wall. A heavy woman with dyed red hair, in her early fifties, sat in the closest desk with her back to them.

"Can I help you?" she asked as she swiveled in her chair and then stood, walking toward them.

Dave handed her the sheet about Algaard.

"Do you know something about this?" she asked, her eyebrows rising.

"No, sorry," replied Dave. "I'm Dave Trask, sheriff of Lake County and this is my brother Don, lead investigator for the BCA." He nodded toward Don. Both men showed their identification. "We happened to see this flyer when we were having breakfast, and, well, we had planned on fishing but, honestly, we're a little bored and thought we might take a look at what you have on this disappearance if that's OK?"

"OK, well then, why don't I just get the chief?"

The woman, whose nametag pinned on her blouse said Officer Judy Little, walked down the aisle between the cubicles and knocked on an open door at the back of the room. She stepped inside, was out of sight for a minute, and then walked out followed by a stocky man of about fifty. He was bald on top, hair shaved close to his scalp on the sides, with bushy black eyebrows and squinty brown eyes. He had beefy jowls with a double chin and hairy, meaty arms. His nametag said Chief Al Fowles.

"Hello gentlemen. Al Fowles." The chief stuck out his hand.

"Don Trask, BCA, chief, and this is my brother Dave, Sheriff up in Lake County," said Don as he shook Fowles' hand.

"Judy says you boys need some work to do," Fowles said with an easy smile.

"Well, actually, we're supposed to be fishing, but the last two days have been a little short on that activity," answered Dave. "If you want us out of your hair, it's definitely no problem; we're just running out of things to keep us busy."

"Not a lot to do here if you can't fish, that's for sure. Where you two staying?"

The men exchanged pleasantries for a minute and then the chief continued.

"I wouldn't mind at all having you gentlemen take a look at the Algaard file," said Fowles. "It's been hanging around my neck for the last three years and I'm afraid it's going to stay there until I die. Why don't you come on back and I'll find a table for you to sit down? You need some coffee?"

Both men declined. Fowles opened the gate for them and led them to a small conference room, one wall lined with tan metal filing cabinets. The table had a couple of manila folders lying open, papers scattered nearby, which Fowles quickly scooped up and set on a chair sitting against the wall.

"You gentlemen have a seat and I'll get the folders for you." Fowles walked to the farthest cabinet and then bent down to pick up a brown cardboard filing box with a cover and punch-out holes for handles. The box was heavy, and he held it low, only lifting it higher to set it on the table. He went back to the cabinet and grabbed a second box as big and heavy as the first. He removed the covers and then pushed the boxes across the table so it sat between the brothers. "I'm grateful for you two taking the time to look at this. Let me get you something to take notes with." He turned and opened the top drawer of the file cabinet behind him.

Dave and Don glanced into the boxes and then at each other.

"Um, looks like you've done a lot of work on this chief. We didn't really expect all of this," said Dave as he pulled a box closer. "You want to give us the abbreviated version of what happened?"

Fowles put two legal pads and pens on the table and then looked at the boxes. "Yeah, we've got crime scene photos, notes, interviews, transcripts of all the calls we've had on it, any tips we've gotten, investigation results. Every time someone puts up a new flyer it seems we get something. It all goes in here." He paused, staring at the boxes, like he remembered something, but then moved on to the question. "Carol Algaard was working alone at the liquor store you probably passed out on 71. Apparently, some time after closing, she just disappeared. Left her purse, car keys, vehicle, and the back door open. No indication of any struggle or anything missing in the store. No sign of her since. Only prints we could identify on the back door were hers and her husband's. It's a paved lot behind the store so no tire tracks. We figure she was probably abducted. Could have been when she took the trash out to the dumpster in back, or it could have been she went with someone she knew."

"You got anybody in mind?" asked Don.

"We looked pretty hard at the husband, Blaine. They had moved to town and purchased the store only a year before his wife disappeared. People had heard them arguing. They went into debt big time to buy the store. Don't think she was too crazy about the idea of owning and running the store. And she was from Minneapolis. Apparently she wasn't exactly excited about living in the north woods either."

"The husband was from around here?" asked Don.

"Proctor." Proctor was only twenty-five miles from Chase.

"And where is he now?" followed Dave.

"Still here. Still runs the store. Got engaged last year but rumor has it he may have been involved with his fiancé before Carol disappeared. She lives with him. Lisa Carter."

"Did he have an alibi?" asked Dave.

"Not really. Says he was home watching TV but no one to say if he was or wasn't. They live out off of 18 east of town about four miles on Jigsaw Lake. No neighbors anywhere close."

"You think he did it?"

"I was sure he did at first but, after all this time, I guess I don't really know. I mean, he didn't report her missing until the next afternoon when he says he found her purse and car when he went to the store. Says he drank too much the night before, didn't hear her come home if she did, and just figured that she got up early to open the store and left before he got up. He never pushed us to see if we had anything on where she might have gone. He did have a life policy on her, but that was required by the bank, and it didn't get paid off yet."

The Trasks looked at each other again. "OK, chief. Thanks for indulging us. We appreciate your time," said Dave.

"No problem at all. Like I said, it's good to get new eyes on things. Just put the stuff back in the boxes when you're done and leave them on the table."

Fowles shook their hands and left the room.

Don looked at the box and then at Dave. "What have you gotten me into now, meathead? I could be sitting in a relatively nice cabin, drinking scotch, getting my tackle ready, and instead I am supposed to spend my vacation doing work?"

Dave stood and pulled folders from a box. "You've been through your tackle six times in the last two days, as well as going through over a fifth of scotch. You could use a break from both."

Chapter 3

The Trasks split the folders inside the boxes, and began to go through them, making notes as they did. After about an hour Dave got up and went in search of coffee.

They continued to work until Don leaned back and stretched and then looked at his watch. "Hey tubby, it's almost noon. Let's go get some lunch."

Dave looked up from his note pad and then to his phone lying on the table next to his pad to check the time. "Sounds good. You had enough of this? Should we pack it up?"

There were no windows in the conference room. Don got up and walked out the door where he could see through the window facing the parking lot. It was lighter, and it looked like the wind was slowing, but there were still raindrops on the glass. He walked back in. "Leave it for now. Let's see how the weather looks after we eat."

They walked by the chief's door, but his office was empty. Officer Little said he had a call and could be gone for a while. Dave said they had left the folders on the table and would be back after lunch. By the time the boys finished the soup and sandwich special at the Lone Pine, washed down with a beer, the rain had been reduced to a mist and the weather radar showed the clouds breaking up just to the west.

"Rain should stop in an hour, two at the most," said Dave as he looked up from his phone. "You think it's worthwhile going back to the station?"

To his surprise his brother replied that they were almost through the files and should give it an hour more. They drove back over to the station, said hi to Officer Little as they passed her desk, and returned to the conference room.

Don sat and then stared at his pad while his brother opened a folder. Dave looked up at Don. "What?"

"Someone has been in here. My pen got moved off of my pad."

Dave looked at Don's pad and then down at his. He didn't think someone had touched it. "You sure?"

"Yeah, I'm sure!"

"So, maybe it just rolled off, or maybe Officer Little was just curious."

Don looked around the room like he expected to see someone spying on them. "Let's just get this done and go fishing."

In an hour they were through the last of the folders and put them back in the boxes. As they walked past Little's desk Don stopped. "I guess we're done. Tell the chief thanks for us."

The officer looked up. "OK, I'll let the chief know."

Don hesitated. "You didn't happen to go into the conference room when we were gone, did you?"

Little looked back at the conference room door and then to Don. "No, you missing something?"

Don just looked at her for a moment until he felt Dave push him on the shoulder from behind. "Um, no. Thanks again."

They fished the rest of the afternoon and into the evening even though the cold front had put the fish into temporary hibernation. A couple of small largemouth bass and two hammer-handle pike were all the men could entice to bite, each fish released. Dave had planned on frying fish so they opted for takeout from Burger King on the way back to the cabin. They sat at the white pine kitchen table eating in silence, Don finishing his Whopper and fries first, crunching the wrappers into a ball and tossing them at his brother. Dave saw it coming and ducked as the wrapper flew past his head.

"Just because I out-fished you again is no reason to start throwing things. You think after all of these years you'd be used to it."

Don was up and behind Dave, bending to pick up the wrapper and toss it in the garbage. "It's sad that you think those three little things you snagged actually counted as fish. But what's even sadder is to see your memory slipping away." Don poured a full tumbler of scotch from the bottle on the kitchen counter, added some ice from the freezer above the refrigerator, and sat back down. He took a long sip and then dragged the legal pads sitting on the table over to him. "You find anything today?"

Dave finished his chicken sandwich, got up and tossed the wrappers in the garbage, and then found one of the two remaining beers in the refrigerator. He popped the top on the can and sat back down, facing Don. "Obviously Fowles thinks the husband did it. The guy was uncooperative in the interviews."

"Yeah, but it seemed like Fowles pushed him too hard and too long. Algaard just got tired of it."

Dave flipped a page on his tablet. "But to not call in to say your wife is missing until the next day, or call any relatives, it just doesn't seem quite right. And why didn't he get to the store until after lunch the next day?"

Don was looking at his notes, sipping his drink, as his brother talked.

"The fiancé, what's her name, Lisa Carter, also bothers me," continued Dave. "Fowles said it was possible they were involved before Carol went missing but I couldn't find anything about her being interviewed. There was a note from Fowles about the engagement and some question marks below his note but that was it."

"The other thing that seems to be missing in this is anything about the backgrounds of Carol or Blaine or his fiancé for that matter." Don put his pad back on the table, pushed it away, and took another sip of scotch. "Christ, what are we doing? I've got no time for this and you have no jurisdiction. This thing is three years old. You know how many of these types of cases there are in the Twin Cities alone?"

Dave looked at his brother.

"What?"

"I thought you were giving up the whiskey?"

"What are you, my mother? I am giving it up but this is a special occasion."

"What's that?" asked Dave.

"I'm trying to survive five days with you." Don threw down the last of his drink.

Don's drinking had been a problem in the past, almost costing him his job, and his current relationship. He promised his girlfriend he would quit, but its grip was too strong.

"After we fish in the morning let's make a quick trip to the liquor store. Maybe we could have a little chat with Blaine."

Don got up and emptied the rest of his bottle into his glass, pulled some more ice from the freezer, and dropped the cubes in the golden liquid. He swirled the cubes as he leaned on the counter. "You do realize that the chance of this going anywhere is about the same as the chance that you will out-fish me tomorrow?" Dave had stood to retrieve a cribbage board from the shelf and did not answer. Don looked back down at his drink, watching as the cubes floated in the whiskey, chilling the liquid. Carol Algaard's face looked up at him from one of the cubes and then melted away.

Chapter 4

The driveway was easily a quarter mile long, winding between poplars and oaks and birch and pine, the brush dense between the trees. The trees reached over the drive creating almost a tunnel that kept the driveway in shade during the day and in complete blackness at night. It was not uncommon to spook a black bear or deer on the driveway, especially in the fall. The gravel roadbed was bad in the daytime but it was a minefield tonight, the ruts and potholes hidden under the standing water, no way to see to avoid them. Five feet of land was cleared on either side of the driveway and was only slightly lower than the roadbed, but the ground was soft, not something you wanted to drive on. The truck moved slow, bouncing along, the driver cursing with each jarring dip. The rain was only a fine mist now, but his wiper blades were old, and did little but smear the moisture across the glass in the enveloping darkness.

His headlights spotlighted the double garage as he pulled into the yard, catching a passing raccoon. It stood on its hind legs and stared at him, eyes shining bright, as if possessed by some evil spirit. The lights flashed across the windows of the army-green stained cedar sided house as he turned and pulled to a stop in front. As he got out of the truck, lights inside the house came on, and then the overhead light above the front door popped on. The front door opened, and a man walked out onto the concrete landing with two steps down to the yard. The driver of the truck took only a quick glance at the man.

The driver walked straight through the house, to a door near the back, pulling it open and then flipping the switch just to the left of the door. An overhead light illuminated narrow wooden steps. He reached for the handrail on the wall to his left, and moved slowly down the stairs, leaning slightly to his left to compensate for the girl. Breathing harder now, he jostled the girl on his shoulder so the weight shifted more toward his neck. He could hear the hollow footsteps of the other man on the stairs behind him. Upon reaching the bottom of the steps he walked across the concrete floor to another door. He opened that too, turning immediately to his left to feel for the light switch.

Recessed lights in thick white foam ceiling panels cast a muted light across the room, two of the six lights not working. A shabby red upholstered sofa bed was directly across from the door and the driver walked to it, dipping and turning to flop the girl on the couch, rubbing his shoulder as he looked down at her. She was awake now, eyes wide with fear, wiggling and twisting, trying to get free, and he laughed when she rolled and fell off the couch onto the floor. She landed on her stomach but wasn't hurt; the floor covered with a dense brown carpet. The other man came and stood next to the driver, putting his foot on her butt.

"Nice rump. You done good." Neese squealed at the touch. "You just scream all you like girl. Ain't nobody gonna hear you down here." After pulling a knife from his front pocket, he opened the blade and bent at the waist, sliding the flat of the blade under the tape that wrapped around her head and over her mouth. He angled the blade out and cut through the tape. He closed the blade on the knife, put it back in his pocket, and then grabbed Neese by the hair on the back of her head, pulling her head up and roughly ripping the tape off. Neese immediately screamed. The man put his mouth next to Neese's right ear. "I'll let you yell for a while girl, but then you better shut up or I'm going to have to kill you. You got that?"

Neese continued to yell and the man stood. "Let's go get a beer while she settles down." The driver turned without a word and started toward the door leading up the stairs, the other man close behind, closing the door behind him. The driver sat at the kitchen table while the other man went to the refrigerator and removed two cans of beer, setting them on the table as he sat across from the driver. The driver pulled a can toward him, popped the top, and took a long swig. The other man did the same, wiping foam from the corner of his mouth with the back of his hand. They sat in silence, listening, elbows on the round oak table, heads down. Muffled cries came from below, but they were barely audible, the room below soundproofed long ago.

"Anybody see you?"

The driver looked up at the other man. The ceiling light put a shine on his bald head, his protruding forehead and recessed eyes in dark shadow, a monster's face. "Not a soul. Think I only saw three cars all the way back here. Ain't nobody out tonight."

The other man tipped his head back and took a long swig, then cradled the can in his lap. He looked out the kitchen window at the blackness beyond; drops of moisture leaking down the glass like tears on a cheek. "Good." He finished his beer in one long swallow and put the can on the edge of the table before he crushed it in his hand. "I'm first if memory serves me right. I got the afternoon shift at work so I'll be taking my time."

The driver finished his beer, set his empty in front of him, and pushed back from the table. "I'm beat. I'm going to bed. Wake me up when you're done."

The other man smiled as he stood. "I'll have her all warmed up for you." He headed back down the stairs.

Chapter 5

Saturday dawned sunny and calm. At seven the temperature was already in the fifties, the weatherman claiming that eighty was on the way. The Trasks were on the water by eight, flipping jigs at the weed line. The bite was slow at first, but as the sun rose and the water warmed, so did the fishes' appetite. By noon they had each landed a dozen bass over sixteen inches, Don claiming big fish with one just over twenty. They motored to the landing and pulled the boat out of the water, planning on going after bluegills or crappies at a different lake after lunch.

They were back at the Lone Pine Café by 12:30 for the lunch buffet. Don filled his plate with fried chicken, fried fish, French fries, and potato salad. He considered an apple but decided he'd come back for it. His brother went healthy with the chicken salad; peaches, a boiled egg and some assorted fresh-cut vegetables and so, upon seeing Don's plate, was quick to comment.

"Should I contact the cardiac unit now or wait until you have the fried ice cream for dessert?"

Don, already with a mouthful, looked back to the buffet. "I didn't see the ice cream. Thanks for pointing it out."

The brothers were in shape but had inherited a high cholesterol count from their father. Both had been told to watch their diets by their respective doctors, but Don had talked to a friend who was a surgeon, who told him that if his cholesterol got too high all he would need would be a pill, and had prescribed Lipitor for him. He didn't like his brother's mother hen words about his eating any more than he did about his drinking. Unfortunately he hadn't found a pill that would take care of the latter. When he felt down, he often found the bottle to be his companion.

The Trasks ate in silence, both men visiting the dessert tray after finishing their initial plates. They had taken an interior booth and Dave looked at the Carol Algaard flyer taped to the wall between them as they finished eating, both sipping at their coffee.

"You think someone staged it?"

Don was putting the last bite of his apple pie in his mouth. "What?"

"The disappearance. Algaard."

Don looked at the flyer again. "Possible I guess, but seems unlikely. According to what Fowles gave us she took nothing with her. In every runaway case I have ever worked they always kept something – cash, a picture, a piece of jewelry – something. I can run a quick check to see if anything has popped up on her since she went missing, but I just get the feeling someone grabbed her."

Dave looked at Algaard's picture a moment longer, and then slid out of the booth, picking up the check. "I feel bad about how much I outfished you this morning so I'm going to get this." He waved the bill in his hand. "Let's go get some adult beverages and get back out there."

Save Big Liquor was two blocks away, on the opposite side of the highway. Two other vehicles were parked in front when the Trasks pulled in, leaving plenty of room for Dave to park the boat on the far side of the lot near the highway. 'SAVE BIG' was in big yellow caps on the front of the white building with 'Liquor' in smaller red script right below like it had almost been forgotten. The Trasks entered the store and went searching for their beverages; Dave grabbing a twelve-pack of pale ale out of the cooler and Don finding his

Jack Daniels. They met at the cash register where a man in a yellow tee shirt with SAVE BIG across the front rang them up.

The man looked worn out with droopy eyelids below bloodshot green eyes, pasty white skin like he rarely got outside, and a two-day beard. His hair was black and thick but had received nothing more than a finger comb. He was about the same height as the Trasks and thin, but there was a thickness to his neck and biceps that said he exercised on a regular basis.

The bell on the front door signaled the only other customer in the store had just left as Don pulled his ID. "Don Trask, BCA, and this is Sheriff Dave Trask. Are you Blaine Algaard?"

Algaard's eyes jumped back and forth between the two men. He stepped back from the counter and folded is arms. "Yeah. What's this about?"

"We're looking into the disappearance of your wife, Carol. We'd like to ask you a few questions."

"Why now? It's been like three years. Is there something new you found out?"

Don looked at Dave and then back to Algaard. "No sir, nothing really new. We just wanted to clarify a few things."

Just then the bell on the front door jingled and all the men turned to see four men file into the store.

"Listen, I'm here all by myself. Can you come back when I close at ten?"

"Sure," said Don as he picked up the bag with his whiskey. "See you then."

The brothers walked back to the truck and got inside after stowing their purchases in the back. "Kid was awfully jumpy," said Dave as he started the truck.

"Yeah."

The bluegills were hungry in the afternoon, no need for the wax worms they had purchased at the convenience store. They dropped small jigs tipped with one-inch plastic tails below slip-bobbers just inside the weed-edge, gave the line a twitch or two, and the floats went under. Bass pulled them deep into the weeds a few times, and two rigs were lost to marauding pike, but otherwise the panfish kept them entertained. The men kept eight of the nicer bluegills and filleted them on a piece of cardboard in front of the cabin. Dave fried the fish along with some chopped up potatoes and onions that they washed down with a bottle of Merlot he had picked up at SAVE BIG. After dinner the Trasks moved to the deck in back, sitting in uncomfortable white plastic chairs, smoking cigars and watching the sunset.

Don looked at his watch. "Almost time to go visit Mr. Algaard. Since he seems a little nervous to be talking to a BCA agent, I thought I'd start out."

Dave watched the sun disappear below the tops of the trees and then slapped a mosquito on his neck. "Sounds good. Let's go."

It was a little before ten when they pulled into the empty parking lot of SAVE BIG. They could see Algaard inside, walking around behind the counter, bending out of sight and then popping back up again. The Trasks entered, and he stopped whatever it was he was doing, watching them approach the counter.

"Just a minute," he said as he moved from behind the counter toward the front of the store. "Let me lock up." Algaard used a key he was carrying on a ring on a belt-loop to lock the door and then flipped a switch there to turn off the store lights on the outside and in the front window. He came back to the men and said, "We can go in back and sit down if you want?"

The Trasks nodded and they all walked through silver metal swinging doors in the back wall to what they assumed was the storage room. Cases of beer and liquor were piled high along the walls and on the floor. They followed Algaard through a maze of boxes until they reached a corner on the back wall of the building where there was a dented brown metal desk from the eighties in front of a couple of metal file cabinets of the same vintage. Algaard sat in a worn upholstered desk chair on wheels behind the desk. The Trasks sat in matching chairs in front of him. Algaard opened the top drawer on his right, pulled out an open bottle of brandy, and poured himself an inch in the coffee cup in front of him. He held the bottle out to the Trasks, but they declined.

"OK, so what can I do for you?" he said as he leaned back, coffee cup cradled in his lap.

"Where did you meet your wife, Mr. Algaard?" asked Don.

"Carol?"

"Yeah."

"UMD. She was a psych major and I was taking business. We met at a party there."

"What year were you?"

"We were both sophomores."

"So what then?" asked Dave.

Algaard scratched the back of his head like he had lice. "So we got married right after school. We both got jobs in Duluth but I never really liked it there and I saw the ad for the store so we decided to give it a shot."

"You ever run a business before?"

"I worked summers at a convenience store back home and I did an internship in college."

"So, tell us about the night your wife disappeared," said Don.

Algaard took a sip from his cup. "Carol came in about five. I did some stock work back here and then I left about six. That was the last I saw her."

"She had worked alone at night before that?"

"Yeah, we switched back and forth. It got to be a drag. We hired somebody for about a month but we really couldn't afford him and let him go."

"And now? You and your fiancé switch off?"

Algaard paused and looked at Dave who had asked the question. "She worked some but she didn't like it. Business is a little better now so I hired some help."

"How long have you known your fiancé?"

"We met in high school. Dated some then. She called after she heard about Carol and then we just kind of started dating again."

"You and Carol ever fight?" asked Don.

Algaard didn't seem offended by the question, pouring himself a little more brandy before he answered. "Sure. Doesn't every married couple?"

"You ever get physical with her?"

Now Algaard got upset. "What the hell is going on here? I thought you were trying to help. I already answered that question about a thousand times. No, I did not hit her! And no, I had nothing to do with her going missing." Algaard stood. "Now you need to leave."

The brothers looked at each other and stood, following Algaard who was already walking to the front of the store. He unlocked the door for them and held it open.

"Thanks for your time," said Dave.

Algaard did not answer, locking the door after they were out.

The brothers sat in the truck, watching Algaard move around inside the building.

"Little defensive, wouldn't you say?" asked Dave.

"Yeah. I can see why Fowles likes him for it." Don watched as the lights in the store went out, wondering if Algaard was sitting in the dark watching them. "I'll run a check on him and Carol and his fiancé."

Don started his car and they drove back to their cabin, parking next to Dave's truck with the boat behind. Don announced he was going to bed as they entered the cabin and Dave decided to do the same. Don was quickly in snore mode but his brother laid on his back thinking about what Algaard had told them, thinking there was more to it, but finally giving up on trying to figure out what that was and rolling to his side and falling asleep.

Dave woke with a headache, feeling a little nauseous. He looked at the clock next to his bed to see that it was nearly three before he swung his legs off the bed and stood to go to the bathroom for an ibuprofen. He felt dizzy, almost losing his balance, thinking he hadn't had that much to drink, and walked toward his door. Dave slept with his door closed when he was with his brother to block out snoring. Sometimes he used earplugs but tonight he had just closed the door. The smell hit him as soon as he pulled the door open. Gas.

He started to reach for the hall light switch but then caught himself. He felt his way across the hall, found the doorframe for his brother's room and shouted Don's name. There was no answer. Dave was feeling faint now, his stomach churning, not sure how much longer he could stay awake. He shouted Don's name again as he entered the room but there still was no reply. By the light of the moon he could just make out the window across the room and he stumbled to it, feeling for the handle. It would not budge. His right hand moved across the top of the panel and found the latch, flipping it aside. He put both hands on the handle again and lifted. The window rose. Dave pushed his face against the screen and breathed two deep breaths before putting both palms flat on the screen and pushing. The screen bent out before finally giving way between his hands, his hands and arms sliding out as it did. He pulled them back inside, the jagged screen grabbing his skin and ripping it open.

Dave's burning eyes had adjusted to the darkness and he could see his brother lying on his back. He moved quickly to him, sliding his arms around him in a bear hug and pulling him up. He dragged the limp body off of the bed, nearly dropping him when Don's bottom and legs slid off, the extra weight pulling Dave down. Dave stood again, pulling Don up and dragging him to the window. He turned so Don's back was facing the window and then let Don's head fall back into the hole in the screen. Dave slid his arms down to the small of Don's back and lifted, pushing Don further out the window as he did, Don's shoulders now through. Dave was struggling for breath now and laid his head on his brother's chest so that he could take a breath of the outside air. He thought he could hear a heartbeat when he did.

Dave left Don halfway out the window and stumbled out of his room, down the hall, and into the kitchen toward the front door. He leaned on the kitchen table as he passed, feeling dizzy, his head pounding, the smell much stronger here. Three more steps and he had the front door open. He raced down the front of the house, ignoring the pain in his arms and the sticks and pinecones cutting his feet, until he reached his brother. He dragged Don's body the rest of way through the window, falling to his butt with Don's head in his lap.

Chapter 6

The driver didn't like being second. The other man liked to get rough with the girls, too rough most times. He'd slap and punch and beat them and by the time he was through there was not much life left in them. Not that they would live long anyway but the driver at least liked to get some reaction from them when he was having fun. Sometimes he'd wait a few hours after the other man was done, give them some time to recover, even talk to them and try to be nice before he had them, but it just wasn't the same as when they were wild and scared.

The man woke the driver when he finished with the girl, but the driver was still tired, and fell back to sleep. The sound of the door shutting as the other man left for work woke him a second time. It was after noon and he was hungry. The driver padded down the hall to the kitchen, poured some cereal in a bowl, and then ate as he stood at the counter by the sink looking out the window to the yard. The other man owned the house and had cleared almost half an acre many years ago, building a shed in the far corner to house his lawnmower and other tools. Behind the shed the man had cut a seventy-five-foot path through the woods and cleared another area, stacking the wood, cut in eighteen-inch lengths, where the trail entered the plot. The cleared acre wasn't visible from the house, except in the winter, and even then it was hard to make out.

The driver finished his cereal, putting the bowl in the sink and running some water in it. The man had left some coffee for him but had turned the burner off, so the driver poured some in a cup and heated it in the microwave. He stood and sipped it until it was about half gone, feeling himself start to wake, and then put the cup on the counter next to the sink. He headed downstairs.

Jackie Neese was lying face-up on the single bed. Steel bracelets were around her ankles and wrists, padlocked to chains attached to steel eyebolts in each of the four bedposts. As the driver approached, he couldn't tell if she was conscious or not. She didn't give any indication that she had heard him and her eyes were nearly swelled shut. The other man had done a number on her. Her face was badly bruised, and tears had left makeup streaked down her cheeks. Her nose looked broken too. Blood ran from her nose to her mouth and from the corner of her split lower lip down her chin. The driver thought she had nice tits but it looked like the other man had nearly bitten her nipples off. He had used the whip hanging from the wall on her stomach and legs too.

The driver shook his head and then pushed his boxers down over his hips so they fell to the floor. He stroked himself as he looked at her. "Better get this over with," he said aloud and climbed on top of Neese.

The girl moaned when he was inside her, and he liked that, even though he knew it wasn't a moan of pleasure. But that was the only reaction he had gotten from her and he decided it wasn't enough to make him want to wait and come back to do her again later. The driver went back upstairs, showered, dressed, and then returned to the basement. Neese looked the same. The driver had brought a plastic grocery bag with him and now picked up her clothes scattered around the room. He picked up her pink panties with a thumb and forefinger. It looked like the other man had used a knife to cut them off. The driver shook his head and put them in the bag. Neese groaned and as he turned to look at her she moved her head. Good, that will make it easier.

The driver took one last look around the floor, and confident he had everything, released the girl from her shackles. He moved her legs so her feet dangled off the bed and then pulled her up. Neese nearly collapsed, but he grabbed her under the arms and led her toward the stairs. "Come on, we're going for a stroll."

It was a struggle to get her up the stairs and he ended up carrying her most of the way. He put her back down and then helped her out the back door into the yard. Half way to the shed her head popped up and she struggled a little. He considered bringing her back inside and having her again, but just as quickly she was quiet again, pretty much dead weight, and he decided to keep going. He was sweating by the time he had her down the path behind the shed and the mosquitoes were after him too. He walked her nearly all the way across the plot and then dropped her to the ground, dropping the bag with her clothes at the same time. She fell to her knees, and then to her stomach, her arms back at her side. The driver bent over at the waist, hands on his thighs, trying to catch his breath. He finally stood, wiped sweat from his forehead, and slapped a mosquito on his neck. He reached to his waistband in back, pulled out his gun, and shot Neese in the back of the head.

The driver walked back to the shed, pulled on gloves he found on a shelf just inside the door, and grabbed the shovel next to the shelf. He walked back to where Neese was laying and dug, putting the dirt from the hole on the opposite side of where Neese was laying. He was momentarily thankful that the other man had cleared the plot where the ground was soft, but then two more mosquitoes bit him, and he cursed the other man for making him do this. When the hole was big enough, he pushed Neese in with his foot, threw the bag in on top of her, and covered her up. Finally, he grabbed a piece of wood from the woodpile, and put it so it was over the girl's feet. He was hot and sweaty and needed another shower but he couldn't help but smile when he looked at all the other pieces of wood in rows on the ground.

Chapter 7

Released from the hospital late on Monday morning, Don was not happy about having to spend all of Sunday there. A burner on the stove in the cabin had been left on, both brothers sure they would have noticed it before they went to bed on Saturday night. Dave felt bad in the off chance that he had forgotten the burner after he had made dinner, telling Don he was sorry, but Don wouldn't hear his apology. Don was certain someone had tried to kill them, he just couldn't figure out why. He was also cursing how long it took him to get released from the hospital as he made his way south on 35W Monday morning. He knew what his desk would look like when he got back and he also knew that Dave knew that once he got in to something he couldn't let it go. He hit the button for the phone on his Lexus and found the connection he wanted.

"Good morning sir," answered Trask's assistant Larry Stoxon in a brisk voice. Stoxon was in his early thirties, gay, extremely efficient and eternally cheery, and the only person who Trask knew that dressed better than he did. Trask knew he didn't pay Stoxon enough for him to dress like he did, and he had almost asked him on more than one occasion how he afforded his clothes but had let it pass.

"Hey Larry, I need you to run background checks on a few people for me."

"I thought you were on vacation, sir?"

"Yeah, so did I, but my knucklehead brother seems to think it's fun to do police work on vacation." Trask gave him Blaine Algaard's name as well as those of his missing wife and fiancé and told Larry he should be in the office in a little over an hour.

The Minnesota Bureau of Criminal Apprehension building is in St. Paul, close to Lake Phalen where Don had his condo. He debated about stopping home before going to the office but couldn't think of any good reason to avoid work, so went directly to the three-story burnt-orange brick building and parked in his spot. His office was on the top floor. Larry stood behind his desk as Trask entered his outer office. Stoxon was dressed in a powder blue Armani suit with a white button-down shirt and silk magenta tie. Trask did a small shake of his head at the sight of his assistant and walked into his office. Stoxon followed with his iPad.

"Welcome back, sir."

Trask felt tired as he sat, weak and worn, wanting to go home for a nap but knowing he couldn't. He surveyed his desktop, Larry taking one of the two chairs in front of his desk. "What happened? Crooks take a vacation too?" There were a few phone messages, papers, and files – all neatly organized by Stoxon – but nothing of the volume Trask expected.

"I guess the poor weather must have kept them inside. Maybe we should be working with the weather service to see if they can make it rain more often?"

Trask picked up his phone messages and began to go through them. "What do you know?"

"Pike would like you to call him about the Delmar investigation. It seems Mr. Delmar is not being very cooperative. Also, the Hennepin County Sheriff's office has requested that the BCA investigate a drug bust they conducted. And, last and probably least, the Superintendent has called a budget meeting for this afternoon at three in his office."

"Great," muttered Trask. "I was so hoping I'd get to see the boss today," said Don with obvious sarcasm.

"I knew you'd be excited about that. Anyway, those are the only urgent things that need your attention. I did run those background checks you requested if you would like to hear about them now?"

"Sure. Fire away."

"Alright, well, Carol Algaard was raised in Bloomington, and went to school at UMD, where she met her husband. Her parents are both living, her father works maintenance at Normandale College and her mother is a school teacher in Bloomington." Stoxon flicked his pad screen as Trask leaned back in his chair. "Lisa Carter is from Proctor, same as Blaine, but apparently did not continue her education after high school. She worked at a couple of different retail stores in the Proctor area after school until she became engaged to Blaine a little over a year ago. Her parents are also both living and still live in Proctor; her father is a dentist and her mother apparently does not work outside the home."

"Did you run a financial check on Lisa Carter's parents?"

"No sir. Would you like me too?"

"Yeah, that would be good."

"Alright, anyway, neither woman had or has much to their name in terms of money. The usual credit card and bank accounts."

"No big money transactions going into or out of Lisa Cater's accounts in the last few years?"

"No sir."

"Interesting. OK, what about Blaine?"

Stoxon looked at his pad. "Also grew up in Proctor, went to school at UMD but didn't graduate. Father passed away several years ago, mother works as an accountant in Duluth. He purchased the Save Big liquor store in Chase about four years ago. Seems to be keeping up on payments on his mortgage on his house and his business but it just doesn't seem to make sense."

Don sat forward. "What do you mean?"

"Well, I did a little math, and the gross receipts and profit he is making from his business seem high."

"Maybe people in Chase are thirsty. Not much to do there unless you drink."

"Possibly. But I compared his business to municipal liquor stores in Duluth and he is doing as much business as they are and his margins are higher. His inventory seems to match his receipts though, so, I don't know, it just seems off to me."

Trask was chewing on a pen, a bad habit he had kept from his college days that had resulted in ink in his mouth a few times. He had come to trust Stoxon's intuition as he had worked with him. "Hang on a second." Trask went to his computer and typed.

"Sir? Are you Googling sir?" Stoxon held his hand over his chest as if he was having a heart attack.

Trask was slow to adapt technology, unless it came to helping him catch bad guys and was more than happy to let others take care of it for him, especially after he had been locked out of his own computer on multiple occasions. "Yeah, I'm thinking of creating a cyber assistant so we can save some dollars on headcount around here."

Stoxon laughed but Don didn't so he quickly went quiet. Trask plugged in a number on his phone that he read off his computer.

"Hello, this is Special Agent Don Trask of the BCA. I'd like to speak to Chief Fowles please." Trask waited as his call was routed.

"Hello Special Agent, how are you feeling?" asked Fowles as he picked up.

"I'm good chief, thanks. Do have a quick question for you though."

"I'm listening."

"You ever notice any unusual activity around the liquor store?" inquired Trask.

"By unusual activity are we talking about drugs?" asked Cowles.

"Probably."

"Well special agent, I'm afraid to disappoint you but there's nothing there. We're a pretty small town and we keep pretty close tabs on anybody that seems to be hanging out when and where they're not supposed to. We caught a couple of kids from the high school doing some cocaine behind the Shell station last year, but we were able to track that stuff to a dealer in Proctor. You got something I don't know about?"

Chapter 8

Don wasn't sure he wanted to bring the sheriff in on where he was but he let him know what Larry had discovered. "It just seems that the liquor store does a very hefty business for a town your size."

"Well, I got to tell you, that store gets a big chunk of my pay check and probably just about everybody else around here. It's pretty important, especially in the winter, which lasts about ten months a year here."

"I noticed that last week."

Both men laughed at Don's comment, they chatted for a moment more, and Trask hung up. "The chief says he's pretty sure Algaard isn't dealing from the store. Seemed like a pretty good way to launder the money though."

Stoxon said "Hmff," looked at his pad a moment longer and then stood. "Don't forget your meeting with the superintendent or to call Pike or Hennepin County."

Don promised he would and Stoxon left. He leaned back in his chair and chewed on his pen, thinking about what Stoxon had said, thinking about Algaard and the liquor store, and thinking that he had missed something. As he chewed his stomach grumbled, causing Trask to look up at the clock on his wall to see that it was almost noon. "Larry! I need a sub!" he yelled.

~~~

Don called his brother as he ate. "Oh good, I'm glad I caught you before you went to see your psychologist."

"My psychologist?"

"Yeah, well, I figured you were pretty depressed after I out-fished you so bad."

"You know, maybe you should go see someone. I think your dementia is getting worse."

"Listen, I want to bring you up to speed on what I know about the Algaards." Don told him about the background information Stoxon had uncovered including the hefty sales going on at the liquor store and his conversation with Fowles. "Also, there's been a drug bust in Hennepin County, and it looks to be something big, so I'm going to be tied up for a while. I thought that maybe since you really have nothing to do you could go interview Lisa Carter's and Blaine Algaard's parents and maybe try Blaine again."

"No problem. You got any other cases I can solve for you with the rest of my day?"

"Number one, this isn't my case, you're the one who wanted to look at it remember? Second, you're a hell of a lot closer to Chase than I am. I will talk to Carol Algaard's parents."

"Alright, I got to look into the disappearance of a woman from a bar down that way anyway. But, what about the little matter of jurisdiction?"

"I just made you part of a special BCA task force investigating the disappearance of Carol Algaard. You should be good to go."

"Swell. When do I get my first paycheck?"

"You're being paid in fishing lessons so last week should cover you for the next few months."

"Good grief. Have Larry send me the contact info."

~~~

Dave and one of his deputies, Tom Chandler, spent the afternoon in and around the town of Knife River in the southern tip of Lake County assisting the local police in their investigation into the disappearance of Jackie Neese. Neese had been alone, closing the bar, and not seen since. From what the police could determine, she was likely abducted from the parking lot after work as the bar was locked and her car was still in the lot. They had questioned Gary Thomas, who was supposed to be working with Neese until closing, but his wife swore he stumbled into the house about one. There were no exterior cameras at the bar, and even if there were, it is unlikely they would have seen much with the storm that night.

Follow-up interviews with family and friends described a girl who was getting her life together, enrolled at UMD for the fall semester, planning to get a teaching degree. She had no steady boyfriends and seemed happy. She had just vanished. The sun was setting by the time they finished. Dave asked Chandler to file a report and send a copy to the Knife River police. He said he would stay the night in Proctor, conducting an unrelated investigation in the morning, but expected to be back to the Two Rivers office in the afternoon.

Dave made it to the Days Inn northwest of Duluth when he knew he wasn't going any farther. He made appointments to see both the parents of Blaine and Lisa Carter the next day. He wasn't able to reach Lisa Carter. He decided he would drop in on Blaine and see if he could get any more out of him later in the day.

Lisa Carter's parents lived in a single-story rambler just south of town on a street of similar homes. Trask parked his 4-Runner in the driveway in front of their two-stall attached garage and took the sidewalk to the front door. Before he could ring the bell, the front door opened. Inside the screen door stood a man with short, thinning gray hair with bushy eyebrows and a matching mustache. Black-framed glasses with thick lenses sat on a short nose. He was probably about Dave's height but stooped and thin, making him look shorter. John Carter.

"Mr. Trask?"

Dave showed his badge and the man pushed the door open, offering Dave his hand. Dave grabbed the handle and then followed the man inside to a small living room immediately to the right. Trask looked around the room. The room had apparently been newly painted from the odor. The furniture was of nice quality but older, the fabric on the chairs that sat in front of the front window faded. A fireplace with blackened brick over the hearth on the wall to his right, and a gold corduroy sofa sat under a large landscape on the wall opposite the front window, an older woman and a mousey blonde in her twenties seated together there. It was clear they were related – same big, blue eyes, same tiny pointed nose, and same full lips.

Carter sat in one of the chairs by the front window, pointing Trask to the other.

"Thank you for seeing me on such short notice," Dave began. "I assume you are Lisa?" he asked as he looked at the younger woman. She nodded. "Alright, as your parents have probably told you I am investigating the disappearance of Blaine's former wife Carol. Did you know her at all?"

"No, not really, just what Blaine told me."

"And what did he say?"

"Just that she was always complaining."

"Complaining about what?"

"That she didn't like it here, I mean, in Chase. And she didn't like the fact that she had to work so much."

"Did he ever mention anything about her disappearance?"

"Not that I remember."

"How long have you known Blaine?"

"Since grade school I guess. That's when we moved here."

"We moved from Duluth when she was seven," added her father.

Dave looked at him and then to Lisa. He had wanted to interview her alone and now feared there would be interference from her parents. "When did you start dating?"

"I think maybe ninth grade. We were pretty serious for a while but we both dated other people in our senior year. Then Blaine went to UMD and I didn't really see him again."

"Not even during the summers?"

Lisa thought about that. "I guess I did see him at my dad's office when he came in for a checkup but that was about it. I think he was working in Duluth."

"Do you know what he was doing?"

"No."

"And how is your relationship with your fiancé?"

Lisa looked down at her hands clasped in her lap; her knees pushed together as her mother put her hand over her daughter's hands.

"Is this really necessary?" asked Beth Carter. "I thought you were trying to find Carol Algaard. What good will this do?"

"It's important that we get to know as much as we can about the people closest to Carol, Mrs. Carter. Now Lisa, how is your relationship with Blaine?"

Lisa continued to stare at her hands. "Not good. I moved out a few weeks ago."

"You're living here?"

"Yeah."

"OK, so what happened?"

She let out a big sigh. "I just had enough you know. When we first started living together, he wanted me to work every day and he was always saying how we needed to save money and he criticized me about every little thing I bought." Tears were coming to her eyes and her mother handed her a tissue. She sucked a breath through her nose.

"OK, then what?"

"Then things actually got better. I mean he hired somebody so I didn't have to work all the time and he stopped talking about money. He even let me buy some clothes. But then, about a month ago, I was working alone during the evening and I felt sick, so I closed up the store and I went home. I found Blaine with another woman." More tears. Mother put her hand on her daughter's back.

"I'm sorry. Had this been going on for long?"

"Not that I knew about."

Trask turned to John Carter. "Did you give your daughter and Blaine any financial support?"

"I tried, but Blaine refused. Even offered an interest-free loan, but he didn't want it. Said he could make the store work on his own. We just didn't like all the hours that Lisa was putting in."

Trask studied Lisa who had regained her composure. There was something more there. "Are you pregnant?"

Chapter 9

Something passed between the two women on the couch and then Lisa looked at Dave through watery eyes and sniffed. "Yeah."

"Does he know?"

"I told him when I went back to get my stuff. He didn't seem to care."

Trask did not like the picture the Carters were drawing of Blaine Algaard. He wanted to hear more from Lisa and her parents but he had arranged to meet Blaine Algaard's mother for lunch and needed to check in with his staff beforehand. He thanked them for their time and said he may have additional questions at some time in the future.

He had arranged to meet Donna Algaard at Jimmy's restaurant on Highland Street just west of Duluth. Jimmy's was small, accommodating maybe thirty-five people at its booths, tables, and the half-dozen round wooden stools along the counter if it was full, which it often was. It smelled of bacon and eggs in the morning and burgers and fries in the afternoon. Businessmen in suits reading papers and college students in torn jeans looking at laptops sat side-by-side each day, enjoying the large portions, low prices, and good coffee.

Trask was early and took a booth. He ordered coffee and spent time getting updates from his staff on ongoing investigations, including the abduction, and then called his brother to update him on what he had learned from Lisa Carter. Don was not available so Dave left a message. He had just disconnected when a thin woman of average height in black slacks and a layered marine blue blouse walked in, scanning the restaurant from the area inside the front door. She was in her mid-fifties, with no-fuss short black hair, silver wire-framed glasses on a flat face.

Dave walked up to her. "Mrs. Algaard?" She nodded. "I'm Dave Trask." He showed his identification. "I'm sitting over there," he said pointing and then leading the way.

The waitress brought menus and asked if Algaard would like anything to drink. She ordered coffee and the waitress left.

"Thanks for meeting me," started Trask. "Hope this isn't too inconvenient."

"No, my office is only a mile from here." She was nervous, fidgety, not sure what to do with her hands, glancing at her purse on the bench next to her like someone might try to steal it at any moment.

"As I said on the phone, I am part of a new task force looking at the disappearance of your former daughter-in-law. I know you have probably been asked several questions about it in the past so I hope you will bear with me while I try to get a little caught up."

The waitress brought Algaard's coffee and she took a sip. "Actually, I received a call from someone from the Chase police department soon after it happened but that is about all."

It surprised Dave but he tried not to show it. "OK, well, I hate to take you through all of this again but maybe you can tell me when you first heard that Carol was missing?"

"Blaine called me. He was upset. He said that she had just disappeared and that he didn't know what he was going to do without her."

"They were very close?"

Algaard looked at Trask with calculating hazel eyes. "I think he meant that he didn't know how he would keep the store going."

"I see."

There was a pause in the conversation when the waitress returned, brought them each cloudy plastic glasses of water, and took their order.

"When did your son meet Carol?

"At UMD, it was in his second year. They seemed to get serious pretty quickly."

"Did you see your son often when he was in school?"

"I guess. He'd come home to do laundry every other week or so. And get groceries."

"He dropped out after his junior year?"

"Yeah, he got a job in the port, and it was paying good money, so he decided not to go back. I wasn't too happy about it, but honestly, tuition was really putting me in a hole. It was kind of nice to have him back for a while too, to have someone at home at night." Algaard gazed out the window while she sipped her coffee, a lost look on her face.

"And then he and Carol got married after she graduated. Is that right?"

"Yeah, well not right away, it was late in the fall. Carol had a job in Duluth and so they got a cheap apartment there. They saved their money and then bought the store in Chase a few years after that."

Dave was jotting notes as she talked. "How did your son and Carol get along after they married?"

"I think OK at first, when they were in Duluth, but things seemed to be a little strained after they moved to Chase."

The waitress returned with their orders, and they were quiet for a while as they ate. "Why do you think things were strained in Chase?"

Algaard finished chewing and took another sip of coffee. "The store I think mostly, although I don't think Carol ever really liked it there. She was from the Cities you know."

"Did they fight?"

The woman looked at him like she was trying to see through him. "You think Blaine had something to do with her disappearance? You're wrong," she said in a raised voice causing the couple in the table next to them to look in their direction.

"I never said that, Mrs. Algaard. The question still stands."

Algaard wiped her lips with her napkin and set it back in her lap. "They argued, but nothing more than that. Blaine would never hit the mother of his child."

Dave held his coffee cup in front of him. "She was pregnant?"

Chapter 10

Donna Algaard confirmed that her missing daughter-in-law was indeed pregnant. "That was something else I heard them arguing about when they stopped for a visit."

"When was this?"

"About two weeks before she disappeared."

"And what did they say?"

Algaard put her hand to her forehead. "I got the feeling that Carol had just told Blaine about it. He didn't know how they would manage the store and a child." She paused and then looked at Trask. "That was all I heard. Blaine would never have hurt that girl."

Algaard appeared to be close to tears. Dave had to wonder how something that could be as important as the pregnancy did not make it into the reports he and Don had looked at in Chase. "Did they actually tell you about the pregnancy?"

Algaard shook her head 'no'. It was a point of pain.

"Not even after she disappeared?"

"No." Algaard sat with a stiff back, trying to be strong, but she was hurt.

"How are things going with your son and his fiancé?"

"OK I guess. I haven't seen them since Easter."

Trask guessed she didn't know about the separation and maybe not even about her new grandchild to be. "I understand that your husband passed away several years ago. I'm sorry." Dave watched Algaard's face but there was little reaction to his comment. "Can I ask how he died?"

"I don't know."

Trask was about to take a bite of his BLT but stopped short. "You don't know?"

"Not really. I mean they found his boat all banged up on the shore so everyone just assumed that he fell out and drowned, but they never found his body."

"On Superior? Was it rough on the lake that day?"

"Yeah, he liked to fish for trout on Superior. It was pretty rough because Blaine had my husband drop him on shore so he could go home because he had a bad stomach."

"How old was Blaine?"

"Oh, just sixteen. He just had his license. He was supposed to go back to get my husband at sunset, but Larry never showed at the landing."

Dave made a note to look at the reports of the disappearance and any statements Blaine had made. People close to him seemed to disappear.

~~~

Don despised it when the BCA was called in to investigate an officer-involved shooting, something that had become standard procedure across the state. 99.9% of the time the BCA was a rubber stamp on what had happened, and it was a time-consuming process; time Don felt was much better spent catching bad guys. But today's request for an external investigation would not be a rubber stamp effort. Request J0723951 came from the Minneapolis Police Department. The MPD requested that the BCA investigate an officer-involved shooting in Minneapolis.

According to the report, the officer involved, Phillip Anders, who was white, stopped a black woman, Lavelle Benning, who was exiting a department store on 7th. Anders was answering a call of a woman shoplifting in the store and Benning fit the description. When Anders approached Benning she was carrying a large plastic shopping bag as well as her purse. He asked Benning to show him what was in the bag as well as her receipt for the items inside. Benning put the bag on the pavement and opened her purse, removing a handgun. The officer viewed what he thought was a gun being pulled from Benning's purse and pulled his weapon. He told her to drop the weapon, at which point Benning told him she had a license to carry the weapon and said she had to get it out of her purse to find her wallet. She raised the gun which Anders took to be a threatening gesture, and he shot her, killing her. Her twelve-year-old daughter who was with Benning filmed all this. The daughter posted the video online this morning.

An immediate firestorm had ensued. In the space of fifteen minutes, the BCA Superintendent - Don's boss, the Minneapolis Chief of Police, the head of the police union, the mayor of Minneapolis, as well as a multitude of media had called Don's office. He had ignored them all.

"Larry!"

Trask's assistant entered his boss's room from his outer office. Don was never short of amazed at his assistant. Stoxon worked long hours, often well past when Don was in the office, and yet he always beat Don there in the morning and looked chipper and ready to go. Today Larry had gone with an off-white linen suit with a vest, pink dress shirt, and a bow tie. He carried his iPad. "Yes sir?" he said with a smile.

Trask was not a morning person. It took several coffees to get him going and happy people irritated him, especially in the morning. "Has the governor called yet?"

"No sir, but my guess is that he has called the Superintendent." Larry sat. "How would you like me to handle the media calls? I was thinking I could say something like 'The BCA does not comment on investigations. You will need to contact the Minneapolis Police Department.'"

Don leaned back. "No, that will put it on Marty Olson." Olson was the commander of the 4th precinct in Minneapolis where Anders worked. He was also a friend of Trask's who had covered for Don more than once. "Just leave it at 'no comment' for now."

"As you wish, sir. By the way, Commander Olson called."

"Damn! He knows I can't talk to him about this." Trask sat forward and looked at the papers on his desk. "OK, I'll take care of it." He glanced quickly at the background information Larry had found the day before and realized he had done nothing on his promise to his brother to talk to Carol Algaard's parents. "See if you can set up a meeting for me with Carol Algaard's parents? Tonight would work for me."

Trask spent half an hour on the phone with his boss listening to how he should handle the investigation into the Benning shooting, and how the governor wanted regular updates. He assigned one of his investigators to look into the shooting, apologizing to him as he did, and spent the rest of the day avoiding calls and completing paperwork. Larry told him he had arranged a meeting with Carol Algaard's parents at six, so Don left early, stopping at a Burger King on 494 for a Whopper meal that he sat and ate by himself, feeling lonely and feeling like he didn't really like his job any more.

Trask pulled his Lexus to a stop at the curb in front of the faded blue rambler in west Bloomington, a southern suburb of Minneapolis, home of the Mall of America. Don hated the Mall of America. Metropolitan Stadium, home of the Twins and the Vikings, and the Met Sports Center, home of the North Stars, had been bulldozed to make way for the mall, burying some of Don's favorite childhood memories of time spent with his dad. Someone had killed his father and mother in a fire in their home, a fire Don was sure was set as retaliation for a case he was working. Nothing had ever been proven and the few leads he had came to nothing. He blamed himself for their deaths.

He walked through grass that was already a crunchy August brown. The shrubs on either side of the front steps looked like they had not been trimmed for a few years, their branches poking through the railings on the steps, and the white trim around the front door was beginning to peel. "A man after my own heart," said Trask as he reached to push the button next to the door.

Nadine Johnson was not what Don had expected. While her missing daughter was tall and blonde and blue-eyed, Nadine was a broad woman, barely over five feet tall, with dark hair and brown eyes. She invited Trask in and led him to the living room where Tom Johnson extended his hand. Trask took the hand of the man who was, in most ways, of the same physical appearance as his wife. His hair was thinning, mostly silver with a few flecks of black, his eyebrows high above his blue eyes, like something had surprised him. He was stocky, with a solid build. He motioned for Trask to sit on the couch and he took the leather recliner to the left, directly opposite a large flat-screen television. Nadine lifted a plate of bakery-purchased cookies that sat on the coffee table in front of the couch and held them out to Trask, but he declined, as he did her offer of something to drink. She sat in the chair to her husband's right, a small table with two coffee cups between them.

The Johnsons perched on the edge of their chairs, elbows on their thighs and hands folded between their knees as if they were praying, which Trask was afraid they might have been doing. "I want to start off by saying that I have no new information about your daughter's disappearance." The Johnsons looked at each other and then back to Trask. Their eyes told him he had given them some kind of hope after three years of emptiness, and then that bit of light died, and he wished he had never agreed to look into this. "I'm sorry. I would like to help you get some kind of closure. We're hoping a fresh set of eyes on your daughter's case can find something."

"What can we tell you?" asked Mr. Johnson, the resignation clear in his tone.

"When was the last time you talked to your daughter?"

Johnson's left hand went to his forehead and he blew out a breath. "Boy, I don't know. Nadine, I got to think it was like two or three weeks before she went missing. Does that sound right?" He looked to his wife for her confirmation.

"I guess so," she replied looking at her husband and then at Don. "Oh no, maybe two. I remember we talked about what she was going to do on the Fourth, so it was probably a few days before that."

"How did she seem to you?

"About the same," Mrs. Johnson answered. "She was pretty down. She was working long hours at the store and she didn't really like it there. They were pretty heavily in debt so I think that weighed on her too. And I'm not sure that she and Blaine were getting on that well."

"Why was that?"

"Well, I don't know. When I suggested that she maybe take a break and come home for a week or two she said Blaine would never stand for it. I really got the feeling she was afraid of him."

"Like physically afraid? Do you know if he ever abused her in any way?"

The Johnsons looked at each other, some kind of agreement being made without words. Nadine turned back to Trask and replied. "They were here the Christmas before she disappeared and you could tell that they weren't getting along – no hugging or touching – in fact they seemed to try to avoid each other. I asked Carol if Blaine was hitting her or anything her but she said no."

"Did Carol ever like living in Chase?"

"I don't think so," answered Mr. Johnson. "Blaine pushed hard for it after they were married and she finally just gave in."

"And why didn't she like it there?"

"She was always a city girl I guess. She was a long ways from her friends and I think she got lonely. Plus, I don't think she ever liked being alone after the abduction."

Don's eyes shot up from his pad where he was jotting notes. "The abduction?"

"Yes. She saw her roommate get abducted in college. It terrified her."

"When did this happen?"

"Her junior year. Her roommate was waiting for her outside the library when this guy pulled up in a truck, grabbed her roommate, and forced her into the truck and drove off."

"And she reported this?"

"Of course."

"Did they catch the guy?"

"Not that we know about."

"And her roommate?"

"They found her body down by the lake a few days later. She had been raped and beaten."

Don didn't see that it had any relation to Carol's disappearance; still he asked for the roommate's name and made a note to check it out. "Have you had any contact with Blaine after the disappearance?"

"We were up there with the search parties, and saw him then of course, but not since then," said Tom.

Trask thanked them for their time and rose. Tom Johnson walked him to the door.

"Mr. Trask?" Don turned as he stood on the step. "Please don't let this drop. We need to know."

Trask looked into the eyes of the beaten man before him. He wanted to tell him that it was highly unlikely that anything would turn up after all this time, and that his office was swamped with active cases, but he didn't. His parents' murders had gone unsolved and it ate at him every day. "I'll do my best."

Trask had left his phone in the center console and retrieved it after closing his door. There was a blinking light and he pressed his finger to turn on the screen. "Shit!" It was the number he did not want to see. He hit the call back icon.

Chapter 11

"Don. Thanks for calling." The voice of Marty Olson sounded tired.

Trask knew what Olson was calling about and he wanted to cut it off. "Listen Marty, you know I can't be talking to you about an investigation."

"Who said I was calling about an investigation? Maybe I just wanted to get a fishing report?"

"Bullshit. You know I wouldn't give you any fishing information either."

Olson laughed, but it sounded forced. "Yeah, don't I know. Listen Don, all I want to say is that this whole thing is a bunch of political bullshit and that this kid is a good cop. Have you looked at the video?"

Trask leaned back. "No I have not looked at the video Marty and I don't expect to until my team has reviewed everything and has a report ready."

"Jesus Don. You got to stop this thing. Look at the video. There's nothing there that says he did anything out of line."

"I told you, I will look at it when the time comes."

"You owe me Trask. I need you to step up here. This kid deserves none of this," replied Olson as his voice raised, his tone stern.

Trask knew Olson was right. He owed him. He owed him big time. He also knew there was no way he could interfere in the investigation. Too many eyes were on it, eyes that mattered. "I'll see what I can do." Trask ended the call and tossed the phone on his passenger seat. "Shit!" He banged the steering wheel with the palm of his hand, and then grabbed the wheel with both hands, straightening his arms as he pushed himself back against his seat. Anger rose inside him like lava in a volcano and he could feel his stomach tighten.

He knew the feeling and knew where he wanted to go. Don wanted a whiskey, several whiskeys, in the worst way. He could taste it on his tongue, feel it on the back of his throat. Last year he would have been on his way to a bar by now. But something held him back. He was in the middle of slowly working his way back into the good graces of his girlfriend and had promised her he would not go on a bender or ever drive drunk again. He had broken things off with her twice, once because he became afraid he was getting too close, and the last time when she caught him drinking. Two strikes. He knew he wouldn't get three. He picked up his phone and dialed. "You eaten?"

Lieutenant Melanie Jenkins of the Stillwater Police Department had not eaten. She liked to eat but she was on a mostly salad diet trying to maintain in her battle against her weight. She was sitting on her couch, her fat cat in her lap, and her fifth salad dinner in a week sitting on the coffee table in front of her – untouched. "Nope."

"What if I bring Chinese and a bottle of wine?"

"Hmm, that sounds good, but where are you?"

"I'm just leaving Bloomington."

"Bloomington! Geez Trask, that's over an hour. I don't think I can wait that long. What if we meet somewhere in between?"

Trask thought about that for a moment but was also thinking that moving their relationship back to a more physical level would be really nice tonight. "Hey Mel. You know me. I'll just drive at my usual speed. Shouldn't be more than forty-five minutes at the most. What if you just open a bottle now and have a glass while you wait?"

Jenkins could hear it in his voice. She knew where he wanted to go and she wasn't sure if she was ready to go back over that line again. Part of her wanted to but another part was warning her that this was not a good idea. But she also detected something else, an urgency not just for something physical. "Are you OK?"

Besides his drinking, Jenkins had made it clear that if they were going to go anywhere, he would have to open up; he would have to talk. Trask had never let anyone in except for his brother, and that had only been on rare occasions. It had played a big part in why his two marriages were measured in weeks. He thought about Marty Olson and what he had promised, he thought about the Johnsons and what he had promised them, and he thought about his parents. "I don't think so."

"Don't get picked up. I'll wait."

~~~

Don called his brother as he drove to work the following day and filled him in on his conversation with the Johnsons. Dave told him about his talks with Blaine's mother, Lisa Carter, and her parents.

"So Blaine doesn't seem to have too many fans?"

"I would say not," replied Don. "Have you had the chance to talk to him again?"

"No. I stopped by his store but he wasn't in so I called but he said he didn't have the time or anything else to say right before he hung up."

"Listen, I don't know that it has any bearing on Carol Algaard's disappearance, but she witnessed the abduction of her roommate when she was in school. Supposedly saw the guy and made a report. Do you think it could be a link?"

Dave thought about it for a minute but came up with nothing.

"OK, I'm going to have one of my guys in Duluth take a quick look at the report anyway. You catch your abductor?"

"No, and the girl hasn't turned up either. I don't have a good feeling about it."

Chapter 12

The summer sun poured into his truck, warming the cab more than he liked, and he pushed the button to turn on the air-conditioning, the first cool blast reminding him of winter. The driver didn't like winter. There was a time when he did, when he looked forward to it. When he and his friends would dig forts in the snowdrifts after a storm or slide down the middle of their road when they cancelled school. They'd play hockey at the rink by school or sneak down to the lake to watch the waves stack the ice on shore high above their heads. When spring approached they snapped icicles off roofs and snowball fights were a daily occurrence. But childhood had slipped away faster than the setting sun in January. Winters now were reduced to cold, long stretches where the temperature never got above zero and the roads, when they were open, were always treacherous, especially with his nearly bald tires. The truck never seemed to want to start, even though he had added a block heater, and even when it did the heater inside the cab couldn't keep up. The house was cold and drafty; the man yelling at him when he would come home and find the thermostat turned up. He felt locked away, cut off. Short days and long nights and drugs and alcohol taking him to places in his mind where he was afraid that he would never escape. He knew he could not survive another winter in the house.

The driver thought about this as he drove along Superior, looking at the lake when the road afforded a view, his window open to feel the air cooled by the water. He stopped at the light in Two Harbors and watched as two girls, not much younger than him, crossed the road in front of him. A powder blue plastic shopping bag dangled from the right hand of each girl, the bags swinging in rhythm to a tune only they could hear. The girl closest to him wore tight red shorts and a sleeveless white terry top stretched over her breasts. Her hair was red and long, tied in a ponytail that fell halfway down her back. She glanced at him as they passed in front of his truck, a smile on her face, and then looked quickly away. He watched her walk until she stepped on the sidewalk and the car in back of him honked. He drove on.

He'd been going further north, past Two Harbors on 61 to Castle Danger, and a little beyond. There were resorts along the Great Lake, crowded this time of year with tourists from the Twin Cities, Wisconsin, and a good number from Illinois. They came to eat at the over-priced restaurants along the shore, shop at the over-priced shops in the towns, and walk the shore looking for agates, sometimes braving the chilled water to wade in, holding their socks and shoes in their hands. But mostly they came to relax, drink, party, and have a good time. It was a beautiful area, hilly and heavily wooded with giant Norway pines and white spruce and sharp granite cliffs where eagles floated on the wind. An ancient place carved by glaciers where what was happening in the rest of the world didn't seem so important. In some ways the crowds made his life more difficult, more people staying out late, more people that might see him. But they also made his life a little easier. He could blend in; get closer to his target and her surroundings without being noticed.

Cliffside Resort literally hung over the cliff on Lake Superior, at least the dining room did. With a wall of ceiling-high windows facing the lake, tables there reserved weeks in advance. The food was nothing exceptional, and the prices tended to be on the high side for the area, but the view of the lake was hard to beat, especially when the wind blew and the waves crashed into the point sitting just to the north. The main lodge was built in the forties and had been remodeled several times. It housed the restaurant and a bar along with a couple of large meeting rooms and an indoor pool. There was no housing in the lodge, rather townhouse units were all to the right of the lodge as you faced the lake, almost two dozen units in all. The entrance to the parking lot was directly in front of the main lodge, the lot long and wide in front of the lodge and the town homes, a lot where the employees parked to the left of the main lodge, and slightly above the main parking area. A single yard light was high on a pole in front of the lodge with smaller street-lamp type lights in front of the town homes. A large pine shaded the employee parking area from the yard light, leaving it nearly black after the sunset.

There were few employees in the small resort, a majority being the cleaning crew that were gone before five pm, the employee parking lot never more than half full. Naturally they all parked as close as possible to the lodge, leaving the dark corner of the lot nearest the highway vacant, except for the old pickup that parked there the last several days.

The driver's truck was partially hidden by low-hanging birch branches when he backed it into the corner of the employee lot, and in four days he had not detected a single glance from any person retrieving their vehicle. A majority of the employee vehicles were gone by eleven, he assumed they were workers in the restaurant that closed at ten, only two vehicles remaining for a pair that worked and closed the bar. Each night at about 1:30 two women retrieved their vehicles, a middle-aged woman with a limp that walked with a cane and drove an older black Jeep, and a blonde in her early twenties that drove a red Subaru. The driver had parked early enough the first night to see the blonde arrive for work. Her hair was long, flowing over her shoulders. The driver liked women with long hair. Her breasts were not large but evident under her Cliffside t-shirt and he liked her walk. She was the one.

Julie Powers was a grad student from Minneapolis attending UMD, working toward a degree in clinical psychology. It was a two-and-a-half-year program with classes in the summer as well as the spring and fall semesters. She was working as a grad assistant at the school, as well as her waitress job at Cliffside, to pay for a tiny apartment in Two Harbors that she was sharing with another student for the summer. She'd move back to Duluth, close to campus, in the winter, but for the summer she wanted to be out of town. Powers was a night person so she didn't mind the late hours at the bar and sometimes stayed up studying even after she got home.

Powers had noticed the truck in the dark shadows of the corner of the lot the first night the driver had been there. There was a reflection of the yard light off the windshield when the wind from the lake blew the birch branches hanging over the truck as she had walked to her car. She could not recall if it had been there when she arrived at work that first night but was sure it had not been there the following days. She could see no one inside the truck but thought it odd that it was parked there only at night. It gave her the creeps, but she had not mentioned it to the other woman who was the bartender, Melissa Hanes.

The night was overcast, no rain, but it felt like it could come at any time. The northeast breeze was cold off the lake and the women both put on jackets before they exited the bar. They walked together up the slight incline to where their vehicles were parked.

By now the driver knew their routine and had moved to a position thirty feet opposite their vehicles, on the far edge of the lot, hidden by the thick boxwood that circled the lot. He could feel his heart rate increase as he crouched in the shrubbery and heard them come out of the bar, their high voices chatting about something he couldn't make out.

Once he selected a location, the driver would watch, night after night, often more than a week. It was most comfortable for him when he could sit in his truck and watch, drinking his Dr. Pepper and eating his Fritos, but he would vary his routine so as not to be noticed, sometimes parking and walking to where he could observe the bar or restaurant without drawing attention. He didn't like the hours of standing so would pass on places where that would be his only surveillance option. Never caught trying to abduct a woman, it had been close a few times, and that had taught him to be cautious, to plan, and be ready to abandon his plan at any time. The man had told him that too, early on, but he had not listened to the man and it had almost cost him.

He did not like the waiting and planning at first, especially when the girl who was his target was attractive, and he had a need. But over time his perception of his work changed. It became a challenge to figure out what people would do and when they would do it. He liked the reconnaissance, planning how he would take the women. He would run 'what-if' scenarios through his head, trying to consider every possibility. From time to time he would enter the bar he was targeting to see its layout inside and to get a good look at the women. He never stayed for more than half a beer and never entered a bar more than once, mostly because he didn't want to be described after an abduction, or caught on video, but also because he made it his practice not to drink on the job. That had been hard too, he liked to drink, but getting picked up for drunken driving was not an option.

The watching, the waiting, night after night, became monotonous though, especially after he had a clear plan of what he would do and how he would do it. To wait for the right night was like a kid waiting for Christmas. He knew it had to be done, that he could leave nothing to chance, but the actual abduction was what he liked best. He held the shock stick in his right hand. He had tested it earlier in the night so he knew it was ready.

The truck was there again; Powers has seen the ghostly white reflection of the yard light in its windshield. She stopped and stared.

"What is it?" asked Hanes.

"There's a truck parked over there in the corner of the lot," replied Powers as she pointed. "See it?"

Hanes studied the area for a minute, thinking the girl had imagined something, and then the branches moved in the breeze and she could see the dark shape. "Yes, what about it?"

"It's been there like every night when we come out but not when we get to work. Don't you think that's kind of strange?"

Hanes continued to look at the corner of the lot, but it was impossible to see much of anything. A few of the employees who worked late, including Hanes, had requested a light for the employee parking lot but the owners had said it wasn't going to happen this year. "Who knows, maybe it's some kid who's sleeping in his truck. Wouldn't be the first time I've seen that."

Powers turned to Hanes. "I suppose. If that's the case it's kind of sad."

Hanes chuckled. "Don't be sad. It's probably some kid that's up here fishing and can't afford a room. Probably having the time of his life."

Powers turned back to look at the truck one more time. As she did the wind died and she heard a noise to her left. She turned to see a bright light coming towards her.

Chapter 13

The driver had caught part of the women's conversation and could hear them talking about his truck. He didn't like that; didn't like the fact that someone might be able to describe his truck. He considered abandoning his plan, finding another place, but then decided that he would take them both. His plan had been to stun them both anyway, and then just abduct the blonde as long as the older woman hadn't seen him, but now he knew he couldn't leave a witness. He'd take them both. Hell, they'd never had two at once before. Wouldn't be any need for one of them to have seconds. Maybe this would work out just fine.

He moved from his cover, turning on the stick as he started towards them, keeping it pointed down so the light wouldn't draw their attention. His steps were nearly silent on the asphalt, the wind off the lake masking any small sound. He was half way to them, crouching as he moved, and they stood talking, unaware of him closing in on them. He decided he would zap the blonde first since he knew the woman with the cane wouldn't be able to move as fast. They were still looking toward his truck and the driver raised the stick, speeding up his pace to close the gap between them, when his heel hit a pothole in the tarred lot. He felt his ankle turn and tried to repress a groan as the pain shot up his leg. The driver went down.

Powers screamed as the man sprawled facedown at her feet, some kind of pole in his hand that was buzzing and had a light at the end. She couldn't move. The man looked up at her and then pushed himself up with his free hand, pulling the lighted pole back, like he was going to stab her with it, when he yelled.

The driver was hurting. He had turned his ankle and skinned the palm of his left hand and the knuckles of his right hand that held the shock stick as he tried to break his fall. He pushed himself up to his knees, surprised to see that the blonde was still standing there, arms across her chest clutching her purse. She thinks I'm going to rob her. He almost laughed out loud at the thought as he brought the shock stick back to poke her when he felt the blinding pain across the back of his head.

Melissa Hanes was not afraid. She served two tours in the Middle East, the last one ending when she had taken shrapnel in her thigh when a mine blew up her jeep. After two months in the hospital she came home to Two Harbors to recuperate and consider what to do with the rest of her life. They told her to rest but that was not in her nature. She liked to be around people, making her solitary recuperation worse, when she had seen the ad for the bartender position. The job required too much time on her feet so soon, but the owner was happy just to get someone, and so allowed her to sit on a stool behind the bar when she wasn't pouring.

She caught the movement of the driver out of the corner of her eye and now, as he raised the shock stick, she brought her cane down on the back of his head. Their attacker's head dropped and he screamed out in pain. As Hanes raised her cane to hit him again, he looked up at her.

The driver couldn't believe it. The old cripple had hit him, and she was going to hit him again. His head was pulsing with pain, so much so that he had almost forgotten about his ankle. He rolled away from the coming blow and then got up and ran for his truck. Every step was agony. Afraid the old woman was chasing him and would hit him again, he didn't dare slow, hip-hopping across the pavement. He found it hard to keep his balance as he ran, thinking that the truck seemed a football field away, wishing he had somehow been able to park closer. The driver pulled open the truck door and hopped in, grimacing as he put weight on his injured ankle, immediately reaching for and turning the keys he had left in the ignition. He slammed the truck into gear and pushed hard on the accelerator. He had backed the rear of the truck off the pavement and the tires spun in the gravel before catching hold and shooting him forward. He did not look to see that the women still stood by their vehicles.

Powers was crying as Hanes embraced her.

"Are you OK?" asked Hanes.

"Yeah," Powers sniffed as she backed away. "Thanks. You saved my life."

"Bastard. I guess I should have listened to you about the truck. I'm going to call the cops."

~~~

The driver took a chance and drove almost to Two Harbors before cutting west. He figured that it would take the cops a while to respond to the women's call at this time of night, if they did call. He was cringing with pain as he drove; his head hurting like it had never done before and his ankle throbbing, pain shooting up his leg each time he had to shift, brake, or accelerate. He reached behind his head and could feel his hair was sticky under his fingers. The bitch! He wanted to turn around, go back, and run her over. Run his tire over her head and show her what real pain felt like.

But he knew he couldn't do that. He had to get home. The man would be waiting and he wouldn't be happy when he heard what happened. He had told the man he thought that tonight would be the night. He told himself there was nothing he could have done about it, that it wasn't his fault. If he hadn't stepped in that pothole everything would have been fine. Hell, everything would have been great. They'd have two women to have fun with. And it was his turn to go first so he would have had first choice. He would have had the blonde. But he wouldn't have her now. He'd wasted a week and was sure that he wouldn't be going out again for a while. "Damn!" The driver slammed the heel of his hand against the steering wheel as he turned left and headed south.

Chapter 14

The driver had been right – about a couple of things. First, it had taken the Two Harbors police over half an hour to respond to the call at Cliffside. There had been a brawl outside a bar in town, and as there was no mention of any injuries or imminent danger in the Cliffside call, the police decided to finish sorting out the bar situation before responding. By the time the police arrived at Cliffside the adrenaline rush from the attack had worn off; the women were tired and just wanted to go home to bed. They had waited outside for a few minutes after their call but then decided they should go back inside the building to be safe in case the man who had attempted to attack them returned. Their description of the would-be attacker was that he was tall and lean, had black hair, and now had a lump on the back of his head and a limp. The officer asked if they had gotten a license number off the truck but they said it was too dark. The women completely omitted the shock stick in their comments. The officer filed a report on the incident when he returned to the station.

Unfortunately for the driver, it would also turn out that he would be right about the man. The driver had taken his time getting back, trying to stay on the pavement so he wouldn't jar his right ankle that was now swelling to three times its normal size. He had gone so far that he had come in from the west, nearly ten miles more than if he had headed straight south. This had nothing to do with driving on a smooth road, both roads were paved; he just wanted to avoid the man if he could. He hoped the man would give up on him and go to bed. He moved as slow as possible up the drive. Every bump was agony, nearly more than he could take. He closed his eyes tight and clenched his teeth each time a pothole jarred his ankle and his head. The truck crawled down the gravel lane in low gear, but still he killed the motor several times, as the pressure needed to engage the clutch was too much for him to handle. Finally, he pulled into the yard under the light and turned off the engine. "Shit," muttered the driver when he saw the porch light turn on. He bowed his head, his hands clutching the steering wheel tight.

The man stepped out wearing only boxers. In the shadow of the light behind him, the stomach hanging over the waistband of his shorts looked even bigger than it was. He stood with his arms folded across his chest, feet spread, like he had been waiting for his teenage son who was getting in late from curfew.

"Shit!" The driver said it louder this time but he still hadn't moved. It was now past three in the morning, and he assumed that the man had been up the whole evening, waiting for his treat. He was also guessing that the man would have to work later in the morning, and now he'd have to go there with almost no sleep and no satisfaction. He was going to be royally pissed.

The driver used his left arm to open his door and swung his left leg out. He slid slowly off the seat, putting all the weight he could on that leg as it touched the ground, trying not to lose his balance by hanging onto the door frame. Finally, as he leaned against the seat and balanced on his good leg, he put his right leg on the ground. It surprised him a little that it didn't feel too bad and for a brief second he thought maybe his ankle was already getting better. Then he took a small step with his right foot and collapsed, yelling out as he hit the ground.

The man's first thought was that maybe someone had shot the driver, probably in the leg. He stepped gingerly off of the step in his bare feet and moved on tiptoes through the sticks and pine needles and dew-laden weeds in the yard to where the driver was still laying. "What the fuck happened to you?"

The driver looked up and said, "Help me inside."

The man grabbed the driver's outstretched hand and then pulled it over his stooped shoulder as the driver made it to a standing position. The driver hopped as best he could on one leg, leaning heavily on the man, smelling the cheap aftershave he used, not liking the fact that he had to touch the man's bare skin. They reached the steps and the man held him tight around the waist, pulling him up, and then walking him into the house. He led the driver to an old armchair and settled him there, leaning on the back of the chair and brushing off the bottom of his feet. "What the hell?"

The driver leaned forward and reached behind his head. His hair was matted and hard there. He pulled his hand away but could see no fresh blood. "I fell."

"You fell?"

The driver glanced up at the man who was standing in front of him, hands on his hips. "Yes, damn it, I fell. I hit some hole in the parking lot when I was walking and turned my ankle and fell." The driver reached down and lifted his pants leg. He could see the swelling for the first time.

The man looked down at the ankle, now grossly oversized and purple. "Stupid shit. And what about your head?"

"I don't know. I must have hit it when I fell," he lied, still looking down at his ankle.

"And that was it? What about the girl?"

"She never showed. Must have had a night off." The driver could feel the burn of the scrapes on his hands now but resisted looking at them. He didn't want the man to see them and question how he could have hit the back of his head and scraped his hands.

The man knew the kid was lying but the excitement he had built up earlier in the night had worn off and now he was tired. He had heard nothing on his police scanner about anything that may have involved the driver so, hopefully, no one had seen him do whatever he did to get in his condition. He looked down at the driver and shook his head. And then he slapped the driver hard across the face. "Stupid shit." He turned and went to bed.

The pain in the driver's head had subsided somewhat before the man's slap but now it was back with a vengeance. It was as if someone had shoved a wire from his head down his spine, hooked the wire to a power source, and flipped the switch. He squeezed his eyes shut tight at the white-hot pounding pain, his hand reaching to the top of his head like he was afraid the pulsing pain would somehow blow his skull open. He touched his palm to the corner of his lip and then pulled it away, a streak of blood evident. He sat like that for a moment before pushing himself to a standing position and hobbling to the kitchen. He leaned on the front of the sink and pulled a glass from the cabinet to his right, setting it on the counter and then letting the water run. There was a bottle of ibuprofen there and he took five pills in his hand, filled his glass, and then threw all the pills in his mouth at once, downing them with one gulp. He guzzled the rest of the water in the glass and then bowed his head in the sink where he lapped water over his head with his hand.

The cool water had a numbing effect as it ran over his head and down his face to his chin. He watched as it dripped red in the sink and thought about the old lady that had done this to him and how he would kill her. He would make her suffer first and then he would kill her. The driver used a dishtowel to dab his head and face, looked at the red blotches that left on the towel, and then tossed it on the counter before hobbling off to bed. As he passed the bedroom door of the man, he thought then that he would kill the man too.

Chapter 15

Agent Danny Carlisle was searching the drawers of her desk for sunflower seeds on the following Monday. She chewed seeds on a regular basis, almost daily, something that did not endear her to the cleaning crew in the Duluth BCA office or when she rode with another agent. She had just given up on her search, standing to make a run to the snack machine, when her phone rang.

"Carlisle, I got something for you."

Danielle Carlisle recognized the voice of Don Trask. Of the two times that they had worked together, they had come close to stepping over the line of no personal relationships with fellow employees. Both recognized it could only lead to bad things, but both also recognized the strong attraction. At the sound of Trask's voice Carlisle could feel her heart rate increase.

"Yes sir. What can I do for you?"

"Danny, I'd like you to look at an abduction that took place at UMD about seven years ago. There was a report of the abduction filed by a woman named Carol Johnson. She was a roommate of the woman abducted. The abducted woman was named Sarah Hollister. She was apparently found raped and murdered by the lake a few days after the abduction."

Carlisle was taking notes. "OK, no problem. What am I looking for?"

Trask paused. "Honestly, I'm not really sure. Johnson disappeared about three years ago and I'm looking at the possibility that the two events may be related. It's a long shot but I promised the parents we'd take a look. By the way, when Johnson disappeared she was married. Her last name was Algaard." Trask spelled it out. "Happened in the town of Chase not too far from you." He filled her in on the details as he knew them.

"Yeah, OK, I remember. OK, I'll check it out and get back to you."

"Thanks, Danny."

Trask disconnected and Carlisle leaned back in her chair, chewing on her pencil and feeling a bit sad. There was no flirting in their conversation. She thought about saying something but wanted Trask to be the one to lead. In fact, there was no indication at all that he was in the least bit interested in her. Somehow, she had held out some hope that maybe there would be a little more there, although it was against policy, something that made it a little more exciting too. She thought about this for a minute more and thought maybe it was God telling her that she shouldn't be going in that direction. She brought up the UMD police department on her screen and called.

The University of Minnesota Duluth sits on about 250 acres on the northern side of the city. There are about ten thousand students that attend the school, a vast majority from Minnesota and nearby northern Wisconsin. The UMD police force comprises ten officers and four clerical staff headed by the Director of Police, Blake Lane.

After identifying herself and explaining her desire to look at the file on the Hollister abduction to the man who answered at the UMD police department, they put Agent Carlisle on hold. A few moments later a low, gravelly voice came on the line.

"Director Lane. Can I help you?"

"Yes Director. I am Agent Carlisle from the BCA and I would like to look at an old case file of an abduction that happened on campus about seven years ago."

"And can I ask what this is about?"

"We believe that it may relate the abduction and another case we are currently working on."

"I see. And what is the name of the victim?"

"Hollister. Sarah Hollister."

"Alright, this should be easy. There was no physical evidence and very little in the file. You can probably save yourself a trip."

"I see. Well, I'd like to see it just the same. Would ten work?"

Lane was silent for a moment and then said, "The file is on the computer. I will instruct our clerk to expect you and set you up on a computer. We will see you a little later."

Carlisle was about to express her thanks but Lane had disconnected. That was a bit odd. She wondered why she had to talk to the head of the department to look at a file and how he seemed to know all about something that happened that long ago.

Carlisle looked at the clock and figured she had fifteen minutes before she had to leave. Time enough for two things. She opened her phone and punched the number for Sergeant Hillary Thomas of the Duluth Police Department.

"Hey Hill," said Carlisle when Thomas picked up. "What's shaking?"

"The kid is teething and I am getting no rest. Someone told me to rub brandy on his gums but it doesn't seem to help unless I drink it."

Both women laughed. They had become good friends at the police academy and had both signed on with the Duluth

Police Department. Carlisle had moved over to the BCA three years ago.

"Listen, I'm working an old case from seven years ago and I'd like to look at your files on it. It was a rape and murder. The vic's name was Sarah Hollister."

"Sure, no problem. I'll see what I can find. When would you be by?"

"I going to UMD to look at their file at ten so I would come by after that."

"You talk to Lane over there?" she asked.

"Yeah. Why?"

"The guy is very protective of what happens there. His number one goal there is to make sure that no bad press goes out about the school. Plus there's something wrong with his head because he can't seem to hold it up when he's talking to a woman."

Carlisle laughed again. "Not someone you're sending a Christmas card to?"

"Don't think so. By the way, he never got a college degree and he's quite sensitive about it so don't bring it up."

"OK, thanks for the warning. I'll see you later."

Carlisle looked at the clock again. Just enough time to see if they had restocked the machine with seeds.

~~~

The UMD police are housed on the first floor of the Administration Building on campus, taking up a good portion of the floor. Carlisle found the room number on the directory and walked down the hall to her left, entering the door at the end of the hall. Inside it looked like about any other office. There were four chrome-framed chairs in the reception area facing a low tan divider topped by a thin laminate counter. Carlisle walked up to the counter and was about to ring the bell when a man in khaki slacks and a UMD Police polo shirt that was being stretched a bit above the waistline walked up to the counter.

"Agent Carlisle?"

The man was not quite six feet tall, with a black goatee sprinkled with silver that matched the thick coarse hair on his head. His face was pockmarked and there were deep furrows in his forehead above his bushy eyebrows and narrow brown eyes. Those eyes did an assessment of the tall woman in front of him. She had shoulder-length chestnut hair and bright blue eyes on either side of a slightly upturned nose. She wore a white short-sleeved blouse over navy blue slacks. The woman was slender but fit, like she was a runner which she was.

Carlisle noticed the survey and how the man's eyes ended up on her chest and she almost giggled. "Yes," she answered holding out her hand. "You must be Director Lane?"

Lane gave her a tight-lipped smile. "You can read name tags. I'm very impressed."

"Reading is usually optional for BCA agents but I'm kind of an exception."

Lane had been looking at her face while she answered, the smile still on his face, and then his gaze drifted back to her chest.

"OK, so I don't want to waste any of your time. If you or someone can just point me to the computer I should use?"

Lane didn't seem to be in any hurry to stop looking at Carlisle and it was giving her the creeps. He moved to his left and pushed a button that made a buzzing sound before pushing open a door next to the counter for Carlisle to enter.

She followed him past several cubicles to one that looked well used, the desktop and edge scarred, several holes evident in the panels surrounding the desk. He stopped and held out his hand.

"Here you go agent. The file you wanted should be keyed up so all you have to do is hit "Enter". There are separate files under the main file so you'll need to click on each one to get it to open. Any questions?"

Carlisle moved past Lane and sat down at the desk. She hit enter on the keyboard and the screen lit up with a main file showing and a connected file below that. "This should be fine. What if I want to print something?"

Lane said nothing for a moment making Carlisle wondering if he had heard her when he said, "I would prefer that you just took notes, but if you need something printed, just ask Gene. He's in the first cube on the left."

Carlisle smiled and thanked him again. He stared at her for a moment longer and then left. Icky. She took out her pad, set it by the keyboard, and moved the cursor over the first file. A summation of the investigation by campus police filled the screen. Her eyes went wide.

Chapter 16

There was nothing there. Well, almost nothing. Carlisle read it twice. The abduction had taken place seven years ago on May 6, 2010. It had happened outside the Lester Library on campus at a little after ten in the evening. The abducted woman's name was Sarah Hollister. She was a junior at the school, majoring in secondary education. Her roommate, Carol Johnson, also a junior at the school, had called in the report of her abduction. The responding officer was Blake Lane.

Carlisle opened up the attached document that turned out to be Johnson's statement of the incident. According to Johnson, she and her roommate had been studying at the library since a little after seven. As the library closed at ten, they exited and walked north in front of the building when Johnson realized she had left a notebook in the library. She turned and went back to see if she could get back into the building. As she reached the front door, she heard her roommate scream and turned to see a man forcing her roommate into the cab of a pickup truck and then drive away.

She described the man as being tall, at least six feet, with shoulder-length black hair, and thin. She did not get a good look at his face. The man had driven a pickup, dark blue or black, with four doors. It looked shiny in the light. She did not get a license plate number.

That was it. There was nothing about any investigation. No interviews or mentions of any other witnesses. She also thought that it was odd that there was no mention of reporting the incident to the Duluth police. There wasn't much here but Carlisle thought she may as well get a copy despite what Lane had said. She went to find Gene.

Gene was Gene Granger, who looked to be about eighteen to Carlisle. She wondered if he might be a grad student but he had his own nametag saying 'Officer Granger' Velcroed to the outside of his cubicle panel. She leaned on the panel and said, "Officer Granger?"

Granger looked at Carlisle and popped up like a spring had propelled him from his chair. His cheeks immediately flushed and he pushed his bangs back from his forehead. He was about the same height as Carlisle, with blonde hair and a husky build. Granger tried to say something but there was apparently something in his throat which he worked hard to clear before saying, "Can I help you," in a high squeaky voice.

Carlisle almost laughed but managed to only smile. "Yeah, I'm Agent Carlisle of the BCA and Director Lane said you could print something off for me?"

"OK, Sure. Um, what is it?"

Carlisle led him back to where she had been working and pointed to the documents on the screen. Granger said that would be "no big deal", moved the cursor to the print icon, and pressed the button. He opened the Johnson interview and did the same. He stood and told Carlisle he would be right back as he turned sideways to move past her, brushing up against her, his face blushing again.

Granger was gone for less than two minutes and returned with the documents in hand, holding them out to Carlisle. "Here you go."

Carlisle looked at what he had handed her and then back at Granger. She guessed he was maybe twenty-three. He was kind of cute, in a teddy-bear kind of way, not that she was interested, but there was no denying that he was infatuated with her. His face was still red and she could see perspiration on his brow gleam in the lights. Carlisle had been feeling a bit old lately but she felt herself perk up now. Maybe I still got it.

"Listen Gene. Can I call you Gene?" Granger shook his head in the affirmative, his eyes opening wide. "So Gene, I'm working on this big case for the BCA, and I'm wondering if you could help me out? I noticed what a whiz you were about getting those documents printed and I was wondering if you could find a couple more for me?" She moved closer to him and could hear his now rapid breathing.

"Uh, yeah, like what?"

"Well Gene, could you possibly search your case files for any rapes or abductions or attempted abductions that happened on campus in the last ten years?"

Granger was locked on her eyes. He swallowed noticeably, his Adam's apple popping up and down. "Uh, yeah, just let me slip by you so I can sit down."

Carlisle was having too much fun with him so she only backed half a step away, forcing Granger to rub against her again as he passed.

Granger sat and, after a few keystrokes, was in the campus case database where he started a search. In a moment a dozen case files appeared on the screen. "OK, there you go," he said as he looked at the screen before standing again, now inches from Carlisle who had been behind him watching. "Um, you just need to click on each file to open it."

"Wow, you're great at this computer stuff," said Carlisle as she looked in his panicked eyes. "You must have been here a long time."

"Uh, no, actually I only started a few weeks ago."

"That's even more amazing," she commented. She stared at him a moment longer but was afraid he might faint. "OK, I better let you get back to work. Can I come over and see you again if I need more help?" Carlisle knew she should stop but she hadn't had a date in over three months and her ego needed a fix. Granger managed to get out "you bet" before he scurried away.

Carlisle was back in the chair and clicked on the top file. It was a report of an attempted rape in one of the dorms that had occurred in the spring. She clicked on the one below and discovered it was an altercation where a former boyfriend had tried to force a girl to go with him the fall before. It quickly became clear that the files were in chronological order and she moved down the list to the Hollister file, clicking on the file of the most recent incident after that. A quick look and she saw the file described the arrest of another disgruntled boyfriend who had been outside of his girlfriend's dorm throwing rocks at her window. It had been over two years after Hollister's abduction.

Carlisle moved her cursor to the file on the list just before the Hollister file. This incident had occurred in the winter before the Hollister abduction. It was after ten on a snowy night, again in front of the Lester Library. A black pickup had slowed and the driver had offered a ride to Mary Zastro as she walked. She declined but the boy in the truck, described as having thick black hair sticking out from a red stocking cap and a partial beard with bushy eyebrows, had pushed her to accept. She had kept walking when he stopped his truck, jumped out leaving the door open, and ran after her. He grabbed her by the arm and tried to drag her back to the truck, only it was slippery because of the snow and both Zastro and her attacker fell. Just then another car swung in front of the library. Zastro yelled for help. The abductor saw the other car, ran back to his truck, and took off. Carlisle took down the details as well as the contact information for Zastro and moved to the next file.

This incident occurred roughly eight months before the Zastro attempt, in March. Again, it was a snowy evening, and again, the incident occurred in front of the Lester library just after it closed. This time the intended victim was a Jennifer Truman from Anoka, Minnesota. As Truman stood outside the front door of the library, a black pickup pulled up and the man inside offered her a ride. The man had a sharp nose over a black beard and mustache and was wearing a dark blue stocking cap pulled low over his ears. He had high cheekbones. Truman had refused his offer and turned back to face the library when she heard the truck door open and turned to see the man coming at her. Peter Bacon, her boyfriend, walked out of the library at that moment and yelled as he saw the stranger moving towards Truman. The man from the pickup saw Bacon and ran back to his truck and took off. Truman was not going to report the incident but her boyfriend insisted. Again, Carlisle took notes and contact information. As she was jotting down Truman's home address, she sensed a presence to her right and turned to see Lane striding toward her. She quickly backed out of the file and then closed the database just as he arrived.

Lane looked at the blank screen and then at Carlisle. "You've been here a long time. Get what you need?"

Carlisle folded the sheet she had been using to take notes, the back of the printout given to her by Granger and tucked it in her purse as she stood. "I've always been slow at taking notes. I sometimes wonder how I ever got a master's degree. How about you? Where did you get your masters?"

Lane looked taken back, a scowl on his face. "Um, I haven't had time to finish yet."

Carlisle put her purse strap over her shoulder and moved past. "Good luck with that. It's really a lot easier than getting an undergrad degree," she said with a smile over her shoulder as she left.

Lane frowned and looked down at the computer screen. Something wasn't right.

Chapter 17

Lane filled the entrance to Granger's cubicle. "Granger!"

The officer immediately pushed his chair back and shot to his feet, almost raising his arm to salute before replying, "Yes sir."

"Granger, did you make copies of the Hollister case file for that BCA woman?"

The anger in Lane's eyes was sharp as razor blades but Granger didn't see it. Instead, he thought about brushing up against the very attractive woman earlier in the day and got a silly grin on his face before snapping back to reality. "Yes sir."

"And that was all?" asked Lane in a threatening tone.

Granger thought about telling Lane about helping the BCA woman look at the files on other abductions but he didn't think his supervisor would be too happy about that and, besides, he had technically only asked if he had copied anything else for her. "Yup."

Lane looked skeptically at his new rookie before he turned and left. He returned to his office and sat back in his chair, coffee cup in hand, looking out the window. Lane was not a computer savvy person by any means, but he knew that Carlisle was not on the same screen she had been on when he left her. She had been looking at something else, or at least trying to. He needed to know what. A few years earlier Lane had looked the other way when he had pulled over a new female employee in the university's IT department who had run a stop sign. He had thought about calling in that IOU for a date with the woman but had never had the nerve. Now it was time for her to do something for him.

~~~

Hillary Thomas retrieved Carlisle from the waiting area and brought her back to her desk. There was a chair at the side of the desk where Carlisle sat while Thomas brought two cups of coffee.

"Thanks," said Carlisle as she held the cup in both hands. It was warm out but the air conditioning in the Duluth PD made it feel like the windows were open and a cold spring breeze was blowing off the lake. She took a sip.

Thomas leaned back in her chair. "So, you and Lane have a date scheduled?"

Carlisle nearly spit out her coffee. "Actually, we're engaged. I was hoping you could recommend a church for the wedding."

Thomas giggled. "I believe that the Church of the Lecherous on second would work for you two."

Both women were laughing now.

"So, is that guy creepy or what?" asked Thomas.

"Way beyond creepy if you ask me. There are some serious problems there not the least of which I may have stumbled on when I was there."

"Oh yeah? And what would that be?"

Carlisle leaned forward. "You know that case I asked you to look into?"

Thomas looked down at the manila folder on her desk and pushed it toward Carlisle. "It's right here."

Carlisle put her hand on the top of the folder. "Thanks, but you didn't happen to have a record of any other abductions or attempted abductions on campus within a year or two of that did you?"

"Hmm?" Thomas turned to her computer and moved her fingers over the keys. "Nope, we have nothing."

"Hill, I found two cases of attempted abductions in the year before the Hollister abduction. Both happened in front of the library just like Hollister, and officer Lane investigated both."

"Are you shitting me?"

"Afraid not. There wasn't much in either file but it was pretty easy to see that the attempted abductor was likely the same guy that took Hollister. Do you know if there is any way to see if the school issued some kind of warning about the abductions?"

Thomas shook her head. "No idea. So you think that the school just covered this all up? That would not be good."

"Well, it sure wasn't good for Sarah Hollister and I'm pretty sure it wouldn't be good for Lane and whoever was his boss at the time. Probably not whoever was in charge of the school at the time either if they knew anything about it."

Thomas whistled. "My, you certainly jumped into a mess with this one didn't you?"

"That wasn't my intention. I was supposed to just do some background on the Hollister abduction."

"So, what are you going to do?"

Carlisle set her cup down on Thomas's desk and picked up the file. "Can I take this with me?"

"Yeah, it's just copies. So?"

"I'm going to look at this file and I'm going to think about it." Carlisle stood and looked down at her friend. "And then I'm going to figure some way to make it someone else's problem."

Thomas laughed. "That's my girl. I predict you will go far."

Carlisle tossed the file down on the passenger seat of her Subaru and drove back to her office. She had just laid the file on her desk when a thought hit her. She pulled out her notes and the printed report from her purse and looked at them again. If it was the same guy that was involved in all three abductions, and it sounded like it was, then she probably had enough information from the three reports to at least get a semi-decent description of the perp. Was it possible that the guy was a student at the time? Or maybe worked on campus? And if so, did the school still have photos of the students that attended then as well as the staff at the time? Then she looked at the accumulating pile in her inbox and put the information on Hollister and the others aside. Tomorrow. She worked the rest of the day on her inbox and then headed home.

Chapter 18

Carlisle's morning run seemed to take forever; her feet felt like lead weights and she could have sworn that the wind kept switching directions so that it was in her face the whole way. She kept checking her watch, thinking she was slow, but when she arrived back at her apartment she was surprised to see she had finished her usual route in one of her better times. She wolfed down her homemade smoothie and a cookie after her shower, finished drying her hair and brushed her teeth, and headed in to work. She was eager to get back to the Hollister file. She had been thinking about it as she ran, and the more she thought about it, the more she felt it made sense that the abductor was a student. The guy knew when the library closed, knew he was just a short distance from exiting campus, and somehow knew the girls were there. Maybe he had even been in the library with them before it closed?

Carlisle sat at her desk and took notes from her UMD notes and the printout supplied by Granger. She was able to get hold of Jennifer Truman but the woman could add nothing to what Carlisle already knew. There was nothing more in the way of a description of the abductor in the Duluth PD report, but she thought she had enough of a description to start her search. She went back to the UMD website and found contact information for the registrar's office. She called the number listed and a girl answered who Carlisle guessed was likely a student.

"Registrar's Office. Can I help you?"

Carlisle identified herself and explained her desire. The girl seemed to think about it for a minute and then asked Carlisle to hold. In a moment another voice came on the line.

"Hello. This is Deputy Registrar Michelle Jones. Can I help you?"

Carlisle again went through her identification and request.

"You know, we probably have what you are looking for, but I don't think you're going to find it on a computer. You're going to need to come down here and look through a few boxes I'm afraid."

Carlisle thanked Jones and said she would be down early in the afternoon. She hung up and opened the file Johnson had given her again, reaching for a bag of sunflower seeds as she did. Her hand came up empty and she realized that the machine had also been out when she had looked the day before and she had completely forgotten that she was going to stop at the store to get a bag on the way home. "Rats!" She reached down and pulled open a lower desk drawer, removing a bag of chips. She would have preferred a bag of cheese balls, but those left her fingers orange. "Plan B."

The police report included the medical examiner's report on Sarah Hollister. The girl had been beaten and strangled. Someone had tied her arms behind her back; her hands, feet and mouth bound with duct tape. She had bruises on her face and scalp and chest. Her hair had pulled out. She had been raped. There were three partial prints on the duct tape but no other evidence. No DNA was found.

Carlisle looked at the medical examiner's photos and wondered why God would let this happen to someone. The crime scene photos and description only increased her loathing of the killer. He had treated this woman like an animal for his own abuse and pleasure and literally dumped her like garbage. He had wrapped her in two large black garbage bags leaving her body near a park by the harbor. The police had no idea how long the body had been there when a park maintenance worker found it after an early spring thaw.

Learning to ride a bike had not been an easy experience for Carlisle. In fact, she had fallen so many times, that her mother had suggested to her father that they should wait until she got bigger to let her ride. But Carlisle was not one to quit. She wanted to cry when she skinned her knee and her elbows but something inside her drove her to keep going. Through all of her falls she never cried, and she did learn to ride. Her father gave her the nickname of 'bulldog'.

Carlisle knew as she looked at the report that she did not like this man, this man who had done these terrible things to Sarah Hollister. And she knew she did not like Blake Lane for letting this man continue to try to abduct a woman. And she knew she would not let this go until she found the man who had killed Hollister and somehow saw to it that Blake Lane would be punished.

Chapter 19

Chris Larson was one of three investigators that reported directly to Don Trask. Larson had an unassuming presence – average height, average build – pretty much an average looking guy except for one distinguishing feature. He had a large mouth. It wasn't clown-mouth large, or pumped with drugs large, but it was definitely bigger than normal. And something he was sensitive about.

Trask had given his three lead investigators nicknames – Pike for Pete Seton because he had a rather long nose, Walleye for Wally Bradley because walleye was close to Wally, and Bucketmouth for Larson. Trask did it because he liked to fish and liked to be reminded of fishing whenever possible. The nicknames were to be only for his use with his assistant Larry. They had, however, leaked out as these things do, and Larson was not happy about his nickname.

Trask had put Larson in charge of the investigation of the Anders shooting of Lavelle Benning. Larson completed his investigation and Trask was looking through his preliminary report. The report said that there was no clear evidence to say that it was an unjustified shooting. On the other hand, the report did not strongly support the officer's use of force. It was essentially a toss-up. Another officer in Anders' position may or may not have felt threatened to the point that they would have shot Benning. In other words, the investigation was non-conclusive.

Don walked down the hall of BCA headquarters to Larson's office. The door was open but he knocked anyway,

Larson, seated behind his desk, looking up from something he was reading.

"Hey, boss. What's up?"

Trask walked in, closed the door behind him, and sat in the chair facing Larson. He tossed the Anders investigation folder on Larson's desk. "Good work on this, Chris."

Larson had worked with Trask for several years. "But?"

Trask looked at Larson and then out the window to his right. Trask had looked at the video of the incident and the report with supporting evidence and had come to the same conclusion as his investigator. Still, he had come here to push Larson to come to a clear conclusion, a clear conclusion that the shooting was justified. It was what the police union wanted. It was what his boss and the governor wanted. He knew there were a lot of guys in the building that had ties to the Minneapolis PD and guessed that they would want the report to show clear support for Anders. And it was what Marty Olson wanted. He figured it was probably what the media wanted too because it would throw more gas on the fire.

Most of the protestors had left the positions they had occupied in front of the fourth precinct to protest the shooting but this report, regardless of what it concluded, was sure to bring them back, and likely bring them to the BCA building too. A clear finding that the shooting was justified was sure to ignite more protests, something Don didn't think anyone wanted. But he had promised Olson. He looked at the report lying in front of Larson and then at his investigator. "No buts. Good job. Send it in." Trask stood and left.

~~~

Dave Trask was feeling sorry for himself. August had arrived. Dave loved August. Sure there were mosquitoes and horseflies, but August also brought warm days and pleasant calm evenings. Evenings when the smallmouth bass on the lake where he lived would feed on the surface. A small floating lure, tossed over shallow water and given just a twitch or two, sometimes just letting it sit, would be more than any smallmouth lurking below could stand. Sometimes they would just slurp it in, but most of the time the fish would explode out of the water, occasionally missing the lure entirely. It was the kind of fishing Dave loved most.

And it was what Dave wasn't doing as he sat in his Two Harbors office, over two hours away from his home on a lake full of bass. Dave had fourteen deputies to patrol the nearly three thousand square miles of Lake County. There were three offices - the main office in Two Harbors, a second office about thirty miles north in Silver Bay, and another in section 30, close to Trask's home. He tried to work from the section 30 office as often as possible, but there were complications.

Most of the population was near Two Harbors and so, most of the crime. This meant Two Harbors housed the most deputies and investigative capacity. That meant if there were a major investigation, like the disappearance of Jackie Neese, Dave would need to be in Two Harbors. There was another complication. Two Harbors was also the location of the medical examiner's office. This should have only been a complication if Dave wanted to be on hand for an autopsy, but there was a related complication. Doctor Linda James. Dr. James was one of the two medical examiners for Lake County and lived in Two Harbors. She was also the woman he had been having a semi-covert relationship with for the last year.

The investigation into Jackie Neese's disappearance had stalled. Interviews with friends, other employees, bar customers, and video had given nothing of any substance. There had been a man with black hair under a baseball cap in the bar a few days before the abduction, but he had neatly avoided the camera and the only two other patrons in the bar at the time. Neese had been the only employee in the bar that night so it was possible he was scoping her out, but no one could say they had ever seen any man that might fit his description, limited as it was.

Trask was convinced someone planned the abduction. Whoever had taken Jackie Neese had waited for her, knew she was alone. There were tire marks in the gravel at the back of the lot that might have been from the vehicle used by the abductor, and footprints near Neese's car, but the rain that night had made it impossible to get anything usable from them. He thought more about the abduction and then he thought about an abduction that had happened years earlier – the abduction of Carol Algaard, and how her husband had thick black hair. Where had Blaine Algaard been on the night Neese disappeared?

~~~

As she pulled up to the Administration Building at UMD Agent Carlisle knew she should probably update Don Trask on what she had discovered but she was like her dad's dog on the scent of a grouse and couldn't stop. There was no question in her mind that she would report in to him to get approval to talk to any of the other victims or witnesses or their families, but she figured it wouldn't take that long to look through the pictures of students on campus at the time of the attempted abductions as well as the Hollister abduction. In reality, the only thing that didn't take long for her was to find out that she was wrong.

Carlisle found the registrar's office on the directory in the lobby of the building and went up one flight of stairs to the first door on her left. She entered the office and was greeted by a girl that she guessed was a student, sitting at a desk behind a beige partition. Carlisle asked for Michelle Jones. The girl said she would be right back and Carlisle watched her walk to the second office behind her and lean in the doorway. A plump woman in a red dress popped out of the door and came up to Carlisle.

"Agent Carlisle?"

"That's me," replied Carlisle as she held out her identification.

Jones glanced at it and then handed it back. She had been carrying papers in her hand and now handed them to Carlisle. "I'm afraid that before I can let you look at our files, I will need you to get this form signed by the vice president of administration, Mr. Walls. You'll find his office on the first floor."

Carlisle looked at the form and then back at Jones. Something had happened since they spoke. She wondered if this was about her trip to the campus police. "OK, I guess I'll be back in a few minutes." But in the back of her mind she somehow knew that wouldn't be the case.

Carlisle went out of the office, back down the stairs, and found the number for Mr. Walls' office. She walked down the hall, found the dark oak door with opaque glass stenciled with 'VICE PRSIDENT ADMINISTRATION', opened the door and stepped in. She was greeted by an elderly woman with no-nonsense short gray hair in a white blouse and navy blue skirt seated behind a similar desk as the one in the registrars' office entry. The name on the plate Velcroed to her panel said Lisa Klang.

"Can I help you?" asked the woman as she removed reading glasses from her nose, letting them fall to her chest where they hung from a gold chain.

"Yes, I'm Agent Carlisle of the Bureau of Criminal Apprehension and I need to look at some old student registration information for a case I am working on." Carlisle had found that people were much more impressed with her title when she used the full name of the BCA rather than just the abbreviation. "Apparently I need to get approval of Mr. Walls to do that." Carlisle handed the woman the form.

Klang looked at the form and then at Carlisle. "I'm sorry but Mr. Walls is not in this week. He is away on business."

Now Carlisle was pretty sure she was being stonewalled. "Uh, OK. So who can I get to sign this if he's not here?"

"I'm afraid that Mr. Walls is the only one who can sign."

Now she was positive. "What about his boss?"

"The chancellor? I don't think so but I suppose you could try. It may not do you any good though."

Carlisle put her hands on her hips. "And why is that?"

"I happen to know that the chancellor is out of the country on a trip to Norway. I don't believe he will return for almost three weeks." Klang was smug, taking pleasure in stonewalling the agent who had tried to impress her with her credentials. Klang prided herself on never being one to be pushed around by anyone.

Carlisle was generally slow to anger, or show her emotions, something that she found helpful in her job. But now she could feel her ears getting warm and she knew from experience that was the first sign that she was about to lose it. "Well, isn't that nice? I've never been to Norway but I hear it's lovely at this time of year. I guess that I'll just have to come back when Mr. Walls returns next week."

"Oh, he won't be back until after next week, and I know that when he returns, he will be very busy. Getting ready for the fall semester you know. I can't guarantee when he'll be able to get to this." Klang gave her a smile that said she had won.

Carlisle could now feel her face going completely red. She seriously wanted to choke the woman in front of her by the chain around her neck. "Well, that's sounds just fine Miss Klang. You just give me a call when your boss has had time to sign the form and I'll just hope that the killer I'm looking for only kills a few more people before then. Maybe you? Who knows? Here's my card and you just have a nice day."

Carlisle flicked her card so it hit Klang in the chest, nearly giggled at the shocked look on Klang's face, and walked out. She went to her car, got in and slammed the door, and then growled. She had never been a screamer. When she got angry, she just growled. It was probably another reason for the 'bulldog' nickname but she never really associated one with the other. She was angry about the runaround she had received and also upset with herself. She believed that God was watching what she did; judging her daily, and that God probably wasn't too pleased with how she had just acted. Carlisle briefly considered going back in the office and apologizing but she couldn't get the smug look on Klang's face out of her mind so she just folded her hands in her lap and asked for God's forgiveness. Then Carlisle picked up her phone and dialed Don Trask.

Chapter 20

Chief Fowles had dismissed Trask's suggestion that Algaard was dealing drugs but what Trask had said bugged him. He didn't like the fact that Trask may have discovered something happening in his town. He also didn't like the fact that Trask had way more resources available to him than he did. And he didn't like Blaine Algaard.

Fowles was 99% sure that Algaard wasn't dealing but he had put the store and Algaard's home under surveillance after Trask's call anyway. That surveillance had revealed nothing other than Algaard liked to sample his own product. But Fowles also knew that there just had to be something going on. Save Big liquors seemed to do a pretty good business, but he wondered how Algaard was affording the extra help he had hired recently, as well as the new boat one of his deputies had noticed at Algaard's house. Somehow Algaard was getting away with something in his town and he wasn't going to stand for that.

~~~

Larry told Don Trask that his brother was on line one.

"What now?" said Don as he picked up.

"And good day to you."

"What do you want?" The disgust in Don's voice was evident.

"Good gracious! The ugly brother of the south is not in a good mood."

"And what was your first clue Sherlock?"

"So what's going on?"

Don didn't like to share with his brother who he felt was always trying to analyze him like he was some kind of shrink. Don was taking heat from his boss and the media for his investigation of the Benning shooting and it was not likely to stop soon, not to mention the fact that his now former good friend Marty Olson had told him he had better not so much as litter in his precinct or he'd have Trask spending time in a cell with people who did not like him. "Nothing. Now what's on your exceedingly small mind?"

Dave backed off and got to the point. "I'm still looking at that abduction we had. The Neese woman still hasn't turned up."

"OK."

"So the only lead I really have is that a black-haired guy was seen in the bar where she was taken a few nights before she disappeared."

"Alright, so you want me to arrest all the black-haired guys in Minnesota?" asked Don.

"Maybe tomorrow. But the only black-haired guy I know that is associated with a woman's abduction in the last few years is Blaine Algaard."

"You think Algaard did this new one?"

"I don't know. Seems a stretch."

"Well, we can agree on that anyway."

"The bar where the Neese woman was abducted is a ways from Chase, but not that far. What I am wondering is if there have been any other abductions or rapes in the last few years around the Chase area?"

Don leaned back in his chair. "Good grief! I don't have time to be running down every little thought that passes through your little brain." He thought about the call he had received earlier from Carlisle. "OK, I'll take a look, but only because for once in your life I think you might have had a thought with something to it." He relayed what Carlisle had told him.

"Interesting. I'm wondering if we put Algaard's picture in front of the victim's or witnesses what they might say?"

"I didn't tell Carlisle about Algaard, at least what he looks like. I want to see what she comes up with. The President of UMD should be calling the registrar's office with his approval for her to look at the files. Let's give her a little time and in the meantime I'll run a check for you."

Dave was silent for a moment. "Thanks brother. How's Mel?"

Don thought about the other night and relaxed. "Good. I think we're pretty good again."

Dave smiled. "I'm sneaking home this weekend. I can hear the smallmouth calling my name all the way from the lake. Interested?"

"Shit. You really are an asshole. I got plans with Mel." Don paused. "I suppose I could tell her that I got called away to a meeting?"

The Trask brothers' meetings had been going on for years and Melanie was well aware of them.

"Why don't you bring her? I'll ask Linda."

"Hmm, not sure that would be a great idea. Mel hates to lose at anything and from what you've told me about Linda, she'll probably out-fish everyone but me. There could be a fight."

"Think about it. I'll call you."

~~~

Two years earlier Blaine Algaard had been in a significant amount of trouble. His wife was missing and the police seemed certain he had something to do with her disappearance. Algaard could handle that, he thought the Chase police were a bunch of idiots anyway, but without his wife to help him at the store the hours he was putting in to keep it open were taking their toll. He felt like a zombie, not sure of the day or time, forgetting to eat and drinking too much of his inventory. Lisa wasn't helping much and he wasn't sure if he could hang on much longer. And it wasn't just the time he was spending in the store. He was running out of money.

Algaard had never been much good at accounting; he had left that up to Carol. It seemed that she was on him about their finances monthly; how they weren't taking in enough to keep paying the loan on the store much less pay the mortgage. But he had thought that was just her. In fact, he was convinced she was saying those things because she wanted to sell the store and move.

He pushed her into buying the business in the first place. She was the frugal one who had saved most of her paycheck, and it was enough for a down payment and a loan. He was sick of working at the docks, taking orders from idiots who were only his bosses because they had been stupid enough to work at the docks longer than him. He saw the ad for the liquor store and knew it was a way out, a way for him to be his own boss.

Carol didn't want to go. She liked her office job and she liked living in the city. In fact, if she had her way they would have moved to the Twin Cities so they could be in an even bigger city. Blaine didn't want that. He wanted to be in a small town and the liquor store had been his chance to go home.

He had lied to her. He told her it would only be for a few years, five at the most, and then they would sell and move to Minneapolis. He'd look for a store they could buy while they ran Save Big. But he had never looked for an opportunity to buy a store near Minneapolis, never even thought about it once he convinced her to go to Chase and spend her savings on Save Big.

But Carol had been telling him the truth about their finances and now he was having trouble paying his bills, delaying payments, and he was late on his taxes. And now his distributor had called him. Algaard was late on that payment too. If he couldn't get any stock that would be the end. He had no way to pay and was thinking about packing up and leaving, not really sure where he would go or what he would do. Just get out from under for a while.

Algaard's distributor was a guy he only knew as Felix. Felix owned Felix Distributing and had always arranged for Algaard's entire inventory. If Algaard was running low on something he just called Felix and whatever he needed was usually there in a day. Carol had set up the whole deal with Felix and Blaine had rarely talked to him. But now Felix was coming to Chase.

Algaard was sure Felix was some guy in an expensive suit with slick-backed black hair that probably went around with bodyguards with biceps like oak trees who broke the legs of anyone who didn't pay Felix what he was owed. Algaard spent the good part of the day watching the clock, on edge about what was going to happen when Felix and his bodyguards showed and he had to tell him he had no money. He guessed the guy would take what was left of the inventory, forcing him to close. If he wanted to sue him for what he was short he could try, but Algaard knew he had nothing more to his name. Algaard mulled it over during the day as he sipped on an open bottle he kept behind the counter, thinking about just skipping the meeting, just walking away, no, running away. But the alcohol fueled his bravado, and he decided he'd stay, at least until he saw the guys who would come with Felix to break his legs.

A few minutes before closing a little man in a Twins ball cap entered the store. He wore thick glasses in heavy black frames and had a gray goatee. His shoulders were slightly stooped like he spent the day looking at the ground. He wore what looked to be a navy blue bowling style shirt with black sleeves and khakis with tan loafers and no socks. He made his way slowly from the front of the store towards the counter in back.

"We're closing in a minute," said Algaard. "Can I help you find something?"

The man stuck out his hand. "I'm Felix."

Algaard was too shocked to move for a moment. Finally he extended his hand while he looked to the front of the store to see if he could spot anyone that had come with the man. There was no one. "Felix, right. I'm Blaine. Blaine Algaard."

Felix smiled. "You owe me some money."

Algaard shouldn't have been intimidated by the diminutive individual in front of him, the small man almost had to stand on his tiptoes to reach over the counter to shake his hand, but he was. There was something in his warbled voice, something about the way he had said that he owed him money that made Algaard think about the movie "The Godfather". He felt his mouth go dry. "Yeah, I know. Um, things have been a little slow." Algaard moved out from behind the counter. "Let me lock up and we can talk." Algaard locked the front door and shut down the lights and led Felix to the back room.

Felix looked at the boxes in the room, many empty. "You need more inventory."

"Yeah, well I know, but like I said things have been slow this year. Um, I'm wondering if it would be possible to set up some kind of credit arrangement?"

Felix could tell that Algaard had been drinking, and that he maybe wasn't well. Algaard's face was a blotchy eggshell white, with deep dark creases under his bloodshot eyes. His clothes were wrinkled and stained, and he did not look like he had shaved in a week. He walked over to look in a box that had held vodka and now returned to stand in front of Algaard. "I don't do credit."

Algaard figured this was it; he'd have to give up on the store. At least the guy hadn't brought any goons with him. He was sitting on a case of wine, bent over, watching as his shoe moved back and forth, making a pattern in the dust on the smooth concrete floor. He was about to tell Felix he could take what was left of his inventory.

"But I can do something better."

Algaard's head popped up. "What do you mean?"

Felix moved a case of whiskey so that it was in front of Algaard, brushed off the top of the box, and sat down. "How would you like to make more money than you have ever made?"

"OK, like how?"

Felix smiled and Algaard got a creepy feeling like maybe he was about to sell his soul to the devil.

"I have a client, Blaine, a client who deals in cash. Now this client, because of the nature of his business, prefers not to deal directly with financial institutions. As a result, he is willing to pay, and pay quite well, business associates that will help him distribute his cash." Felix smiled again. "Are you following me Blaine?"

Algaard may not have been the one doing the books in his business but he was smart enough to get where the conversation was going. "OK, I think so."

Felix was still grinning. "Good. So the way it works is that on a monthly basis I will send you a bill for your order, just as I have before, only now that bill will be slightly higher than in the past, let's say thirty-five percent. With that bill you will also receive a cash amount equal to the thirty-five percent plus another ten percent. Are you following?"

Algaard nodded.

"Good. So you would then include that cash in your receipts that you take to your bank. Then write me a check for the full amount of your monthly invoice as usual. Is that clear?" The little man was leaning forward, his elbows on his knees, his arms spread like he was waiting for a hug.

Algaard got it. "What if I can't sell everything I order like now?"

"That's not a problem. I will adjust your order to fit the invoice, but I will only ship you what you order."

"So, the more I order, the more I make?"

"Just like now. Of course I reserve the right to limit that amount. Don't want things to look too out of whack for your accountant now do we?"

Blaine was thinking about what Felix had said. He knew there had to be a way to make more money with what Felix was talking about but he couldn't figure it out, at least not right then. He could figure out that this was his ticket to keep the store and maybe have something more.

Felix knew he had him but he wanted to seal the deal. "Listen, I know that you've been struggling here. Why don't you just try it for a month or two and see how it works? Hell, I'll even cover your shortfall from last month."

Blaine was smiling like he hadn't smiled in a long time and was thinking he may just get into a little of his private dope stash to celebrate. He stuck out his hand. "Deal!"

It was now nearly two years later. Save Big was bringing in enough, with the help of Felix, to pay for help and a little more, like a girlfriend and a new boat. But Algaard wanted more. He had tried once to increase his order but Felix had turned him down, said Algaard didn't need tax auditors looking at his books. Algaard argued his books were fine, he had followed the plan, and there was nothing there to see. But Felix refused. Now he had called Felix again, demanding a meeting. He knew Felix had to be running the same deal with other store owners, like some kind of Mary Kay pyramid scheme. Algaard wanted more.

Chapter 21

Lane had smiled when he saw Carlisle stomp out of the Administration Building three days earlier. She looked pretty hot to him and when he realized the double meaning he laughed out loud. He had found out that she had been looking through the old files, the files that would show that he had essentially done nothing about a potential killer on campus. But he had not acted alone in that regard. Dave Walls had been head of the campus police department and his boss at the time and still was. After each abduction attempt, and the abduction of Hollister, Walls had conferred with the former president of the school, and it was decided that the reports would not be made public, shared with the Duluth police, or be made known to the students and faculty, in the event that the attacks may negatively influence the perception of the institution. Walls and Lane had both received promotions to their current positions as a result.

Lane guessed that Carlisle would want more information about the students involved in the incidents and would return to look at their files. He had alerted Walls of the possibility and Walls had taken the necessary steps to see that Carlisle would not get what she was after.

Lane was feeling good the next morning and stopped at the bakery just a block from campus on his way to work. He couldn't decide between a cream-filled chocolate éclair or a glazed donut, so he had purchased both. Lane's cholesterol was high and he had promised his doctor that he would try to control it with his diet but now he thought that maybe drugs would be a better idea as he bit into the éclair. He was driving past the Administration Building when he glanced over and recognized the car the BCA agent had driven the day before. He nearly choked on his pastry when he saw Carlisle get out, some of the cream from the éclair that he was holding dripping onto his slacks. Lane swore as he looked down at his pants, then looking up just in time to see a student crossing the street in front of him. He slammed on his brakes and the student gave him the finger. He looked back to the front of the Administration Building to see Carlisle opening the door to go inside. What the hell is she doing here?

~~~

The driver lay in bed. He was naked and on his back; the sheets pushed into a rumpled mess at the foot of the bed, hands behind his head. He had listened to the man move around the house before he left, making noises in the kitchen and in the bathroom, one time coming down the hall and standing outside the driver's door. The hallway was carpeted and quiet but the driver knew the man was there. He could hear him breathing, sense him.

~~~

The driver knew when someone was close, when someone was coming. When he was a boy he had developed a keen sense of detecting someone's presence. Long before his doorknob would turn he knew his father was coming, coming to touch him, to do hurting things to him, to beat him if he'd resist. And he had resisted at first, fought him, but eventually gave up.

The boy's father was a hunter, and in the fall after his eleventh birthday, his father announced that he was going hunting as usual but that this year he would take the boy with him. He knew what would happen in the small cabin they owned and ran to his mother, begging her not to let him go, but her meek protest was ignored. They arrived at the cabin in the afternoon, sighted their rifles, and had dinner. The boy said he was tired and going to bed, his father's eyes telling him that he would be in to see him. He lay on his back in the dark, knowing what was going to happen. He listened as the man mixed himself a drink in the kitchen, heard the ice cubes clinking against the glass, knowing his father was standing by the counter sipping, getting ready, calling up the demons that drove him.

The cabin had wood planked floors with spaces between the planks where mice and cold air got in. It was easy for the boy to hear his father coming down the hall, his hunting boots marching toward him. The old knob squeaked as he turned the handle and the door hinges gave a high-pitched cry as if they knew what was about to happen. The man stood in the door, a giant figure of black in the dim hall light, then took three steps into the room, his arm waving in the air as he searched for the string hanging from the light on the ceiling. He pulled the string, pausing momentarily as his eyes adjusted to the light, the sick, diseased eyes of a predator.

He shot his father in the chest. The man's hands went out to his side and then he fell backwards. The boy got up and walked over to where his father lay on his back, blood spreading from the center of his flannel shirt, eyes wide open but never seeing again. The boy looked down at his father with a blank stare. He did not feel happy or frightened or sad. He felt no remorse for what he had done, no sorrow at seeing his lifeless father, just a detached curiosity. He set the gun down against the side of his bed and left the cabin, walking four miles to a county road where he met two hunters that took him to their place where they called the police. The boy accompanied the police back to the cabin. He told them how his father was explaining to him how to clean the rifle when it accidently discharged. The police noticed how little emotion the boy showed in explaining what had happened but a child psychologist who examined the boy later assured them it was just shock.

~~~

The driver was feeling better. The swelling had gone down on his head and his ankle and he could walk with only a slight limp. The pain in his ankle was still there, still sharp, but it was tolerable. He would take a ride tonight. He wanted to go after the older woman at the resort. He had feared she or the other woman might be able to identify him somehow but his concern lessened daily as he healed. While he was recuperating, he imagined what he would do to her and his initial anger had now turned to a longing to put things right. But something told him it was too soon. The woman would still be leery, and he needed no more trouble now. He would wait on her. But he would be back.

While the driver recovered from the Cliffside attack, he found an ad in an online paper for a bar not far north. He Googled the bar and looked at it on Google Maps. It was outside of the town of Devon about a mile, cut out of the pines just off county road four, nothing for at least half a mile in any direction. Hard to tell from the photos, but the parking lot, although it was paved, seemed to have only one light. There was a dumpster to the side of the bar, but not much room for more than one vehicle to get around the side and get back there. Might be a good place to park.

He knew he was going out tonight no matter what. The man had been without for several weeks now, ever since Neese, and after the trouble at Cliffside he was getting crabby. It seemed to the driver that the man needed the women more often than ever, maybe more than him. He thought you were supposed to slow down when you got older but the man seemed to be going the other direction. The driver padded slowly down the hall to the kitchen and found the man had left the coffee on. The driver sipped it now, looking out at his truck in the yard through the window over the sink. Better go look at the map again.

~~~

Trask had given up trying to beat Larry into the office. He had also given up trying to think that he could dress better than his assistant. Not that Don still didn't try to dress well. He liked looking good. Liked the feeling he got when people noticed, especially women. But that was somehow changing too. He didn't seem to care as much if women looked at him now that he and Melanie were, well, serious. That thought perplexed him as he walked into his office to see Larry in a dark green gabardine designer suit with a button-down white shirt and lime-green tie and stopped momentarily in front of Stoxon's desk. He wanted to ask Larry where he got his suit, completely forgetting why he had been perplexed only a moment ago.

"Are you alright sir?" asked his assistant.

Trask shook his head as if he was waking up. "Yeah. Um, get me some coffee would you please."

Trask sat at his desk and Stoxon followed with coffee and his iPad in hand. After placing the coffee cup in front of Don, Stoxon sat in the chair facing Trask.

"I'm afraid you have a busy day sir," started Stoxon as he looked at his pad.

"Nope!"

Stoxon looked up, confused. "Nope?"

"That's what I said. It's Friday so I have decided to give all of the crooks in the state the day off."

"I see," responded Larry with hardly a smile. "Well, anyway, you'll need to be at the courthouse for the Benning hearing this morning. You may want to wear a disguise." The brother of Lavelle Benning was filing a wrongful death suit that included claims of collusion involving the Minneapolis PD and the BCA.

"Right, what else?"

"This afternoon at two the boss has called a meeting with all department heads – and that includes you."

"Christ! Friday afternoon? That could take hours. I am supposed to be at a task force meeting this afternoon."

"Sorry sir. Should I call and say that you can't make it?"

Trask thought about that. There was no way he could make a meeting at his brother's place with a Friday afternoon meeting in the Superintendent's office. And he had already told Mel. He also knew that the Superintendent suspected his task force meetings were not what he said they were. "Damn!" He tried to think of any other way to skip the meeting but came up with nothing. "No. I'll be there." He looked down to see a file lying on his desk. "What's this?"

"That is the information you requested on abductions and rapes in northern Minnesota."

Trask opened the file. "Get me a map of northern Minnesota – and Wisconsin."

Chapter 22

Carlisle's jeans seemed a little snug. She looked at herself in the mirror, turning from side to side as if that would change anything, and then scrunched her lips together. She ran her thumbs inside the waistband but that didn't seem to help either. She knew the jeans weren't new so she didn't think she could blame shrinkage from the wash for their tighter fit. Something bad was happening.

Carlisle ran every other day, along the lake when the weather allowed, but many mornings ended up at the YMCA because it opened early and it was never too crowded. She also liked the fact that she could use some of the weight equipment there on days when she didn't run. She had never run a marathon, or a shorter race for that matter, running satisfied her need to do something physical. As she buttoned her blouse, she thought about the bag of chips she had devoured at the office the day before.

Danny Carlisle walked in the Registrar's office and was greeted by a different female student than the one who had been there the day before, this one with no make-up on a sleepy face and blonde hair hastily balled on top of her head. She identified herself and asked for Michelle Jones as she had done before.

The student blinked twice, staring at Carlisle like she had spoken a foreign language. Danny was about to repeat her request to see Jones when something worked its way up from the memory of the sleepy student.

"Oh yeah, Agent Carlisle. OK, I'm supposed to take you to the Records Room."

The girl stood and came out from behind her panel, walked past Carlisle, and out the door. Carlisle grabbed the edge of the closing door, and hustled to keep up with the girl. They went down two flights of stairs to a hall lined with smooth concrete walls, painted a shiny gray, and a floor of worn brown linoleum. The women turned left, walking past two opposing oak doors to a second set. The hallway was poorly lit, the air cool and damp, almost like they were in a cave. The girl stopped and produced a key from her front jeans pocket, opening the door and flipping the switch on the wall to the right. The two ceiling lights didn't help a great deal, their glass globes yellowed and lined with dead bugs. There were no windows. Several rows of tan metal shelving ran the width of the room, three rows of shelves on each, each shelf stacked with blue and white bankers boxes, many of the boxes sagging and yellowed with age. The shelves reached nearly to the ceiling.

"Um, like I've only been in here once, so I guess you need to look at what is written on the outside of the boxes to see what's inside."

There was a corridor running against the wall to their left and one on the other side of the shelves against the far wall. Carlisle tried to do a quick estimate of how many boxes there were but gave up, math never being her strong suit.

"OK, where should I look at the files?"

The girl had been holding the door open and now looked behind it. "There's a desk behind the door," she replied.

Carlisle tried to see around the girl but there wasn't enough room.

"OK, so here's the key," she said as she gave the key to Danny. "Just bring it back when you're done." With that she squeezed by Carlisle and left.

Danny held the door open and watched the girl walk down the hall and disappear up the stairs. Guess I'm not going to get too many clues as to what's in here. She checked to see that the door would open if she let it close and then moved all the way in. She took a deep breath.

The room had that musty smell like her grandma's basement, one that permeated her clothes when she had to sleep there when they visited, not a smell she liked. It was cool in the room too, with the same damp feeling there was in her grandma's basement, and she wished she had brought a sweater or jacket. She used her phone's light to get a better view, sweeping the floor and corners of the ceiling, thinking she would see the same bugs and spider webs that had lived in her grandmother's basement. And then there were the sounds. She remembered lying awake in bed, covers pulled to her chin, listening to the sound of people walking above her. There were boards that creaked and the sound of the flushing toilet would always startle her before the pipes began to rattle and sing. This place was the opposite. There were no sounds here at all. And she thought that was probably scarier than the creaking boards and poor plumbing.

She put her purse and notebook on the desk and moved to the first shelf. She shined her light on the box and saw the content of the box was labeled on the side facing her. Carlisle had decided to start with those attending UMD at the time of the Hollister abduction. Her plan was to look at the photos of the male students in attendance at the time, which would have been roughly 5,000, including graduate students. It was going to be a job.

In the third row she found her starting place, records for students entering the school in 2008. They would have been juniors in 2011. She had asked about admission records for

2007 through 2012, and those were on the computer, but unfortunately, there were no images with those records, that hadn't started until 2013. The admission records with images were in the boxes she now faced. Hopefully the killer was in here somewhere. Carlisle dragged the box back to the desk, set it on the floor, used her hand to wipe off the cracked green vinyl seat of the chair by the desk, wiped her hand on the side of her leg, and sat. She lifted off the top of the box and pulled the first section of papers from the box.

There were five or six sheets of paper on each student – application form, SAT and ACT test results, transcripts, and copies of student ID's and drivers licenses, as well as acceptance letters. Carlisle was happy to see the records appeared to be alphabetized as she looked at the first student record. The first student was a female as was the second. The third, Bradley Aalman, was a freshman from Duluth. She was glad to find a color image was from a drivers license that also revealed hair and eye color, height, and weight. Aalman was a blonde and she moved on to the next student.

It was here she discovered she had two problems. James Aakley was a junior, a transfer student. The records would not all be freshmen. And then she looked at Aakley's picture. He looked older – because he was. Kids changed their appearances as they went through school, some dramatically, depending on their growth spurts. Crap! There could be 2000 boys with black hair in the 2008 class. She stared at the image of Aakley, thinking her wild goose chase had just gotten a lot wilder, when she noticed that Aakley's picture was from a student ID he had submitted from Hibbing Junior College. It showed him listed as a second-year student. What if UMD had a student directory with photos from student ID's?

She picked up her phone to call upstairs and saw she had no reception. She decided she was happy to get out of the room anyway, maybe grab a sweater and something to snack on if she had to come back. She picked up her purse and was putting her phone away when she was distracted by a sound. Someone was trying to open the door.

~~~

Lane was on the phone to Walls immediately after Carlisle entered the Administration Building. Walls didn't answer so Lane left a message for him to call, saying it was an emergency. He wiped the cream off of his trousers as best he could with a napkin but he knew he'd have a stain on his crotch that would look like he peed in his pants. He finished the donut as he waited for Walls' call, watching the Administration Building for Carlisle for fifteen minutes, finally deciding that he would go home and change. He just started his car when Walls called.

"This had better be good news. I'm trying to entertain a potential heavyweight donor here."

"We got big trouble. The BCA agent is back."

"What do you mean she's back?"

"Just what I said. I am sitting outside of the Administration Building and I just saw her go inside."

"I stonewalled her. There's no way she's getting to look at those records."

"Then what the hell is she doing here again? What if she got a warrant or something?"

Walls thought Lane was an idiot, but now he had planted a small seed of doubt in Walls' mind. "Sit tight. I will call you right back."

It was another fifteen minutes and Lane was thinking he could have been home, changed his pants, and been back again, when Walls called.

"This is bad Lane. Somehow she got the chancellor to OK her looking at the files. She's in the Records Room now."

"Fuck!" Lane had his window down and a female student walking by heard his exclamation and gave him the finger.

"Fucked is more like it. You and I are toast if she finds anything out. You need to take care of this Lane."

"What do you mean, 'take care of it'?"

"Just make sure that BCA agent does not find out anything more than you've already let her find out."

"And how am I supposed to do that?"

"I don't care, that's up to you. But if you don't do something, we could both be sitting in a prison somewhere. Do you get that?"

"Yeah, I got it," replied Lane in an almost dejected tone.

"Don't screw up. You and I got a good thing going here."

Lane was still holding his phone to his ear after Walls disconnected. He slowly brought the phone down and thought about what he needed to do. Did Walls want him to kill her? He thought about it some more and couldn't think of any other way to keep her from finding out any more. He had never killed someone, but now he had no choice. He unlocked the glove compartment and removed the pistol he stored there. He held the gun in his hand for a moment, looking at it, thinking about what he was going to do, what he had to do. He hadn't brought his briefcase home with him the night before and didn't want to carry the gun under his belt with his knit UMD Security sport shirt pulled out. It just wouldn't look good. He picked up the empty donut bag on the passenger seat and put the gun inside.

Chapter 23

By the time Don marked the location of the third abduction on the map he was tired of it. Trask liked to be doing things. He wanted to be chasing down leads, or hunting bad guys, or fishing. He did not like being in the office and he had no patience for the never-ending paperwork that came his way. He hated doing employee reviews, and had finally resolved that by having his employees fill out their own reviews, which he signed. But he didn't even like the type of investigative work he was doing now, and which was a major part of his agents' lives. He just couldn't stay focused on it.

"Larry!"

Stoxon bounded in to Trask's office with his pad in hand. "You rang?"

"Yeah, listen, I need you to do something for me." Trask told him what he wanted done, handed him the files and the map, and then called Jenkins.

"Hey, we got a change of plans for the weekend."

"OK, like what?"

"I don't know, but unless you want to drive north late on Friday, which will be a major traffic pain, or early on Saturday, also a traffic pain, I think that the weekend north is off. I got an afternoon meeting with the boss that I am sure will run into the evening."

Jenkins didn't feel that bad. She wasn't crazy about fishing, although she didn't mind doing it if they were biting, she'd just as soon sit in the boat with a cocktail and read a book while Don fished. Besides, after the other evening when he had opened up and she had almost invited him to stay, she thought that maybe it was time. "That's OK. Why don't you just come here after your meeting and then on Saturday morning we'll just do stupid tourist stuff? Maybe take a paddle boat ride on the river?"

"Ah Mel, you know those boat rides make me crazy when I've got to be on the water and I can't fish."

"Hello, earth to Trask. Did you hear what I said?"

Don was perplexed, which was pretty much how he viewed most of his adult life when it came to trying to understand women. "Um, yeah you said come over tonight for dinner and then on Saturday morning we'd...Oh. OH!"

"It truly amazes me how someone who is supposed to be such an astute detective, leading the largest investigative agency in the state, can totally miss clues that are right in front of his nose."

Trask smiled. "Sometimes it amazes me too."

Jenkins pulled her phone from her ear and looked at it. Humility was not a word used to describe Don Trask – by anyone including her. "Uh, are you OK?"

He smiled again. "I think I'm getting there. I'll call you when I'm on my way."

Don called his brother to tell him he wouldn't be there for the weekend.

Dave had known his brother to drive all night just so he could make the early morning bite. "You OK?"

"Why does everyone keep asking me that? I may have something on the abduction locations later today but it will probably be Monday, no Tuesday. You can call me this weekend if you're not catching anything and need a few tips."

"You been drinking breakfast again?"

"See you."

~~~

"Hello? Is someone there?" Carlisle stared at the door. The rattling of the doorknob stopped but there was no answer to Carlisle's call. She thought maybe she was hearing things. "Damn, now I'm spooking myself." She picked up her purse and notebook and stood, deciding to leave the file box in case she would have to come back. She walked to the door and pulled it open.

Lane filled her vision. He was holding a donut bag. He looked warm, perspiration on his forehead, stains evident under his armpits.

"Mr. Lane. What are you doing here?"

Lane's eyes narrowed. He didn't like this woman. She thought she was too smart for him. "That's Director Lane."

Lane seemed tense to Carlisle. She could see him squeezing the rolled up top of the donut bag in his hand. "Oh, right, Director Lane. Did you bring me a donut?"

Lane glanced down at the bag, like he was thinking about whether he was going to offer the agent a donut. She had stepped all the way into the hall and the door shut behind her. Lane knew the door locked automatically, and he also knew how quiet it was inside the room when the door was shut, almost soundproof. Lane had a key for the room as he did for most of the rooms on campus. Getting back in would not be a problem. He could force her at gunpoint into the Records Room and shoot her there. But then what? If he killed her here, how would he get rid of the body? And her car? No, better wait. He looked back up at her.

"Agent Carlisle?" It was the girl who had showed Carlisle into the Records Room. "There's a call for you upstairs."

The girl stood in the hallway at the bottom of the steps waiting for a response. Carlisle turned back to Lane and cupped her hand to her mouth. "You may want to think about changing your pants before you go into the office, Director," she said in a hushed tone and then turned and walked toward where the girl stood waiting.

Lane's face burned red as he watched her go.

~~~

"Hello, this is Agent Carlisle."

"My, don't you sound official," replied Hillary Thomas. "How are they treating you there?"

Carlisle looked around the registrar's office to see the girl who brought her up looking at her as well as Michelle Jones peering around the corner of her office door. "Just like my mama's cookies."

Thomas laughed. Carlisle's mother had brought them cookies nearly every week they had roomed together at the academy. Only trouble was that Carlisle's mother was an awful cook, and her cookies, when they weren't covered in icing thick enough to make you ill, were like eating ground cardboard. "That's nice. Say, I couldn't get you on your cell. I remembered you said you might be at the school so I thought I'd try you there. Hope that's OK?"

"More than OK. I was in a cold musty dungeon they call the Records Room and there's no reception." Carlisle could see Jones still hanging out her door and gave her a big smile. Jones skittered back in her office.

"Sounds fun. Anyway, I took a quick look at the records for abductions around the time that you were looking again. Like I said before there were none on campus but I did find one in the area. I also found two missing person's cases, both women, but both were after the Hollister murder."

"Any suspects or witnesses?" she asked as she sat.

"Afraid not. The woman who was abducted, or I should say almost abducted, was grabbed by a guy wearing a ski mask. She said he was kind of tall and skinny. He tried to pull her into his truck but she fought him off. No witnesses on the missing women."

"What kind of truck?"

"Um, don't know. Let's see, she said it was dark, maybe black, and a pickup with a cab."

"Hmm, could be the same guy. Mind if I look at the files?"

"Mi files es su files."

"Gracias. I'll call you before I show. Thanks for calling."

Danny was sitting at the vacant cubicle across from the receptionist while she talked. "Excuse me. Do you get a new student ID every year?"

The girl looked up from her phone. "Yup. Kind of a pain."

"Oh, why's that?"

"You got to go get your picture taken and then they make you pay ten dollars. My God, don't they get enough of my money?"

"So, is there like a directory of all of the student ID's each year?"

The girl had gone back to whatever was so interesting on her phone. "Yup."

"And can I use this computer to look at it?"

"Umm, I guess so." She walked over to Carlisle who slid away from the computer on the desk in front of her so the girl could access the keyboard.

Carlisle peeked around the partition behind her to see that Jones didn't come out of her office as the girl worked.

"OK, like here it is. You can see the files for each year. Just click on the year you want and then on the name. You can search for a name if you need to." She walked back to her desk, sat down, and returned to her phone.

Danny found the file for 2008 and clicked on it. She typed 'Sarah Hollister' into the search bar and pressed enter. Carlisle panicked. All it returned was Hollister's name, birth date, and current year at school. There was no picture. She felt crushed. She did not want to go back to the Records Room. Maybe she could just call Trask with what she had and see if he really wanted her to do it. For all she knew it could take her weeks.

As she leaned back in her chair to consider her options, she inadvertently moved the cursor over Hollister's name. The name became highlighted. Carlisle sat back up and clicked on it. There she was in color. Now to find her killer.

~~~

The work was tedious. By noon she had only two potential matches and a growling stomach. The receptionist had left a few minutes earlier without a word and Carlisle was about to get up and go find something to eat when a shadow appeared at her shoulder.

"Are you finding what you need?" asked Jones.

Carlisle stood and stretched. "Slow going. Afraid I'm going to be here for a while."

"I thought you would be working in the Records Room?"

"Yeah, and I may have to go back there, but this is a better place to start."

Jones frowned. "How long do you expect to take? This is quite disrupting."

Carlisle had only seen two other people besides the receptionist working in the office that had at least eight workstations. "OK. Sorry to put you out, but like I said this might take a while."

Jones looked at the screen on the computer and then turned and walked back to her office. She picked up her phone and dialed Walls' number.

Chapter 24

Larry finished with Don's mapping project and laid it on his boss's desk. Trask thanked him, and was about to open the folder when Stoxon said, "I wouldn't do that sir. You need to get going to your meeting or you will be late."

Trask looked at the clock that hung on the wall to his right and snorted. He stuffed the folder in his briefcase, stood, and started to exit his office. "OK, see you Monday."

"That will be a delight for both of us I am sure."

Trask had passed Stoxon but now stopped and looked back at him. Stoxon smiled. Trask got a puzzled look on his face before continuing his exit. He could trade sarcasm with the best of them but he just couldn't figure Stoxon out. By the time he reached his car he had forgotten about Stoxon and was thinking about the meeting with the Superintendent. Don hated these meetings with all of his being, and he didn't feel much better about the man himself, who Trask considered nothing much more than a political backstabbing opportunist.

Meetings with his boss invariably put him in a sour mood, one that could linger for hours if not days, making him wish he had a drink – or three. But as Trask parked and then walked up the steps to the Department of Public Safety building where his supervisor had his office, he felt something unusual. There wasn't the feeling of impending gloom that usually accompanied him to this office, he actually felt happy. He entered the office to find that he was the last to arrive as usual, found the remaining chair, and said, "Sorry I'm late sir," with a smile.

This confused the Superintendent greatly. Trask never apologized and he certainly had never seen the man with a smile before. "Are you OK Trask?"

Don sat back and folded his legs. He was thinking about tonight. He was thinking about Melanie Jenkins. He was thinking about a naked Melanie Jenkins. "Excellent sir. Thank you for asking."

~~~

Walls was having lunch in the dining room of Big Bear Lodge in eastern Ontario when Jones called. He was sitting next to the vice president of Latmore Industries, Eli Blankenship. Walls had invited Blankenship on the trip after discovering that Blankenship loved to fish at about the same time he discovered Blankenship would be the one to make the recommendation to the board of Latmore Industries on a possible donation to UMD. It was not until the flight to the lodge that Walls discovered how much Blankenship loved to talk.

It was now the fourth day of a planned five-day trip. For the first three days of the trip the wind had howled out of the northwest bringing cold temperatures and unfishable conditions. Today the wind had switched to the south, and the temperatures had climbed back to normal levels. Unfortunately, with the change also came thunderstorms, keeping all boats on shore for the fourth day in a row.

Walls chit-chatted with donors and potential donors on the phone and at events set up by his staff, not because he wanted to, but because it was part of his job, a job he only tolerated because it was his ticket to a higher-paying position, most likely at some other school. But now he was seriously questioning if he could hold out for another day of having to entertain Blankenship and have him spout off about every topic under the sun. He thanked God he didn't have to share a cabin with the man.

Walls excused himself from the table when Jones' call came in and walked into the adjoining room. He listened to her report, thanked her for the information, and then turned back to the dining room where he could see Blankenship boring the man next to him. Walls walked back to where he had been seated, told Blankenship he had to take care of some business, and smiled at the man who was now regretting his choice of a seat next to Blankenship.

Walls slipped on his rain jacket, put the hood up, and ran from the main lodge to his cabin. He had no problem running the short distance, he was in good shape for a man of forty-five. He took advantage of his position at UMD to spend a good deal of time using the pool and other health facilities, often during the workday. He had also used his position to take advantage of a few coeds, something that lead to his divorce.

Walls hung his jacket on the wooden peg just inside the door of his cabin and dialed Lane.

"Lane."

"She's into the directories now."

"Aw, shit."

"Yeah. Why haven't you taken care of her yet?"

Lane thought about his confrontation with Carlisle outside the Records Room. "The time hasn't been right yet."

Walls shook his head. The guy was an idiot. "This needs to be done. I'd do it myself but I'm stuck here for at least another two days, and with this weather, I may not get back even then."

"Yeah, yeah. I've already got it figured out. I'm going to go over to her place and take care of it this weekend. It'll look like a robbery that she tried to break up."

Walls was sure Lane would screw this up some way, but he couldn't be there, and he didn't really care if Lane screwed it up and Carlisle caught him. Unless he talked. "Damn it Lane. Don't screw this up!"

"Relax. I got this."

Lane hung up just as Carlisle was getting in her car to go find some lunch. He hated her but she sure looked good in those jeans. Maybe have a little fun with her before I kill her to show her she's not so smart. He smiled. He had decided he would take care of her tonight.

Chapter 25

The driver cruised past the Passer By Bar about a mile east of Big Lake just before sunset. The bar near Devon had been closed for remodeling so he had gone on to his second choice. The shadows from the tall pines lining the road in front of the bar had crawled over it nearly two hours earlier, and the yard light in the parking lot was already attracting bugs. He slowed as he passed, like he was maybe thinking about turning in to the lot, checking out the bar. There were six vehicles parked in the lot in front of the building, and two on the south side that he guessed were employees. Arborvitae had grown unchecked in front of the bar window facing the street, the bottoms of the trees eaten away by deer, the remaining upper branches effectively blocking any view of the road.

The bar's redwood-stained siding was faded and peeling, the shingles drooping and moss-covered. A lighted outdoor sign that no longer lit showed the name of the bar and announced 'Happy Hour' just below. Weeds had found homes in the cracks in the surface of the parking lot as well as around the base of the building. Two pressure treated pine steps bowed with age led to the aluminum-clad red door in front.

The driver decided not to go in; there were too many people. Instead he did a U-turn after he passed the bar and parked roughly a block down the road. He pulled off the blacktop onto the gravel; barely able to get all four wheels off as steep ditches with visible water lined either side of the road. He stopped for a moment and looked out his passenger window, the truck tilted on the shoulder enough so he could see into the ditch. Then he pushed open his door with his foot, climbed out, and walked on the road to the back of his vehicle. He was only an inch or two off the gravel but he didn't dare drive any further off. Concerned that the gravel under the wheels nearest the ditch might give way, as well as someone coming along in the dark and clipping him, he climbed back in the truck and pulled back on the road. He headed back towards the bar. He slowed again just before he got there and this time saw there was space for his truck on the side of the building opposite the two vehicles he had seen.

Pulling in front of the building, he backed around in a U-turn so that he was on the side of the building and facing the road. He turned off the truck and sat looking around. There was good and bad about this place. There were no windows or doors on this side of the bar and the dumpster was on the opposite side so there was no real need for anyone to come over here. And there was just enough space for him to park and fully open his doors on either side, the building on one side and thick brush and forest on the other. He thought the brush grew up close to the building in back as he looked in his rearview mirror, maybe only enough room for someone to walk around the corner, but it was hard to see in the fading light and he would have to check that out. That was all good.

What he didn't like was that he couldn't see much in front and nothing in back, or on the other side. He could catch headlights of vehicles as they came and went, and he'd be able to see them if they entered or left the lot from the north, but that was about it. If he really wanted a good look at what was happening, he'd need to be on the southeast corner of the lot in front where it met the road. The driver got out of his truck and walked to the edge of the building in front, peering around the arborvitae, trying to get a look at the far corner of the lot. There were two trucks blocking his vision, and he was about to step out and walk around them, when he heard talking and two couples came walking out of the bar. He ducked behind the corner. The two couples got in an old Chevy Suburban and backed out of the lot onto the road before heading south.

The driver hoped he may be able to get around the back of the building and move around the other side without crossing in front of the bar and headed that way. He had almost been right. The brush had grown close to the corner of the building behind where he had parked, only it wasn't really brush, at least it wasn't at one time. He guessed that someone had planted a few shrubs next to the building's northwest corner in back at the same time as the arborvitaes, but these shrubs hadn't been appealing to the deer and so had grown thick, now just a foot or two from the encroaching forest in back.

He turned sideways and slid between the shrubs and the brush and stopped. There was a small window on this side, up high, and a door close to the far corner. The dumpster was pushed up against the brush. The gravel angled from where he was to the spot where the dumpster stood about twenty feet behind and forty feet away from the corner of the bar. The driver moved slowly along the building until he was next to the door. He could hear music, country music. He never liked country music, thinking it was something that belonged in the south, and frowned.

There was a small glass pane in the door, about eye-level for someone his height if he was inside, hazed over, and a light to the side of the door on the building. He moved past the steps leading up to the door, looked around the side of the building where all he could see was the two vehicles he had noted there before; there were no windows on this side of the building either. He memorized what kind of vehicles they were so he could match the person getting into each vehicle with a vehicle after the bar closed. Making a dash for the woods that looked like they were about to overtake the lot at any moment, he hustled along them until he was only a few feet from the road. He backed through the brush and stood under a misplaced box elder tree. He was breathing hard from the short sprint, his ankle aching. An image of Julie Powers came into his mind and he cursed the woman under his breath.

About the only light now came from the yard light in front of the bar and one over the front door that he hadn't noticed earlier. He could see the front and side of the bar opposite where he parked. The vehicles parked in front of the bar somewhat obscured his vision of anyone coming or going but he didn't really care about that. The two vehicles parked on the side of the bar were at an angle to it, and they would block most of his vision of anyone who exited in the back and came around the corner to get their vehicle. That could be an issue. At that moment he also slapped himself hard on the back of the neck. The mosquitoes were coming out in force and they would get worse. That could also be an issue but bug spray should take care of that.

He watched from that location for another fifteen minutes until the bugs became unbearable and ran from his hiding place, around the back of the building, and back to his truck. He slapped himself a few times more as he sat in the cab, scratching bites on his arms and legs, grimacing at the pain in his ankle. It was cooling off now, and he cracked his window, enough so he could cool off from his sprint and not let too many bugs in. He reached into the cooler behind the passenger seat and pulled out a Dr. Pepper. Now he would wait.

An hour later there were only two vehicles left in the lot. The driver needed to see who was working, what they looked like. This was the tricky part as far as he was concerned. Most bars made you walk a long distance to get to the bar once you entered. That would be the time someone might look, might see him, and might have enough of a memory to tell the cops. The driver walked to the front of the bar and pushed the door open, taking in the inside as he entered. There were two couples in a booth to his left and a man behind the bar. He walked straight to the bar so he was sitting with his back to the booth. The bartender, a man with stringy long hair and a wrinkled weathered face, asked what he'd like to drink. The driver ordered a tap beer, Miller, as he looked down at the bar, his ball cap pulled low over his head. He was trying to figure out if the bartender was the only employee working, despite the two vehicles on the side of the building he thought should be employee vehicles, when a swinging door at the end of the bar opened and a woman walked through.

She was a strawberry blonde, with long straight hair pulled back in a ponytail. She wore khaki shorts and a yellow Passer By Bar t-shirt, the logo on front stretched over her ample breasts. She was short, under five and a half feet, but well-proportioned and well-rounded in back as he watched her walk to the booth with a tray carrying chips and salsa. She turned away from the table and he turned his attention back to his beer. She would do. The bartender was older, sixty at least, tall and boney, almost like he starved himself. The driver could see he had a limp as he moved behind the bar tidying up, leaning on the bar from time to time to rest. The driver watched as the bartender moved to the opposite end of the bar and then finished his beer in a gulp, dropped a ten on the counter, leaving before the bartender could get back to him and ask if he wanted another.

The two vehicles remained in front of the bar at closing time, but they were gone minutes after his watch said it was one. Now the driver started his own truck but left the headlights off. He pulled out of the lot, but he did not go far, backing into a gravel drive that was almost directly across from the bar. It was almost impossible to see where he was going as he backed up, forcing him to hang out his window, his left hand with the light from his phone shining on the ground, branches slapping him as he slowly maneuvered down the driveway.

He had noticed the driveway when he drove by earlier and considered using it as his observation point, but decided against it in case whoever lived down the drive came or went. The driveway was grown over, and there had been no activity on it in the time he had been there, so he felt secure parking there for a short time. From this vantage point he could see down the side of the building where the two vehicles were parked, but could really only see the dark shadows where they blocked what little light there was from the front lot and the faint light from the door in back. Forty minutes later he couldn't understand what he was seeing.

It looked like two lights came out from around the back of the building, one stopping, and the other moving away towards the woods. The light that had moved towards the woods stopped and then the driver heard a bang. That light returned to where the other one waited and they both moved to the vehicles, one higher than the other, bobbing slightly up and down. The lights seemed to go into the vehicles and then disappeared. He was trying to figure out what he had witnessed when the cars both started and their lights came on. Later he realized it had been the two employees holding flashlights, probably lights from their phones, one taking the trash to the dumpster before they walked to their vehicles. He watched as the car closest to him backed away from the building so it was facing the road and then driving out, the second doing the same immediately after. The first car went north, the second south. He now knew which car was the girl's and how he would take her. The driver finished his Dr. Pepper and tossed it on the floor in the back seat. He'd be back tomorrow.

Chapter 26

Danny Carlisle's apartment was in a newer complex west of campus. There were two buildings in the complex, three stories high, with an area cleared for two more. The buildings were L-shaped, the L's in opposite directions, facing each other, creating a large courtyard in the center of the two buildings. Her apartment was on the second floor of the building closest to the entrance to the complex and faced a vacant lot.

Lane had surveilled her apartment Friday afternoon after he saw Carlisle return to the Administration Building. He parked in the lot on the south side of the complex, walked through the courtyard, and hung around in the cramped security entry that housed mailboxes for the residents. Carlisle's name was on the box for apartment 206. Lane loitered, and even became slightly nervous when he recognized the faces of a couple of students thinking they might remember him, eventually grabbing the security door before it shut and sneaking in. He went up the stairs to his left and opened the door.

The door opened into a hallway that went in either direction. He walked down a sort distance to find apartment 210 and then 211 opposite. He turned and went in the opposite direction, eventually stopping in front of 206. Lane looked at the apartment door and then up and down the hall. He was alone and tempted to see if he could work the lock. He tried the doorknob, thinking that it might be fun to be in this woman's apartment, and he could feel himself get a little jolt of sexual excitement. The handle wouldn't move and he backed away. Lane thought about how he had gotten in and where this apartment would be on the outside of the building. He walked to the end of the hall, standing between the doors for apartments 201 and 202, and looked out a floor to ceiling window studying the view.

He exited the building and walked around the outside of the building until he was sure he had the same view as he had when he stood between 201 and 202. He looked up behind him to see the window, and then walked around the corner of the building counting off the apartments as he went, until he was standing below Carlisle's. She had a balcony like the rest of the second and third story apartments. Her's had two black mesh-covered patio chairs, a small glass-top table between, and a clay pot of flowers in the corner. The sliding glass door leading onto the balcony had its beige curtains drawn. The balcony faced an open lot that Lane guessed was ready for another building at some time soon.

He walked back to where he parked and got in his car. There was a long line of parking garages going off to the north and Lane figured that Carlisle probably had one but had no way of being certain. Hard to tell if she was or wasn't here by looking for her car. He started his car and drove to the edge of the lot and stopped. From this spot he had a good view of her apartment balcony. It would be easy to see when the lights came on in her apartment.

He had already decided how he would get in – it was simple. He would buzz her apartment saying he had information for her. She was bound to let him in. And then he thought about it some more. He couldn't just show up. She wasn't stupid. She'd want to know how he knew where she lived. Lane leaned back in his seat, momentarily dejected, pondering. He had to have a reason to go to her place....or maybe he didn't? He'd get her to come to him. Say he had a file she needed to see, one he couldn't show her on campus. Arrange a meeting at some place where it would just be the two of them, like up at Rocky Point. But he'd want to be sure she was home when he called, make sure she was alone.

Lane decided to think about it some more but he was getting excited about this now. He had thought he would wait until Saturday night but now he was getting anxious. Maybe tonight? He would come back in the evening and watch anyway. He wouldn't mind looking at her some more. He could decide then.

~~~

By three-thirty Carlisle had two more possible candidates, and still more to look at. She glanced at the clock on the wall, shut down her computer and stood to leave. She went to Jones' office, leaned in, and told her she was leaving but would be back Monday morning. She exited the building, drove out of the lot, and made her way to 35W south. As she accelerated down the exit ramp, she plugged in a CD of greatest hits by Queen. Tonight she and her sister would go out to dinner in St. Paul and then attend the Queen concert at the Xcel Energy Center. Tomorrow would be spent with her mother and her sister's family. Bohemian Rhapsody came on and she turned up the volume.

~~~

Lane thought he might have the wrong apartment for a while, going so far as to sneak into the building again, but staying on the first floor this time. He walked to the end of the hall where he could see out the window to the lot where he parked and then looked at the apartment number on that side. It was 102. 202 would be above it and two balconies down would be 206. He had the right one. It was midnight now and he was steaming, pacing around his car like a junkie waiting for his dealer to show. He'd get back in the car for a while but then would be out walking. As it passed one the pacing had stopped. He was leaning on his car until he finally got back in. Now he was more tired than upset that Carlisle hadn't shown. He leaned back in his seat and could feel his heavy eyelids dropping before he forced them open. He took one more look at the dark apartment. Tomorrow bitch! He started his car and spun his tires as he left.

~~~

Rain moved in on a strong northeast wind Saturday evening. The waves rolled in to shore on Superior like they were angry, trying to break down the barriers man had built to keep them at bay, exploding as they hit the breakers. The driver slowed as he passed the bar at midnight, his wipers at full speed, opening his window as he tried to get a look, squinting as the rain pelted his face. There were half a dozen vehicles in the lot, two that he thought he remembered from the previous night. He rolled up his window and wiped the rain from his face with his hand. Shit. There were three vehicles parked to the side of the bar but he couldn't tell if her car was one of them. You never knew the work schedules and now he was wondering if there were three people working tonight. Shit.

He was thinking as he drove that the weather would be a help to him, make it easier to take the blonde, but now it was just a pain. The driver did a U-turn where he had the day before and then drove back. He took a chance on the drive across from the bar and backed in, his head hanging out the window trying to see into the impossible darkness behind him, nearly going off the side in the process. A wet birch branch slapped him in the face and nearly knocked off his cap as he felt his back tire dip and he stepped on the brake. He pulled ahead slightly, cranked his wheels to the left and moved cautiously backwards again until he felt he was well hidden. He rolled up the window, shut down the engine, and then wiped his face with the front of his shirt. He pulled a Dr. Pepper out of the cooler on the floor in back and popped the top, savoring the bubbly sweetness. In the next ten minutes one vehicle left but he wasn't really concerned about that. He had to know if she was here.

The driver set his half-empty can on the dash, made sure his overhead light was off so he wouldn't be seen when he opened his door, and stepped out. The rain had let up some, but it seemed like it was colder, and the driver wished he had brought a rain jacket. He dashed across the road and moved along the side of the lot to where the three vehicles were nosed up to the building side by side. They were only dark shadows, the two vehicles parked farthest from the road completely engulfed in the darkness, the light from the front of the lot blocked by what was some kind of large pickup that had not been there the night before. Rain ran off the bill of his cap obscuring his vision even more. He'd need a closer look.

He reached into his front pocket and removed his phone as he crossed the lot to the back of the vehicles. He thought about putting on the flashlight but decided the light from activating his screen would be enough. He put out his left hand until he felt the back of the vehicle while at the same time he pressed his right forefinger to the back of the phone, holding it in front of him, and then rotating it between the vehicles. It was enough. The car the blonde had driven the night before was not here. He hurried away and back to his truck.

The driver tossed his soaked cap on the passenger seat and wiped the rain from his face with his hand. His finger lingered on a bump on his right cheek near his sideburn. He scratched at it and he knew that it was bleeding. The bump had shown up nearly a year ago, red and dark. He had used a razor to shave it off but it grew back, bigger than before. Now his hand seemed to go unconsciously to it, his fingertip feeling the rough surface. He had looked up types of skin cancer on the Internet and he didn't see any that looked like his bump, but it concerned him. He had an uncle who had lost half his nose to skin cancer surgery and still died.

His shirt was wet; especially his shoulders and back, and he hugged himself trying to fight off the chill. He looked at the temperature control on the dash and slid the knob to red, starting the truck immediately after. His truck was not loud but he did not want to attract any attention, deciding he would run the engine only long enough to warm the cab. He guessed those in the bar would hold out until closing or close to it, still an hour away. He held his palms up to the vents on either side of the steering wheel, feeling a shiver as he waited for the heat to kick in.

He was getting chilled, sniffling, thinking he should just go when the heat came on and he decided to wait again. The rain continued to lessen and he thought it was possible that the blonde had driven another vehicle. It would also be good to know if there were more people working on Saturday nights. He let his motor run until a quarter to one. Twenty minutes later he watched the patrons exit the bar as a group. They stood on the porch momentarily, looking like ghouls in the shadows, and then ran for their vehicles in the rain like some dark creature had come up behind them. They ran with their heads down, some with the hoods of their jackets held in place below their chins with their hands, others simply shielding their faces with their hands. All went to the vehicles in front except a large man who took off around the side of the building. Headlights came on, the rain silver streaks in front of them, and the vehicles began to leave. The driver heard the roar of an engine through the window he kept cracked so his windshield wouldn't fog up, much louder than the others, and saw the big pickup back away from the side of the building.

Only the two vehicles remained on the side of the bar as the night before and the driver reconsidered his options. He was certain he could make out the drivers of the vehicles with the light from the parking lot, even with the rain, and if she was one he could still take her tonight. He knew in the back of his mind that it was too soon, too risky, but he had become anxious. It had been a long time since the last. The driver reached behind the passenger seat and grabbed the stun stick. He tested it before he left so he knew it was charged. He stroked it feeling the smooth cool surface, like it was an obedient pet, and returned it to its place. He badly wanted to use it.

Just before two he picked up lights bouncing through the dark and soon the headlights of the vehicles shined on the faded siding of the bar. The vehicle closest to the road backed up first, the second as soon as the first had pulled away. The first vehicle was a silver sedan, with four doors, and a tattered Minnesota Vikings flag on the antennae. As it passed under the light the driver could see a gray-haired man drove it - the bartender from last night. He turned north. The driver turned his attention to the second vehicle, a small pickup, dark blue or black, he couldn't tell exactly. The driver reached for his ignition, ready to turn the key so he could follow, as the truck approached the umbrella of light cast by the yard light. The headlights of the truck flashed over the driver's truck. The driver held his damp cap in front of his face and peered over it. As the truck passed under the yard light, the driver could see it was not the blonde. The bar was closed on Sundays. He would have to come back on Monday.

Chapter 27

Blaine Algaard was three grades behind Randy Palmer in high school. Palmer was the stud at school, a three-sport star with the hottest cheerleader as his girlfriend. Palmer never knew Algaard, or knew of him, but Algaard knew of Palmer. It was hard not to know of him. He put on a show walking down the hall in his heavily pinned letter jacket, his girlfriend hanging on his arm. He also put on a show when he was on the football field or basketball court although the teams did not do well as there was little athletic ability or size in his teammates. Still, Palmer was single-handedly able to keep many basketball games close, and even engineered a few upsets on the court. He was a local hero and parents of the other boys used him as an example of what their boys could do if they just tried harder.

While there were whispers of scholarship offers from major conference schools, and Palmer was a good athlete, he was not that good. He did receive and accept a partial scholarship to play football for Mankato State University, a division two school in southern Minnesota, but it was clear that even the freshman schoolwork was going to be a struggle. This turned out to be a moot point anyway when he blew out his knee in a scrimmage late in the fall, ending his college football career and his scholarship. Palmer came back home and enrolled in the law enforcement program at Mesabi Junior College, eventually landing a deputy job with the Chase police department after graduation.

Palmer was the one Chief Fowles assigned to watch Blaine Algaard on Tuesday, Thursday, and Sunday evenings. At first Palmer was pretty excited about the assignment. He had never been involved in anything close to a stakeout before but he had seen them on television and knew that they almost always lead to a shootout or car chase. He took his assignment seriously, carefully choosing locations where he could get a good view of the back of Save Big or Algaard's house when he was there. Watching Save Big was easy. There was a big dumpster in the back of the Sunco station next to Save Big where he could park with a good view of the back of the store where Algaard parked.

Watching Algaard's house was not so easy. Algaard's place was in a clearing at the end of a two hundred-yard gravel drive off the county road. The clearing was a high spot on property surrounded by woods and thick brush, much of it a low bog area of dead timber covered by moss, thick dogwood, elderberry, winterberry, and bog birch. Jigsaw Lake was a hundred yards behind the house but essentially inaccessible, except in the winter when the bog was frozen and you could walk or snowmobile. The drive snaked through the woods, the woods so thick you could not see cars on the road, even in winter. This was good for Palmer, but the county road was straight, with fairly steep ditches on either side and no other driveways on either side for at least a quarter of a mile in either direction from Algaard's place. This was not good for Palmer. If he parked on side of the road, Algaard or anyone else that happened by would easily spot him, and it concerned him that with the limited shoulder someone driving by after dark would plow into him.

Nearly a quarter of a mile to the west of Algaard's drive, Palmer found an old access that had been built across the ditch. It was so grown over that he didn't spot it at first, and it abruptly ended in dense woods on the other side of the ditch. He got out of his car, looked it over, and decided it would have to do. He went home and came back with a handsaw and a lopper, clearing enough of the brush away that he could park.

On the first Tuesday of his surveillance Palmer followed Algaard home, driving past his place after Algaard pulled in, and then going to park on the access. It was still light out, but he stood outside of his car and doused himself with bug spray before grabbing his binoculars and phone. He hurried along at a trot, not wanting to be seen in the open if Algaard happened to leave. He was breathing hard by the time he reached Algaard's drive, out of shape and carrying forty extra pounds since his high school days. The driveway went in straight for the first fifty yards but then angled to the left and then back to the right, avoiding a large oak at that point. Palmer moved quickly down the drive as far as the oak, the gravel crunching under his feet, and then stepped into the woods behind it. His boots, black jeans, and long-sleeved black shirt offered some protection from the thorny brush, but heated him up quickly and he stopped to wipe the sweat from his brow with his sleeve. He could hear nothing so stepped back on the driveway and made his way nearly to the clearing, keeping low as he went. He stepped off the driveway and into the woods surrounding the house, then kneeled behind a spruce, parting its branches for a good view of the house and clearing.

The house was an unremarkable single story cedar-sided affair, stained a faded alabaster, no basement below, cement steps leading to the front door. The shingles were moss covered and there was a red brick chimney on the west side, the mortar and a smattering of bricks missing in spots. An unattached double garage was on the other end of the house, siding and roof matching the house in color and condition.

Parked to the right of the garage was what Palmer perceived to be a fairly new Lund fishing boat, seventeen feet long with a full windshield and a 115 Yamaha on the back. Palmer wished he had a boat like that and made note to include mention of the boat in his report to Fowles.

He watched the house for a full fifteen minutes after the lights went out on the first night. His bug spray kept the mosquitoes at bay initially, but as the darkness filled in the spaces where the light had been, the mosquitoes joined the biting flies attacking him even through his shirt. Palmer struggled to find his way back to the driveway, stepping in puddles and falling over a downed tree, afraid that using a light would give away his position in the heavy gloom of the moonless night. He fell again as he stumbled out of the woods, his hand reaching to break his fall, skidding across the gravel of the driveway as it tore at his skin. The bugs were persecuting him as he moved slowly down the driveway toward the road, and he joined in by slapping himself repeatedly while he tried not to step off into the ditch. When he thought he was out of sight of the house, he pulled his Maglite from his pocket, shining it on the gravel at his feet, and took off running. By the time he was back to his car he was sweating profusely, his shirt soaked and hand bloodied, scratching himself all over. He decided he'd take a chance on using a light to get out of the woods next time and find some better bug spray.

Algaard spotted Palmer on Thursday. He had taken the trash out and had noticed the white car behind the dumpster in the adjoining lot. He thought it looked like the same Ford Palmer drove when he had stopped in to buy liquor in the past. He thought no more about it until he spotted the same vehicle following him as he drove home that evening when he had to slow for a doe and two fawns. This time he was sure it was Palmer because it had the bright blue Mankato bumper sticker on the front, and he remembered thinking it was odd to see a bumper sticker on the front of a car when he had watched Palmer park in front of the store.

Algaard pulled into his yard, leaving the car in front of the garage, and then went in his house. He pulled his recliner away from the picture window in front of the house and sat down to watch. The sun was getting low and casting long shadows across the yard, the drive completely in the dark. Algaard had grabbed a beer on his way through the kitchen to the living room, leaving a light on in the kitchen but keeping the living room in the dark, and now sipped as he watched the shadows lengthen. He thought he saw movement near the big spruce by the corner of the drive but he wasn't sure at first. Then he picked up the reflection of light off the lens of Palmer's binoculars and was sure he was there. He continued to watch, hidden from the outside, thinking about Palmer. He couldn't figure out why he would be spying on him unless maybe he was thinking about robbing him, but that didn't make much sense because Palmer knew when he worked and could come out here then. No, he was definitely spying on him for some other reason.

Algaard sat in his chair until the sun was long gone and blackness swallowed the house like a black marble dropped in an inkwell. He got up and moved to the window staring out at where he knew Palmer was hiding. He thought about going out and sneaking up on the deputy, confronting him about what he was doing, but then decided he'd think about it some more. Maybe something would come to him. Suddenly there was a light by the spruce. A flashlight or light from Palmer's phone dancing through woods like some giant firefly. He was leaving, moving through the woods back towards the driveway.

Chapter 28

As the week went on Algaard spotted two other deputies watching him at work and at home in the evenings. He had only worked until three on Thursday afternoon, but no one was behind the gas station watching when he left, no one had followed him home, and whoever watched him that night hadn't shown until an hour before dark. He still hadn't figured out why but at least he knew it was the Chase police for whatever reason.

Algaard was meeting Felix at a vacant second-hand store four miles south of town on Sunday evening. He decided he didn't need any deputies following him on Sunday, so he left his home a good three hours before they had been showing up. He ended up driving to the diner in Black Lake, three miles southeast of the second-hand store, and had the patty-melt special with mashed potatoes. The mashed potatoes were smothered in gravy and he cut his patty-melt in pieces, coating each bite in the potatoes and gravy before he ate it. He had three beers while he ate. Normally a big dinner and the beer would make him sleepy but he found he was hyped. He was nervous about meeting Felix.

The second-hand store was two miles west of County Road 11 at the intersection of Barge Road and Old County Road 11. When 11 was moved east five years earlier, the owners of the second-hand store tried to hang on, but the traffic was gone, and so was their business. When Algaard pulled into the gravel lot in front of the store, the sun was already at the treetops, shadows working their way up the side of the store like the fingers of some giant invisible monster. A large FOR SALE sign with red letters on a white background was screwed into two treated four by four posts in front of the building, like it was a permanent part of the property. He could still read the faded hand-lettered signs painted on the exterior plank walls for ANTIQUES, COLLECTABLES, and CONSIGNMENT SALES, but he didn't think that would be the case for much longer. He was surprised to see that vandals had left the place untouched, even the larger display window, now so covered with dust that it was hard to distinguish from the plank walls, had not been broken. He got out of his car and waited, leaning on the front of the hood, feeling the warmth, a comforting feeling. A horsefly landed on his head and he waved it away just as he heard a vehicle approaching.

It was big and black and shiny with windows tinted so dark it looked like someone had painted them over. He envisioned a hearse and knew then the meeting was a mistake. The SUV glided through the four-way stop and into the lot next to Algaard's Escape, the dust it kicked up surrounding it as it stopped, washing over Algaard like a fog that he tried to wave away. The passenger door opened and Felix climbed down, using the running board as a step. He walked up to Algaard and stuck out his hand, a closed-lip smile on his face.

"How you doing?"

Algaard was looking at the man in the driver's seat of the Escalade, but with the shadows it was hard to see anything except that he had a shaved head, a large shaved head. Algaard looked at Felix. "OK."

Felix was wearing dark, black-framed sunglasses that he removed now and looked at the second-hand store. "This place doesn't look like it's doing too well."

Algaard looked at the building. "Nope. I think it went out of business when the county road got moved. Nobody much comes by here anymore."

Felix took in the area around the store. There was a concrete slab kitty-corner from them, cracked and crumbling with weeds living in the pour lines, the remains of something he guessed had been a store or restaurant behind the slab, only portions of two charred walls remaining. Trees and brush on the corner across from them had nearly swallowed an abandoned mobile home. The other corner had been cleared at one time but there was no visible sign that anything had ever been done with it. He looked up at Algaard, his eyes so dark they looked almost black.

"So, you think you're not making enough money?"

Algaard had been so sure of himself on the way over, how he'd tell the little man to fork over more or he'd find a better deal, but now he wasn't so brave, not with the bald guy in the dark glasses staring at him. "Um, well, you know, I can do more. It would help you too."

Felix never let his gaze move from Algaard's face. "What do mean, help me too?"

"You know, I could run more money through for you, so you'd make more money too."

Felix looked over Algaard's shoulder. "This is a very complicated business. There are a whole lot of moving parts, and all those parts have to work together or the business just doesn't work. Do you get that?"

Algaard had no idea what Felix was talking about. It was simple to him. If he runs more money, he makes more money, and Felix makes more money. But Felix's voice had turned hard and something about it scared Algaard.

Felix looked back at Algaard, putting his sunglasses back on. "Let's go for a ride. I want to show you something." He turned and stepped back toward the Escalade, climbing back up and getting in. The window rolled down and Felix looked at him.

Algaard hadn't moved.

"Come on. Get in. It's not far."

Algaard knew he shouldn't get in the SUV, knew he should run. Maybe he should just tell Felix to forget the whole thing. "What about my car?"

"I'll bring you back. Shouldn't be more than half an hour."

Chapter 29

Carlisle arrived back at the Administration Building at nine-thirty Monday morning. Things had gotten late at her sister's place on Sunday, and she had a few beers, so she spent an extra night. She had a tough time getting going, but once she cleared the Cities and stopped for a coffee and Egg McMuffin she was feeling better. She stepped out of her car with her notebook in hand, pushed the lock button on her remote, and stepped up on the curb. Something caught her eye and she turned to her left to see Lane leaning against the hood of his car. "Morning, Director Lane," she said with a perky smile as she waved.

Lane did not smile back; he only stared. Carlisle could see that Lane did not look well. His knit shirt hung out of his wrinkled khakis and it looked like he had some kind of red food stain on his left thigh. There were dark circles under his eyes. His hair had maybe had a hand-comb job and he definitely had not shaved this morning.

She stopped in front of the steps to the Administration Building. "You do a little partying this weekend?"

Lane pushed himself up. "How long you going to be poking around here?"

"Hard to say. Everybody's been so friendly it's just hard not to keep coming back." Carlisle gave him her biggest pushing up the cheeks smile but it didn't seem to have any impact.

Lane stared for a moment longer, a hard look, like he was thinking he'd like to strangle the perkiness out of the woman in front of him, which he was, before walking around his car and getting in. He started it and backed out, giving Carlisle one last look before he changed gears and drove away.

Carlisle watched him go. "Creepy."

There was another new student working in the Registrar's Office, a boy this time, who did not look to be in much better shape than Lane. He was leaning over his desk, elbow on the desktop, holding his head up, and Carlisle thought he might be asleep when she walked through the door but he perked right up at the sight of the tall woman with chestnut hair in a ponytail with long legs below her jean skirt.

"Uh, can I help you?"

Danny smiled. There were some crabby people here but at least a few of the men were giving her ego a lift. "Nope. I'm Agent Danny Carlisle from the BCA and I'm going to be working in the station right next to you today." Carlisle cut around his desk and sat at her workstation, aware of his eyes following.

"Um, OK. Well, if I can help you in any way let me know." He was practically drooling.

"What's your name?"

"Jeff."

"OK, Jeff. If I need some help, you will be the first one I call."

Jeff wasn't sure he got the meaning of her remark, forced a smile, and turned back to his desk.

Carlisle went to work. By one she had a list of six probable and a dozen possible men who fit the general description of the man she was after as well as a list of all of the administration and professors on staff each year. She turned off the computer and leaned back in her chair and stretched, her arms out to the side, giving Jeff an eyeful of her breasts as they pushed the fabric of her blouse. Glancing over to see him staring, she smiled, and then folded up her notebook. She got up, pushed in her chair, and then started to leave, stopping in front of Jeff's desk. "You know Jeff, I have handcuffs."

The boy's eyes grew large and he swallowed hard.

"Just saying." She winked and walked out.

Carlisle picked up the files from Thomas on her way back to the office. She dropped the files on her desk and put her notebook next to them. She thought she should call Trask and let him know where she stood. He was the kind of guy you wanted to keep informed. But what did she have, really? A bunch of names and faces of people who she would just have to look at further and some files from the Duluth PD she hadn't even opened. Nothing, really. He'd probably just tell her to keep digging. She decided that's what she would do.

~~~

Lane had spent three nights outside of Carlisle's apartment and he was feeling it. After he had seen her in the morning he had gone home to shower and change. A decision to lie down for just ten minutes before getting cleaned up had turned into a two-hour nap. After a shower and shave and late lunch on the way back to school he felt better on the outside but on the inside he was feeling anger like he never had before. The BCA woman had somehow evaded him all weekend and now, this morning, she had ridiculed him. He hated this woman with every fiber of his being and wanted her dead. Badly.

He also knew that Walls would be on his way back and would want to know that she had been eliminated. In fact, it surprised him he had not heard from Walls. No matter, it would be over tonight.

~~~

The man had been the most upset that the driver had seen him when he got back early Sunday morning. The driver tried to explain what had happened, why he had come back empty-handed, screaming his reasoning at the top of his lungs, but in the end he had just given up. He knew it was no use trying to talk to him. The man was tired, strung out, and on the edge. The man needed his release. His face was tomato red and his eyes looked like they were ready to jump from their sockets. The driver thought they would maybe come to blows when the man threw a half-full beer can by his head, beer spraying the wall and window before the can landed in the sink, but eventually the man went off to his room. The driver sat at the kitchen table and watched him go. He wasn't sure he could take the man, at least in a fight. He was a little taller than the man, but the man was big, husky, with forearms like pot roasts and fists that he didn't think would fit in boxing gloves, and the driver had no doubt the man knew how to fight. The driver guessed he would be quicker but was pretty sure that wouldn't cut it in a fight.

Didn't matter. If the man came after him he'd find out about the knife. The driver kept it sheathed in the small of his back. The blade wasn't that long but it was sticky sharp, honed for hours by hand. The driver had started carrying it after he had shot his father. He had used it to convince a girl in high school to do what he wanted, just pricking her nipples to show her how sharp it was in case she decided not to let him have his way with her, but that was the only time. He had never killed anyone with it. Some nights as he lay in bed he thought about pushing the blade into the fat gut of the man, moving the stone over the blade again and again, thinking about how he would pull it up and then back off, watching the guts of the man spill out. It seemed to him that he was thinking about it a lot more lately.

~~~

Monday evening was clear, the breeze light and from the south, a little humidity still in the air. Lane had followed Carlisle from her office. She stopped at a grocery store, came out with two bags and a half-gallon of almond milk, and then drove to her apartment. Lane watched her as she walked to and from her car, following her long legs, her athlete legs, with a nice top. He let his mind wander thinking about her, thinking about her naked, struggling under him, and he could feel himself start to get excited. He reached down and briefly touched his crotch, got what was an evil smile, but then shook his head as he brought himself back to reality. There would be no fun with this woman. Tonight she would die.

Chapter 30

Lane knew where she parked now; there was no way she would leave without him knowing. For the next three hours he watched and waited for the sun to go down. He moved his car frequently so as not to draw any undue attention, always keeping Carlisle's car in sight. One time she came out and sat on her deck with a glass of wine, sipping it as she leafed through a magazine, but he could see her slapping herself and it wasn't long before the bugs chased her inside.

It was hard to be patient. Lane was not a patient person. His teachers said he lacked focus in school, which he had, but the things he had to do in class always seemed to take too long. The reality of it was that he had a mild case of ADD, but his parents were ignorant of it, and so he went without treatment, barely escaping high school. His condition had lessened over the years but at times of stress he could feel the jitteriness course through him. He badly wanted to kill her when she came out on her deck, or sneak in again and go to her door, getting into her apartment some way and killing her there. But he waited, finally parking on the road that bordered the vacant lot across from Carlisle's building. He waited until after sunset, watching as the lights in the apartments came on, until he was sure he would not be seen. He removed his deer rifle from the trunk and hurried to the woods next to the lot. He had dressed in camo and stayed just inside the tree line as he approached the back of the building.

Standing in the corner of the woods, Lane was actually closer to Carlisle's apartment balcony than he had been as he sat in his car on the far side of the lot. He estimated he had about seventy yards to her apartment as he raised his rifle and looked through the scope. He could see the blue light of the television through her open curtains highlighting a bookshelf and floor lamp that were against the wall beyond the sliding doors. He could also see one other thing - her sliding door was open. There was a screen door to keep out the bugs but the glass door was open. He knew she would come to close it at some point. Lane grew tired of holding his rifle up and found a low branch off an oak and laid his gun on it. He peered through the sight. He had a perfect shot.

Lane was a deer hunter. He loved the shooting, the stalking; he even liked to butcher his animals. And for some reason he found that when he hunted, he had no problem being patient. He could sit in a deer stand for hours at a time waiting and watching, feeling only patience for his quest. Now that patience returned.

He had seen her shadow pass a few times as he watched, and one time had a quick glimpse of her as she moved past the far wall of the apartment. He was stifling a yawn when his senses went on high alert. A light had come on in the apartment. He caressed the barrel of the gun now as he again peered through the site. The blue light of the television disappeared and it seemed that another light had been added to the one he first saw. She passed quickly through his vision again and he saw a light come on behind the curtained window next to the balcony. He guessed it was her bedroom.

Danny had a second glass of wine as she watched a movie on Netflix. She wasn't really interested in the show, playing solitaire on her iPad as she watched, but she just didn't feel tired. She knew she should be dead on her feet after working all day and being gone all weekend, but she kept thinking about the faces of the men she had identified at the school. One of them was maybe a killer, a rapist, and every day he was out there more women could be in danger. She had been so tired at the end of the day at the office that she had lost focus and left a little early, but now her brain wouldn't stop cranking. She needed to nail this guy and do it soon.

She finally gave up on the movie before it ended, changed into her pajamas, brushed her teeth, and then returned to the living room to shut off the light there. As she was about to flick the switch the sound of a loud truck driving past drew her attention to her patio. She had thought about leaving the door open for the night but decided she didn't need any drunken college boys climbing in, but then thought maybe one wouldn't be too bad. She thought about a boy she knew in school and wondered what had ever become of him. Danny walked to the screen door, peered into the darkness of the night feeling lonely, and then reached for the door handle.

Lane could hardly believe his luck. She was back-lit against the screen door wearing what looked to be only a t-shirt, a sheer one at that. She was so hot. He released the safety. "Sorry baby."

Carlisle wasn't sure what had happened. When she had looked down to find the handle on the sliding door she had noticed something sparkling on the floor at the base of the door. She immediately bent to pick up whatever it was when the vase in the cubby on the wall next to the kitchen exploded. Carlisle knew a shot when she heard it and immediately dived to her right behind the glass patio doors. As she did the doors exploded, glass raining down. She rolled further to her right behind the wall, crouching under her oak desk, hands wrapped around her knees, waiting for the next shot.

Lane took off. He didn't think he had hit her but he wasn't sure. She had lucked out in the Administration Building coming out of the Records Room and now here. The damn woman had nine lives. He was breathing so hard he thought he was having a heart attack, sure everyone in the complex could hear his heart that now sounded like a warning gong trying to burst from his chest. He ran back along the edge of the woods to his car. He threw his rifle in the back seat, took a deep breath, and then willed himself to drive slowly away.

Chapter 31

By the time the driver was approaching the Passer By Bar at midnight his windshield appeared to have been used as protection in some miniature paintball war, the result of driving through a bug hatch for the last few miles. As he cruised past the Passer By, he counted only one car in the lot. He quickly glanced to the side of the bar where it appeared there was also only one car parked and he was almost sure it was the blonde's car. He felt a jolt of excitement as he doubled back, turning off his headlights as he turned in to park on the side of the bar where he had been the first night, and hustled around the back of the building. He moved past the door in back and around the corner to where the car was parked, risking a quick pass of the screen on his phone over the vehicle. It was hers.

The driver reversed his path, scooted past the door in back of the building, through the shrubs on the corner, and back to his truck. He climbed into the cab and reached for his stun stick, sitting with it in his lap, thinking about how he should take the woman. He thought he would have to follow her, get her to stop, but now, unless the car parked in front was another employee, he would grab her here. He was deciding where he would position himself when he heard a car start and saw the headlights of the vehicle in the parking lot. Its lights passed over the woods to the left in front of him as it backed up and then turned toward the road, the light unable to penetrate the thick undergrowth more than a few feet.

He looked at the time on his phone then leaned his head back and drained his soda. No time to waste now. No telling how long until she would leave – she could have been cleaning up while she waited for the last customer to go. Maybe close early. The driver was out of his cab again; stun stick in hand, moving through the shrubs again. He decided he'd wait by the dumpster, just behind it. Someone had carried the trash out as the employees were leaving on Friday and Saturday so he assumed it was part of their routine. He'd have a view of the back door, know when she had deposited the trash, and turned toward her car. He would take her then.

The driver ran across the back lot towards the dumpster keeping low, bent over, like he'd seen soldiers do in the war movies, the light from his phone flashing across the ground in front of him. He reached the side of the dumpster closest to him and knew he had a problem. The dumpster had been dropped with the back up against the heavy brush that surrounded the lot in back. He could work his way in but there was no way he wouldn't be heard trying to get out. Crouching by the side of the dumpster, he looked at the bar. He could clearly see the back door but would easily be seen when she brought out the trash. He moved around to the other side. This was better, but it still posed a risk. Because of the way the dumpster was angled, he would not be exposed to anyone approaching the dumpster. The problem was with the dumpster. It had four doors on top. If she chose one of the two doors on the side of the dumpster where he was now she would likely spot him, especially if she went for the door to the rear. She'd practically have to step on him to get to the door. He slapped a mosquito on his neck and then one on his arm as he considered his other options.

~~~

Justine Blake started closing down before the last customer was out the door. His name was Tim Connors and he had been sitting at the bar nursing a beer for the last hour before he left. Tim worked construction, painting, and just about anything else that turned up, and had the hots for Justine. Tim was a nice enough guy, and Justine was a little flattered, but she wasn't interested. As far as she was concerned Tim was in the same category as her current boyfriend, Mike Evers.

Blake began working at the bar a year and a half ago, moving in with the manager, Evers, after six months on the job. It impressed her that he was a manager, and he talked about his plans to buy the bar or another one, maybe even looking at something in Duluth. But Blake discovered that managing the Passer By mostly meant scheduling work and ordering stock and supplies, and that Evers consistently drank and smoked away any money he made, with no sign that he was going to do anything more. He was good with her almost two-year-old son, watching him occasionally when she had to work, but as far as she could tell, all she had done was make his life easier by taking care of his house and being available to work anytime he felt like scheduling her.

Blake knew it would upset Evers to see her home before one, knowing she had closed the bar early, but she no longer cared. She just hoped the arguing wouldn't wake her son. She had decided the week before that this would be her last week at the bar. It was time for her to take her own advice and show a little ambition. She'd be starting as an assistant manager in a restaurant in Duluth the following Monday, moving in with a girlfriend until she could find a place of her own. She felt a little bad about leaving Evers on such short notice, but not too bad.

She locked the door behind Connors and finished the dishes before collecting the trash. Blake took a final look at the inside of the bar, decided it looked fine but that she really didn't care anymore, turned out the lights and opened the door in back.

~~~

The driver was thinking that maybe he should move back to the building, next to the back door, and zap her when she came outside. He would be on the opposite side of the door from the light and the door handle and there was a shrub there that would provide some cover. He stood to make a dash back across the lot to the building when the back door opened. He squatted back down, moving as far toward the back of the dumpster as he could, feeling the branches poke at his back, trying to push him away like they were refusing to let him enter their private sanctum.

Blake held the screen door open with her hip, the trash bag between her feet, as she stood on the stoop and pulled the inside door shut. She twisted the door handle to be sure it was locked and then turned toward the dumpster. Blake didn't like the short walk to the dumpster. With only the single bulb by the door it was pitch black only a few feet from the bar. After she had frightened off a large black bear in the spring, she had complained to Evers about it and he had promised to get a motion detector light installed. He had made it a policy that the trash be emptied into the dumpster from the bag and then the bag tossed in empty so that the bears wouldn't drag a whole bag of trash out if they got in, but he had never inquired about the installation of a light.

Blake removed the phone from her purse and selected the flashlight from the pull-down menu on the screen. The light came on and she pulled her purse strap farther up on her shoulder before reaching down to pick up the trash bag with her free hand. She shone her light in the direction of the dumpster and walked that way.

The light the woman was using was like a spotlight, casting a sharp shadow from the dumpster that cut just in front of him. He scooted back a little more, a sharp branch poking him in the neck, cutting him. He reached to push the branch away and got a thorn in his palm for the effort. He gritted his teeth and winced, trying to hold back a cry.

It was a calm night, warm, with a clear sky but no moon, and the woman had heard a movement in the brush by the dumpster. "Shit" she muttered, hardly more than a whisper, stopping a few feet short of the dumpster. When she had surprised the bear before she had flashed her light on it and it had taken off running. She listened to it crashing through the woods until she couldn't hear it anymore, amazed at how much noise it made. Now she wondered what she would do if the bear didn't run, if it came after her? She panned her light over the dumpster and the surrounding area. She could see nothing and it was quiet. Maybe just a raccoon? Still, she stepped farther to her left, leaning now, as she tried to see on the far side of the dumpster, just to be sure nothing was there.

But there was something there. The driver tensed as her light began to move in his direction. He tried to back up further but it was no use, the brush blocked his attempt at entry like a thousand small, intertwined arms and hands holding him back. The darkness cast by the dumpster slowly disappeared like a shadow on a sundial until the light caught his right knee and then his shoulder. He looked up and the beam shined on him.

She wasn't sure what she was seeing. It looked like it could be someone's leg in dark jeans. She shuffled a little more to her left, leaning as far as she could, trying to get a better look. There was a shoulder in a gray t-shirt and now she caught just a flash of the arm that came from the shirt. There was definitely someone there. Something inside of Blake told her to run but she had broken up a few fights in the bar in the last year and didn't scare easily. She wondered if it was someone she had caught dumpster diving. A little farther over she could see most of the person crouched by the dumpster, their head bowed so she could see the top of a cap. She took a small step closer and the head came up. For a brief instant she looked into the eyes below the bill of the cap, dark consuming eyes, eyes of the devil. She dropped the garbage bag and ran.

The driver was up and after her, turning on his stun-stick as he ran. The woman reached her car and had her light shined in her purse, frantically searching for her keys. Surprisingly she found them immediately and pushed the remote button to unlock the door. She chanced a look back as she pulled open the driver's door and saw a strange light coming at her accompanied by a buzzing sound. She turned her back to the light to step into her car when she felt the shock between her shoulder blades. She lost all control of her muscles and dropped to the ground.

The driver was breathing hard from the quick sprint, hands on his knees, adrenaline flowing, looking at the girl on the ground. The light from inside her car poured out over the doorframe leaving most of the girl in the dark; her head and upper torso had landed towards the back of the car, the light only showing a portion of the back of her legs. She had dropped her purse and phone when he zapped her, falling on the purse, the phone ending up face down just under the car. He pushed her car door closed with his hip. He could just make out the phone glowing on the ground and bent to his knees to retrieve it, shining it over the girl as he stood. He wanted a better look but that would have to wait. Didn't want someone driving by and seeing him. He used her phone to light his way back to his truck and then drove it around the front, lights off, to the girl's car. Putting his hands under her armpits, he hefted her up until she was almost upright, and then quickly slid his hands just above her waist. He moved her over to the cab door of the truck and shoved her in, found the duct tape he kept in the mesh pocket behind his seat, and then taped her arms and legs and mouth. He trotted back to the girl's car, picked up her purse, and then hustled back to the truck. Time to go home and have some fun.

Chapter 32

Carlisle waited a full two minutes before making any move, and it seemed like a lifetime. She prayed, thanking God for causing her to bend over to look at whatever it was on the floor by the patio door, and then asked that she not get shot at again. Not a coward and wanting badly to go after whoever was shooting, she couldn't be sure if whoever was shooting at her was waiting to take another shot or maybe they were coming after her. Her phone, her keys, and her gun – they were all in her bedroom. She made a dash for her kitchen that was separated by a wall from the living room. After hurrying through the kitchen she peeked around the corner, looking out of her shattered balcony door. She half expected another shot but there was nothing. She reached around the corner to turn off the lights and then bent low, took a deep breath, and sprinted to her bedroom. Nothing, no shot. Whoever did the shooting was gone. Or they were still coming.

There was a window in her bedroom facing the same direction as the patio door. Carlisle stayed low, crawling along her bed until she reached her dresser where she had set her purse and gun. She stretched to get them and then sat with her back to the side of the dresser and called 911. She also called her supervisor.

Carlisle had changed by the time the Duluth police arrived, Hillary Thomas showing up shortly after two uniforms. She rushed up to Carlisle, holding her by the shoulders, scanning her up and down.

"Are you OK sweetie?"

"Yeah. I got to stop wearing those pajamas with the deer on them. Gets men excited in the wrong way."

Thomas smiled but she could see the tiny smile on her friend's face was forced and she was upset. She led Carlisle to the couch and they both sat. "OK, so tell me what happened."

Just as Carlisle was about to speak her supervisor, Bob Farmer, walked into the room and stood in front of them. "Danny. How you doing?"

Carlisle looked up at Farmer. Farmer was in his early forties with marine-cut black hair on a round head. He was two or three inches shorter than Carlisle and stocky. He was in jeans and a t-shirt, looking like he was still not quite awake. He always seemed a little cold to Danny, but he had been a good boss, willing to spend time with her when she needed it and also willing to let her run with her ideas.

"Hey, Bob. I'm fine. This is Sergeant Hillary Thomas, Duluth PD."

"We've met," he replied as he shook Thomas's hand. Carlisle got the feeling there was some background there but lost that thought quickly when Thomas spoke.

"So, Danny was just going to give me a rundown on what happened," looking up at Farmer.

"Yeah, that would be great. Go ahead Danny."

Carlisle went through what had happened while Thomas scanned the room. By the time Carlisle finished her explanation she was too worked up to sit any longer. She walked over to her patio door and looked at the flashing lights of the vehicles in the parking lot. "I need to get out there."

Thomas stood and grabbed Carlisle by the arm. "Listen. I know you're a big tough BCA agent and all, but maybe you need to just take a break for a second."

"The asshole who did this is getting away. I need to do something!"

"OK, so tell me who the asshole is."

That stopped Carlisle. She hadn't really thought about it.

"Could this have had anything to do with what you came to see me about? What about other cases you have been working on? Or maybe someone you put away?"

Carlisle looked down at the glass scattered on the carpeting and then at her boss who had come up behind Thomas. Her adrenaline rush was ending and she felt tired, worn out. "Um, I don't know."

"OK, listen. The crime scene guys will be here for a while and you're not going to get any rest at all. Grab some clothes and whatever you need and you can stay with me tonight." She turned to Farmer. "That OK with you, Bob?"

"Sounds like a good idea." He looked at Carlisle. "Get some sleep and come in to the office when you feel ready. Doesn't have to be tomorrow if you're not up to it. We can talk more then."

Carlisle nodded and then returned to her bedroom for a bag and packed. She could hear Thomas and Farmer talking as she was in her bathroom grabbing a toothbrush and makeup. She walked back into the living room.

"I'm ready." She saw a silent look pass between Thomas and Farmer again.

"OK, let's go." Thomas put a hand to Carlisle's back and steered her into the hall. As they drove out of the complex Carlisle looked again at the flashing lights, seeing police walking the woods with flashlights. She unconsciously moved her hand to the door handle. She wanted badly to join them.

Chapter 33

Instead of taking the way he had come the driver went east into Lake County on 14. He knew it would add another fifteen minutes to his trip but he didn't want to chance it that someone who had seen him going north would also see him going south. Besides, he knew that County 14 had fewer homes along it and virtually no stop signs until he would turn south, not much of anything really. He could make good time. Hell, he was already way ahead of schedule.

He had gone about ten miles, cruising at a little over sixty, when he took a glance in the back seat. It was hard to make out what she really looked like. He had just brushed against her breasts when he had pushed her in the truck and they felt firm, full, and he wanted a better look. He thought about reaching back between the seats just to see if he could get a feel but then thought he better pay attention to the road and turned back – almost too late. The driver slammed on the brakes, skidding to a stop inches from a large doe that gave him an annoyed look before calmly walked off the road and into the ditch.

The driver's eyes were wide and he gripped the steering wheel hard, pushing himself back in his seat with extended arms and releasing a big breath. If he wasn't awake before he was now. He felt the girl slam against the back of his seat when he braked and then the clang of pop cans. She was now on the floor of the truck in back. He thought about just leaving her there but then he figured he better make sure she hadn't broken her neck or anything else. He stepped out of the truck and opened the back door, reaching in to turn on the overhead light. The woman had ended up almost on her stomach, her legs and shoulders wedged against the front seats. He reached in and grabbed her legs, trying to pull them up, but then thought he might break her neck for real if he hadn't already, and reached in grabbing her by the waist. He got her hips rolling up on the back seat and then her shoulders and head followed. He pulled her legs up.

"Sorry about that. Fucking deer. Hope you're OK."

Her eyes, so wide open they looked like they might pop out of their sockets, stared at him in terror.

"Maybe I should just do a little examination to be sure you're alright?" The driver leaned over her, reaching for her belt, when she kicked out, nearly knocking him over backwards. "Whoa! Well, I guess you got a little spirit to you. I like girls with spirit." He smiled at her, a full smile showing his stained teeth and pushing up his cheeks below his dark eyes, and at that moment she knew she was going to die. He pulled a Dr. Pepper from the cooler, popped the top and took a sip as he leered at her, wanting to take her right then. Instead he turned off the overhead light and shut the door before climbing back in the driver's seat.

He hadn't gone two more miles when he felt it, knowing right away what it was. He pulled over, found the flashlight in the console compartment, and got out of the truck. He walked to the back on the driver's side and flashed the light. Flat tire.

"Damn it!" he shouted as he kicked at the tire. He had told the man to get the drive graded, and the man said he would, but of course he never did. He was just too damn cheap. And now he had a flat. He knew that the skid stopping for the deer had been the culprit but he also knew that the driveway had contributed. "Damn you old man!"

The bugs were eating him alive, and he was sweaty and greasy as he finished tightening the lug nuts. He had just reached for the handle of the jack to lower the truck the rest of the way when he saw the lights. This could not be good. He did not need any do-gooder stopping to see if he needed help, someone who could identify him to the police. He stared at the lights as they approached and slowed, finally pulling off the road behind him. He was about to crank down the jack, toss it in the back, and take off when the flashing lights came on.

"Fuck!" muttered the driver.

He worked as fast as he could and had the jack off, putting it in the bed of the truck through the window of the topper, when he heard the car door behind him open. The driver turned as the officer approached, flashlight held high, light on him like he was on a stage.

"You OK?"

"Yes officer. Just a flat. All done." The driver closed his window and started to walk around the side of his truck. The officer followed.

"Can I ask what you're doing out here at this time of night?"

The driver had now reached his door and pulled it open. If the officer shined his light in the back seat, he was screwed. "Had a long weekend with a friend. Just on my way home. Got to work in the morning."

"Where do you live?" The officer kept his light on the driver's face.

"South of Two Harbors," he replied as he got in the truck. The driver didn't like the fact that the officer had seen him. He hoped the cop hadn't seen his plate number when he pulled up behind. "Well, thanks for stopping anyway." The driver started his truck.

The officer paused, flashed his light in the driver's face once more, the driver holding up his hand to shield his eyes from the light. He turned away. "Have a safe trip."

Blake heard the men talking outside the truck. She knew there was a police officer there but now it sounded like he was just going to leave. She couldn't let that happen. Blake kicked out, banging the inside of the door.

The officer was two steps past the back door but now came back and flashed his light inside the back seat. He saw the woman bound with tape and was reaching for his gun when he felt the shock, dropping to his knees, his face hitting the side of the truck as he fell, knocking him out cold.

The driver had already decided that he needed to kill the cop when he heard the woman kick the inside of the door; all that did was give him the distraction he needed. He picked up the officer's pistol after he shocked him, stuck it in the waist of his pants, and then bent and grabbed the man by his ankles. The driver dragged him between the back of the truck and the police car and down into the tall witch grass in the ditch. He pulled the gun from his pants and shot the officer in the head, then wiped the gun down and tossed it in the woods. After walking back up on the road he got in the still running police car. He heard nothing on the radio asking about the officer's location or situation, so assumed that the officer had called nothing in when he stopped. He drove the car roughly half a mile down the road to where he found a property access over the ditch and drove the car as far into the woods as he could before it got stuck. The driver used his shirt to wipe down everything he had touched on the car and hiked back to his truck.

Chapter 34

Don Trask was feeling better, relaxed. He had spent a long weekend with Jenkins. They had walked through Stillwater like tourists, looking through the antique shops, watching the lift bridge, and visiting the new brewery. He had turned off his phone and not thought about his parents, his boss, Marty Olson, or anything else work related. They had not watched the news on television or looked at it on her computer. He could not remember the last time he had taken two days off, totally off, when he was in the Cities. Sure he had done it when he had been on fishing trips, or tried to unless his brother brought something up, but never when he was in town had he totally shut down.

He returned to his condo overlooking Lake Phalen in St. Paul Monday night, set his phone on the gray granite counter top in his kitchen, and went to the liquor cabinet. The bottle was there, his companion since he started drinking as a teenager, a companion that had cost him several relationships and nearly cost him his career. It had taken him to dark places for days at a time, leading him down a path where he had nearly killed, and almost been killed. He'd upgraded his companion over the years, now a 28-year-old single malt pushing $200 a bottle, but all that had done was make it more endearing to him.

Mel wanted him to quit and he knew he should. When he got down he drank, and the more he drank, the more depressed and angry he became. Most times, a tumbler was fine - soothing, relaxing. But when he came to the bottle upset, a single glass was never enough, and more than once he had totally lost any recollection of what he had done when he was drunk.

He pulled down the bottle, found a glass in the cupboard, and poured an inch. He swirled the liquid as he leaned on the counter, the phone just to his right. He was severely tempted to turn it on. In some ways the phone was as bad as the scotch, maybe worse. It seemed to only bring bad news, upsetting information; words that made him grind his teeth. All of it demanding his attention, draining him like a vampire sucking the life from him. But he loved it, needed it. He knew he would have to stop some day, or at least slow down, but he wasn't ready for that yet. Trask ran his finger over the dark screen and then walked to the window overlooking the lake. Couples walked along the shore and a fisherman was packing up his gear. He sat in his leather recliner and watched the sun slowly set as he sipped.

Trask looked at his messages as he munched on a bagel and downed coffee the next morning. The Superintendent wanted him to call as soon as he was in; Minneapolis wanted to reopen the investigation into the police shooting. Seton was taking a team north to Anoka to investigate a domestic situation that involved a woman being stabbed by her ex-boyfriend and child's father, and then the police shooting the ex-boyfriend. He listened to the other messages, brushed his teeth, and headed for the office.

Stoxon met him at the door with coffee, telling him he needed to call the boss and Trask telling Stoxon he already knew. Trask sat at his desk and looked at a map spread across it.

"What's this?"

"That's the map of the abductions that you asked me to do last week," replied his assistant.

Trask started to look at the map before looking up at Stoxon. "Well, aren't you going to tell me what all these marks mean?"

Stoxon was about to answer when Trask's phone buzzed and he looked at the caller ID. "Trask."

"Don, it's Bob Farmer."

"Hey Bob. What's up?"

"I tried to get you last night but your phone must have been off or something. Anyway, somebody took a couple of shots at one of my agents last night, Don. She's OK, but I thought I better let you know."

Don leaned back in his chair and swiveled so he was facing the window behind his desk. "OK, well, you catch whoever did it?"

"Not yet, but we're working on it." Farmer paused and Trask sensed the concern in his voice. "Listen Don, the agent who was shot at was Danny Carlisle."

Trask had almost forgotten that he assigned Carlisle to look into the abduction at UMD. "You think this has something to do with what I have her working on?"

"Don't know. Just thought you should be aware." Farmer was cautious with what he said to Trask. He had jumped to a conclusion one time, a conclusion that had proved correct, but Trask had been all over him for doing it.

"OK, I'd like to talk to Carlisle myself about this. I'll be up later today or early tomorrow." Don thought about Carlisle as he paused. "You sure she's OK?"

"Yeah. I told her to take the day off but she's been here since a little after six."

"Thanks Bob. See you later."

~~~

Walls was back in his office Tuesday morning. The floatplane could not get out until Monday, and even then the ride had been so rough that three of the six men on the flight had become ill, Walls being one of them. The coffee he was timidly sipping told him that his stomach had not fully recovered. Jones and Klang tried to see him after he arrived but he waved them both away and closed the door to his office. He needed to think.

The news on Channel Four had video of police cars with flashing lights at an apartment complex north of the school. Apparently there had been shots fired into one apartment shattering a balcony door. Police had not made any statements regarding anyone being injured or a motive. No suspects had been detained. An interview with one resident of the apartment complex speculated that the occupant of the apartment was a police officer.

Walls knew Lane had screwed up again. The guy had been a screw-up since day one and now he was in deep – and he would most likely drag Walls down with him. If Lane were caught he would talk, no doubt. Walls had looked at the reports on the abductions again. Lane's name was the only one on the reports. He figured he could claim that Lane acted on his own, never came to him, but he knew that would be a stretch. Still, it seemed his only way out right now. He'd have to take care of Lane.

~~~

Danny Carlisle had a hard time sitting still when she was growing up and she was feeling the jitters this morning. Besides "bulldog", her parents had also referred to her as "Energizer Bunny II". Her teachers described her as "high energy". She recognized the restless feeling that she experienced as a youth but this was different, more intense, more internal. She guessed it was mostly due to not sleeping the night before combined with the three large cups of coffee she had consumed this morning – not to mention being shot at. And now her boss had informed her that Trask was coming to interview her and go over what she discovered in her investigation.

As Carlisle had lain on her back in Thomas's spare room the night before, listening to a screaming baby and wondering how her friend survived, she was also making a list in her head. When Carlisle had been in junior high school her grades were less than stellar. Tests showed she had the smarts but her inability to sit still and focus was causing her to fail, and was a distraction to other students. Her parents had come to the end of their ropes, ready to submit her for a psychological evaluation, when a counselor at her school suggested that Danny make lists. Lists of what school assignments she had to complete, of what jobs she had to get done at home, of what she needed to do each day. It didn't entirely rid her of her inability to stay focused, she would take prescription medicine through high school, but it made a difference, and Danny had been a list maker ever since.

She discovered her lists were most effective when they were written, and so she put a pad on her desk when she got to work, and started the list she had thought about the night before. The list of who would want to kill her. Number one on the list was 'An Accident' although she didn't really believe it. Still, she surmised it was possible that someone had mistaken her for someone else. She would eventually go back to her apartment and check for herself, but she didn't doubt that the lighting would not have been especially good for someone to ID her, especially at a distance. She would have been back-lit. It would have been hard to see her face. That made her think about which of her neighbors someone would want to shoot and why. That would be a long road.

Number two was someone from a prior case, someone she had put away or helped put in jail. She jotted down a few names. One in particular stood out. Jose Reyes. She underlined his name. Reyes was a drug dealer. She had gone undercover and gotten friendly with him, part of a task force operation. Reyes and his group had been smuggling heroin through the Duluth harbor. She was sure he was still inside but he had sworn to get even with her when they took him down, claimed his family would be paying her a visit.

Third on her list were her active investigations. There was another suspected smuggling operation, this time involving jewels, also at the harbor. Her involvement had been mostly surveillance from a distance and she was certain that neither she nor the other agents involved had been made.

There was an investigation into a shooting north of Duluth. A husband and wife were dead. Initially the Duluth PD had thought it to be a murder/suicide, but the autopsy had placed doubt on that, and they had called in the BCA for assistance. Cocaine was found in the system of both of the victims, and a large stash of cocaine found in the home, as well as cash and several weapons.

The remainder of her work was at her desk, doing research and collecting background information.

Fourth on her list was the only thing at work that didn't fit in the first three categories – the Hollister murder. She supposed it could have been considered research, but it had turned into something a little more than that, although she wasn't sure if it was supposed to. Trask was updated one time on her findings but she'd carried it a little farther, well, a lot farther. She felt like she was on to something and she was after it like her father's dog after a grouse. She hadn't tried to contact anyone on her list after last week at the school, but she had made no secret about the fact that she was looking at Hollister. Could someone have put the killer on notice? That would imply that there was some kind of relationship between someone at the school and the killer. Possibly a relative or girlfriend - some kind of accomplice. She started to make a list of the people she had talked to at UMD but quickly realized that any of them could have mentioned her and what she was doing to someone else, someone who did not want her looking into the murder.

Carlisle finished making a list of all of the school employees she had been in contact with, including the students in the registrar's office, and then blew out a big breath. There was one more possibility for her list. Number five would be 'Personal'. She was poised to write but then put down her pen. She had nothing. Her last steady boyfriend had dumped her almost a year ago because she was too involved in her work. As far as she knew she didn't really have any enemies, certainly no one that would be interested in taking a shot at her. Well, her mother did threaten to kill her if she ever got shot on the job, but she hadn't been shot yet so she was pretty sure she could leave her mother off the list. The fact was, when she thought about it, she didn't have much of a personal life. She thought about Hillary and her family and her sister and her family, and felt sad, a little lonely, and maybe a little sorry for herself.

But only a little. She picked up another list and studies the names of the dark-haired male UMD students at the school when Hollister was killed. There was a killer there, and she would find him.

Chapter 35

Dave Trask was standing in the road, hands tucked in his pockets, looking down the weed-covered gravel access where the rear of Deputy Gary Barton's car could just be seen in the brush. He'd been down to have a closer look, standing next to the car until the mosquitoes drove him out. There was nothing on or in the car that had told him anything.

He looked to the east to see the sun just starting to push the darkness away, the tops of the trees a black cutout against the brightening sky. There were no clouds on the horizon. Trask knew they had forecast rain and hoped any rain would hold off long enough for them to get the car to the lab and do a thorough search of the area. A light was now bobbing up and down as it approached, the beam tracking across the road in rhythm; a flashlight in someone's hand.

"Sheriff, we found him sir. About half-a-mile south."

The deputy said something else but Trask didn't hear. He had already started walking.

~~~

Don Trask was on his way north on 35W when he called his brother.

"You catch anything last weekend?"

"A case of the humbles. Linda absolutely smoked me on the smallmouth," answered Dave.

"OK, so a preschooler could do that. Frankly, it's getting a little boring the way I out-fish you every time."

"I suppose."

Don wasn't sure he had heard that right. The resignation in his brother's voice was evident. "What's going on?"

"I've got a dead deputy. Located his car early this morning. It had been driven into the woods, hidden. Looks like he was shot with his own gun."

"Oh shit. I am sorry, brother. I am on my way to Duluth right now. One of my agents was shot at last night."

"OK, I heard about that."

"So, I'm going to talk to her and then I'll call you."

"Any idea who did the shooting?"

"Not yet, but I had her looking into the Hollister murder."

Dave paused, remembering. "You think it had something to do with the Algaard disappearance?"

"Could be." Don was never what one would call sensitive, but he knew he had said the wrong thing at the wrong time when he got no response from his brother. His brother took things deeply, he had fought depression, and now he knew Dave was thinking that the shooting was his fault for getting Don involved. "Um, I'll call you before I come up. See you."

~~~

Lane hadn't slept. He finally gave up at six and shuffled into the kitchen. He made coffee, dumping out the grinds from the day before, putting in a new filter and coffee before pouring water into his machine. He stood leaning on the counter, listening to the water slowly trickle through the coffee maker, his eyelids too heavy to keep open. He caught himself as he fell forward, forcing his eyes open and straitening up. He moved over to the small television on his counter and turned it on.

It took only a moment for him to recognize the video being played on the news. Police cars with flashing lights filled the screen and then the shattered patio door of Carlisle's apartment. The camera panned to police searching the woods where Lane had stood only hours ago before moving to the reporter on location. Lane hurriedly walked to his bedroom, picking up his pants off the floor. He patted the pockets of his pants until he felt a hard lump and then put his hand inside and removed the shell casings. He knew he had picked them up but the video made him nervous and he had to double-check. Lane looked at the casings in his palm knowing he had to get rid of them but unable to think how. He walked back to the kitchen where the coffee was now ready and the traffic guy was talking about a backup on the freeway going south. He put the casings on the sink, poured himself a cup, and looked out his window.

Lane had heard every sound the night before, certain the cops would come, but they never did. Three times he had gotten up to look out at his backyard and to the street, each time seeing nothing, and each time thinking he was pushing his luck and should pack up and run. But he hadn't. Lane was inherently a lazy person, and his lack of sleep had done nothing but reinforce that trait. He knew he should probably run but the lazy side of him reasoned that he should just let the authorities come, deny any involvement, and then get a lawyer so he wouldn't have to deal with them. So now he stood in his kitchen, sipping coffee, looking out at his weed-covered, fenced-in backyard, just as the sun was providing the first light, deciding that in the new light his backyard didn't look so bad after all.

He poured himself another cup, the first one sour on his stomach, but knowing he would need more to get through the day. Walls should be back today and he wouldn't be happy. Damn Walls. He did all the dirty work while Walls went to his administration parties and fly-ins with donors. Walls never got his hands dirty, not once. Well, damn it, it was time he did. The Carlisle woman needed to be taken care of but there was no way he could do it now. Walls would have to make sure she was silenced. But Lane didn't trust Walls. Walls was sneaky, slimy, always sucking up to people. Lane knew that if it weren't for the Hollister abduction, and the others, that Walls would have dumped him long ago. That was why he had kept the emails from Walls telling him to bury the reports and not notify the police. Lane picked up the casings and decided he would need to take a drive over the bridge on his way to work and toss them in the lake. Then he'd set up a meeting with Walls that evening. And he'd bring his revolver.

Chapter 36

The sound of the slamming door as the man went to work woke the driver. After he was through with the woman he'd laid in bed listening to her scream accompanied by the old man with that high, crazed laugh that he got when he was having his fun. The driver wasn't sure if he could go to sleep, he was so buzzed after killing the cop, but taking his turn with the woman had relaxed him and eventually the sounds from the basement couldn't stop him from checking out.

On his back now, staring at the ceiling, the early afternoon light was trying to burn its way through the blanket he hung over the shade that covered his window. He didn't want to get up. His back was sore and his body felt tired, worn out. He felt the scratch on the back of his neck and lightly rubbed his palm where the thorn had poked him. Both spots were tender. He rolled to his side and put an extra pillow over his head but he could sense the light had invaded his room, and he knew it was no use. The light had found him and it would not let go.

~~~

It had only been in the last few years that he was able to sleep with even a hint of light. His mother had forced him from bed each morning at first light regardless of the day or time of year, saying that the light was a gift from God allowing us to be outside enjoying his creation. In the evenings she would turn on every light in the house, claiming the darkness was evil, insisting that the lights remained on all night. Her obsession had resulted in huge arguments with the driver's father, ending only after the driver had killed him. Five years later his mother started seeing the man. Two years after that they were married.

The driver kept his distance from the man, staying at friends' places as often as he could. After his mother and the man were married, the man still stayed at his place during the week because he was working nights, so it surprised the driver to see him one snowy Thursday evening near his twentieth birthday. The man rang the bell but then let himself in before the driver could get there, stomping the snow off his boots in the entryway.

"Where's your mother?"

"She's not here," the driver replied as he brought a beer to his lips. "She went to stay with my aunt in Proctor. My aunt is sick."

The man turned and looked out the window in the door. Only the hood and windshield of his car were clear of snow. "Damn, I should have called." He looked at the beer in the boy's hand. "You got any more of those?"

The driver indicated there were more in the refrigerator and returned to the living room where he had been watching porn. The man came into the room with a beer and stood next to the sofa watching. There were two girls on the screen who looked to be barely sixteen. The driver became uncomfortable with the man in the room but the man surprised him saying," Boy, I'd sure like to get me some of that."

The driver leaned back in his over-stuffed lounge chair and took a long drink, looking at the man who had now made himself comfortable on the couch. "I can get some."

The man looked at him and grinned. "I ain't talking about any hooker boy. I'm talking about fresh meat."

The driver sat forward. "That's what I'm talking about. But we'd have to share."

The man wasn't sure he believed the kid. From what his mother told him the kid was lazy, a pot smoker, who had just dropped out of college. But the man also guessed that the girls would find the kid attractive. After two more beers the kid left, he and the man agreeing that he'd bring back a girl for them to share, if the man paid him a hundred bucks. The man watched the kid disappear into the snowy night; not expecting to see him again and then helped himself to another beer. He jumped from the couch less than an hour later when the back door to the house banged open and the kid came in, dragging a girl in after him, dropping her on the floor of the living room. She looked to be in her late teens, with long blonde hair and blue eyes wide in fright, her feet and arms and her mouth taped.

"Jesus kid, you really did it."

The driver didn't smile. Instead he gave the man a look that made the man reevaluate how he thought about the kid. "You're first. You can use my room," said the boy as he pointed down the hall. "And I want my hundred now."

The man looked down at the girl squirming on the floor. "Nobody saw you?"

"Hell, you can hardly see a thing out there it's snowing so hard. I don't think I would have seen her except she stopped under a street light."

The man raised his gaze to the kid. He pulled his wallet from his back pocket and pulled out two fifties, handing them to the driver. "I won't be long."

And he wasn't. The driver had another beer and turned up the volume on the movie so he wouldn't have to listen.

The man walked into the living room less than half an hour later, buckling up his pants.

"Your turn."

The driver tipped the neck of his beer to the man, chugged what remained, and headed for his room. Five minutes later the front door burst open.

The volume was still up on another porn movie when the driver's mother marched into the living room without removing her coat or boots. Snow covered her cap and the shoulders of her black wool coat like a very bad case of dandruff. She looked at the television where two naked couples were writhing, and then at the man.

"What's going on? What are you doing here?" she shouted.

At that moment she heard a muffled scream from the boy's room and dashed down the hall to his open door to see a naked, bloodied woman lying on her back, tied to the bed. Her son was at the foot of the bed quickly trying to get into his jeans.

She raised her hand to her mouth, and was about to let out a scream, when the man came up behind her and put his hand over her mouth. He put his free hand on the back of her head and then sharply twisted her head. There was a snap and she dropped to the floor.

The man looked at the boy and then at the girl. "Finish up quick and then we'll take care of 'em."

The boy watched the man drag the body of his mother away, listening to him open the front door, the storm door banging shut as he pulled her outside. He thought he should feel sad, but he felt just the opposite, almost elated, like he just got his best birthday present ever. He leaned over and pushed his door shut and then turned back to the girl.

The boy strangled her with his belt when he had finished with her. They loaded the body of the girl into the man's trunk. The boy's mother, her face ashen and eyes bulging, was already there, lying on several black plastic bags. The man slammed the trunk shut and they walked back into the house.

"Your aunt know that your mother was coming?"

The driver thought back to the conversation he had overheard in the kitchen earlier in the day. "No. I heard her tell my aunt she'd maybe stop by tomorrow if the weather got better but then she just decided to go anyway."

"OK, you go clean up your room, I'll get the rest of the house. Wipe down anything the girl may have touched and bring your sheets. We'll burn them. You follow me to my house and stay with me. We'll come back Saturday and report her missing."

The boy did as the man said. He didn't like being told what to do but the man seemed to know what he was doing. The police only questioned him one time after they reported his mother missing, the man telling him beforehand what he thought the police would ask and what he should say. For the most part, the man had been right. The boy moved in with the man after that.

~~~

The driver leaned against the kitchen counter, sipping his coffee, staring at the door to the basement. He heard nothing and guessed the girl was probably dead. The man liked to be rough, liked to slap the girls around, make them cry and scream. The driver was pretty sure that was why the man liked to go first. He wanted them when they still had some spirit and fight, before they gave up, resigned to the fact that there was nothing they could do that would save them.

He turned back to the counter and was refilling his cup when his phone rang. He looked at the screen to see that it was the man.

"Yeah?"

"Did you kill a cop?"

Chapter 37

Don Trask marched into the Duluth office. Carlisle and Bob Farmer were waiting for Trask in the conference room, seated together on one end of the oblong table. Carlisle had made two copies of what she had and placed one set intentionally in front of the chair on the opposite side of where Farmer was seated. She did not feel comfortable near Trask – personally or professionally. Carlisle and Farmer rose, shaking hands with Trask.

"How are you doing Danny?"

Carlisle could hear the concern in Trask's voice but there was something more. He seemed distant. "Fine, sir. A little tired. Not much sleep last night." She waited for some response but Trask was silent. She pointed to the file on the table where Trask would sit. "I've put together a list of possibilities for us to go through."

Trask looked at the file and its location. He took one more glance at Carlisle and then moved around behind them to his chair. He sat and opened the file.

"Danny, why don't you take us through this," said Farmer.

After Carlisle explained what was on each sheet, Trask leaned back in his chair putting his hands behind his head, staring at the wall across from him. A picture of the governor stared back. "Does that guy ever blink?"

Farmer and Carlisle looked at each other and then at Trask.

"Don?" said Farmer.

"The governor. I've been in I don't know how many meetings with him and he never blinks. I don't know how he does it." Trask seemed lost in thought, trying to solve the non-blinking governor puzzle, when he leaned forward and put his elbows on the table. "I think we can all agree that this attack on Danny has something to do with the assignment I gave her."

Carlisle and Farmer nodded.

"So that leaves us with the two possibilities Danny has outlined, that the Algaard abductor has somehow gotten wind of what she was doing and that he is afraid he will be found out, or, that someone at the school, or connected with it, feels threatened enough to want her dead. Danny, what do you think?"

Carlisle could feel Trask looking at her but she stared at the file in front of her. "No doubt Lane did a shoddy job on the investigations of the abduction and abduction attempts, and I suppose it's possible that was part of a request by higher ups at the time to keep it quiet, but, I just don't see him as a killer. I mean the guy tries to appear menacing but mostly he's just creepy. I think it's got to be one of the former students I identified."

"Bob?"

"I guess I agree."

"You have any ties between your suspects and staff at the school now?" Trask asked Carlisle.

She looked at her notes. "Nothing I have found so far."

Trask looked back at the portrait of the governor. "Who was Lane's supervisor at the time of the abductions?"

"Sorry, I haven't got that information," answered Carlisle.

Trask seemed to drift away again. Carlisle leaned forward to watch him.

"It's always good to listen to your gut, but in this case, I think you may be wrong." Trask turned to Carlisle. "Think about it. Whoever did this had to get word of what you were doing from someone at the school. If it was the Algaard abductor, and possible Hollister killer, then whoever got word to him had to be carrying the secret of what that person did for an awfully long time. Who would a killer trust with that kind of information for that long?" Trask leaned on the table again. "I think you may have our killer and or abductor identified, and we need to get after those suspects, but I just don't think they are the ones shooting at you. Lane followed orders before. Now he's got a lot more years invested. We need to find out who his supervisor was, and who was on the administration at that time, but let's stay focused on finding out more about these suspects you've identified for now." Trask turned to Farmer. "Bob, I'd like you to assign another agent to help Danny check the backgrounds on her suspects. I'll pass the list on to my assistant and see what he can find. Might as well see if we can locate them and see where they were Monday night."

"Right."

Trask stood. "Danny, I'm sorry about this. I really had no idea this would happen. And frankly, except that Blaine Algaard is on your list of suspects, I still don't see a clear connection to the Carol Algaard disappearance although my gut tells me you have the Hollister murderer on your list." Trask moved to the conference room door. "Good work Danny, but no Lone Ranger on this. If they're smart, they'll know you've shared your information by now, and hopefully they'll back off, but don't take any chances. The killers I have known haven't been the smartest people. Let the Duluth PD handle it for now." He turned and left.

Danny looked at the empty doorway Trask had filled. That was it. There was no chitchat, no mention of maybe a lunch or dinner. They were done. He had lost interest or found someone else, but either way 'it', if there ever was an 'it', was over.

"Danny?"

Carlisle had forgotten about her boss and turned back to him. "Yeah?"

"I'll get Dave to give you a hand on these background checks." He paused and saw the lost look on her face. "Danny, Trask may not be right about the shooter being someone associated with the school, but he is right about one thing. You need to be careful."

Carlisle stood and picked up her file. "I will." But as she left the room, she thought that maybe Trask could be right, maybe it was someone at the school. But could it really be Lane? She remembered meeting him in the basement of the Administration Building. How had he known she was there? She decided she'd have to pay Lane a visit.

Chapter 38

Don called his brother as he drove north along Superior, looking out at the lake. The wind was calm and the big ore ships were pushing their cargo across the water. It was a beautiful day, one that should have him itching to get on the water, especially in this area, but his mind was far from it. There was evil here, an evil that had somehow gone unnoticed but now was making itself known. Evil that needed to be stopped.

Dave picked up right away. "You close?"

No smart comment. His brother was feeling it too. "Ten miles to your office."

"I'll be here."

Don heard Dave disconnect, glanced at his phone to see that the conversation had indeed ended, and put down his phone. Dave was definitely feeling it. As he pulled into the Lake County Sheriff's parking lot, his phone rang. He pulled into an open spot and turned off his car. "What's up?"

"I wasn't sure if you knew of this or not but there was another woman possibly abducted up your way last night," Larry Stoxon informed his boss.

Trask was at full attention now. "Where?"

Stoxon gave him the details.

"OK. Can you send me that map? Also, I'm sending you a list of possible suspects that I need background checks done on. I'm especially interested in knowing if any of them have any ties to UMD and or to Blaine Algaard."

Stoxon said he would take care of the requests and hung up. Trask walked into the sheriff's office and signed in. He found his way back to Dave's office and looked through the long window beside the door at his brother. Dave was staring straight ahead, looking right at Don, but did not appear to have any idea he was there at all. Don walked in.

"Brother."

Dave looked up at Don and watched him take a seat in front of his desk before he spoke. "You were right."

"About what?"

"That I was an idiot for taking this job. You were right."

Don looked at Dave. His brother's brown eyes were sunken, bags under them. His hair was disheveled, his shirt wrinkled, like he had worn it several days in a row. He could see him sinking. He knew what was happening. Depression trying to get hold, trying to pull him down. Their dad had suffered from it as his sons did. None of them had ever talked about it but Dave had sought treatment, Don refusing to go that far.

"Finally. After all these years. I can die happy now." Don thought that would get some reaction from Dave but he saw no change in his expression. "OK, so tell me what you got."

Dave took his brother through what he knew about the killing. "We're still going over the car. The autopsy is happening now. That's about it."

"So he didn't call in a plate, get any video?"

Dave shook his head. "No. I had talked to Gary about it but he had a habit of trusting everyone. This time it cost him his life."

Don sat back. "OK, so Barton didn't have an enemy in the world. He was mister friendly. So, for some reason, he crossed paths with a bad guy in the middle of the night in the middle of nowhere and he had no idea it was a bad guy."

"Had to be. No sign of a struggle that we could see, either on the body or in the areas where we found his car and his body. His upper lip had been cut but it didn't look to me like anything hard had hit him. Could have been tricked to stop some way but that would mean that the killer wanted him to stop and Barton likely would have called something in. Doesn't make sense. Seems most likely he came across the killer who had stopped for some reason, and whatever it was, it seemed harmless to Barton. Maybe the killer had car trouble?"

"So you're a bad guy out in the middle of the night with engine trouble, under the hood trying to fix whatever is wrong, and Barton pulls up behind you. Barton gets out to help the guy. Why does the guy panic and shoot Barton?"

"He didn't shoot him in the road, he shot him in the ditch. Looks like someone dragged him in. But as for your question, Barton either recognized him, or he may have seen something in the killer's vehicle. Drugs maybe?"

Don looked at the picture on the wall behind Dave. They were holding a muskie Don had caught on Lake Vermillion, biggest muskie he had ever caught. The fish made two long runs but Don had his drag set right and the fish eventually came to the boat. But it had been a team effort. Dave had the net ready when the fish came close, scooping it up just as the hooks popped free. They needed a team effort now. "So how'd he knock Barton out?"

Dave could feel himself coming out of it a bit now. His brother's question was important. He picked up his phone and dialed the coroner's office.

"Doctor Adams." Adams was a thin man in his late fifties with an unflappable, analytical personality.

"Hey doc, it's Dave Trask. How is the autopsy going?"

"Just finishing up sheriff."

"Anything interesting?"

"The officer died of a single gunshot to the back of the head. I have recovered the bullet and will send it to the BCA for analysis."

"OK, anything else? Any other wounds?"

Adams looked at his notes. "Two items seem to come under that category. There was a cut on his upper lip and the columella on his nose was bruised."

"Columella?"

"Yes, the underside of the front of the nose. I would surmise that he sustained some type of blow to the area before he was shot in the ditch."

"Why before?"

"Well, there was only tall soft grass in the ditch. His nose and lip had come in contact with something hard."

"Enough to knock him out?"

"From the limited damage I could see, I'd say no."

Dave shook his head. There was nothing the doctor had found that seemed to be of any help. "OK, thanks doc." Trask was about to hang up when he heard Adams say something. "Pardon?"

"I said, don't you want to hear about the other thing?"

Dave was confused. "What other thing? You said there were two things, the lip and the nose."

"No, no. The lip and nose are one thing. The other item is a small burn I found on the victim's neck."

"A burn?"

"Yes, just on the side of his neck below and behind his right ear. There appear to be two small points where something burned him and then a small bruise around the area."

Dave sat up. He wanted to see the mark for himself. "I'll be right over doc. I want to have a look at that burn." He hung up and looked at Don. He did not really want to see the body of Barton again but he felt this could be important. He stood. "Let's go see the ME."

~~~

Melissa Hanes had called the Two Harbors police three times in the nearly two weeks following the attack on her and Julie Powers at Cliffside. Each time someone told her that the investigation was open and ongoing but that there was no new information. Each time Hanes hung up she thought BULLSHIT! She was fed up with the inattention given to her and called the Duluth Police Department.

"I'd like to speak to a detective please," she said to the man who answered.

"And what is this in regards to mam?"

"It's in regards to an attack on two women. Now let me talk to a detective!"

"One minute please."

"Yeah?" answered Hillary Thomas.

"Um, I got a woman who wants to talk to a detective. She says it's about an attack on two women."

"Fine, put her through." There was a click and then Thomas answered. "Sergeant Thomas. How can I help you?"

"Sergeant, my name is Melissa Hanes. I am a retired sergeant with the United States Army and currently am employed at the Cliffside Resort just north of Two Harbors. A man wielding what I believe was some kind of shock stick attacked on the evening of August ninth, a coworker and myself."

"Um, OK. Did you report this to the Two Harbors police?"

"Yes mam I did, that evening, only I had a feeling our report was not taken too seriously. I have since called Two Harbors three times for an update but have been given the same line about the case being open but nothing new to report."

"I see. Well mam, I understand your frustration, but what you have been told may be all they know. Regardless, we cannot overstep their jurisdiction, but you may want to contact the Lake County sheriff's office which also operates in Two Harbors."

Hanes wasn't pleased about being brushed off but she thanked Thomas and hung up. She considered dropping it but it was against her nature. She looked up the Lake County sheriff and dialed.

"Lake County Sheriff. Can I help you?" said the woman answering.

Hanes went through the same introduction and explanation after someone transferred her to a deputy who took down her information. He promised to contact the Two Harbors PD and said he would let her know of any developments. Hanes remained frustrated but felt somehow better that she had at least attempted to spur some action. She made a note on her calendar to call the deputy back in a week.

~~~

The man had been royally pissed. The driver tried to tell him there was no way for the cops to trace the killing to him, that he was careful, but the man wouldn't listen and just kept screaming. The driver finally told the man to "fuck off" and hung up. The man called back immediately but the driver didn't answer, just stood staring out the window, drinking his coffee. Work to do.

The driver flicked the light switch next to the basement door, opened the door to the basement, and reached for the handrail as he took the first step down. The steps were steep and short, the ceiling over the stairs low enough that he turned his head to the side as he descended. He found Justine Blake on her back on the bed in the basement, wrists tied to opposite sides of the bed frame. Her eyes were open and hazy, her skin already a mottled gray. She was dead. There was significant bruising around her neck and blood that had run from a split lip and her nose had left a dried dark trail over her cheek and onto the mattress.

The man had choked her to death. When he found he couldn't get the response he wanted from the women, the look of fear that really got him going, the man had found that choking the women when he was on top of them would sometimes do the trick. As their air was cut off, and they suddenly became aware that they were on the precipice of breathing their last, the women would make one last attempt to save themselves. Their eyes would open to their fullest, and they would struggle under him, pulling at their restraints and shaking their heads. He wasn't quite sure what it was that really got him off the most, and he had thought about it, almost trying to analyze it. He thought about them struggling to save themselves, the look of utter fear in their faces, and the ultimate feeling of power it gave him to know that he held their life in his hands. In the end he decided that it was just the whole experience.

The smell hit the driver before he was halfway down the stairs, the girl's bowels had given way, and he figured she'd be gone. What he didn't count on was that the man hadn't put down any plastic. The man had brought a big industrial roll of plastic home several months ago from Home Depot. He told the driver they should use it over the bed so they wouldn't have to get a new mattress every time they had a woman. But last night he hadn't used the plastic. The blood and urine stains were easy to see.

"Fuck!"

Now he'd not only have to take care of the girl's body, he'd also have to haul the mattress outside and burn it. The driver stood at the foot of the bed looking at the dead woman. "Fuck!" He turned his head and looked up the stairs at the sound of a slamming door.

Chapter 39

Dave led the way as the two brothers strode down the brick-lined hall of the county coroner's office. Don hadn't been in the building before and the shiny tan-flecked linoleum floor, red brick walls, and brown metal doors with small square windows made him feel as if he was in an asylum, or maybe his grade school. Dave opened the third door on the left after a quick knock. A man in a white lab coat with thin wire-rimmed glasses perched on a small, slightly rounded nose swiveled in a chair in front of a large cluttered desk and stood. Dr. Joshua Adams was just past sixty, thin, with thinning black hair streaked with gray. He extended a bony hand to Dave and then stopped when he saw Don close behind.

"I take it there is some relation between the two of you?"

"Doctor Adams, this is my brother Don, lead investigator for the Bureau of Criminal Apprehension."

Adams shook Don's hand. "Well, let's go take a look." The Trasks followed Adams out of his office through a connecting brown metal door into his examination room. He stopped at a desk to the right, putting on gloves, and offering the box to the Trasks to do the same. He picked up a magnifying glass on the desk and then led them to a white sheet-covered body on a table at the center of the room, pulling down the sheet to reveal the victim's head and shoulders.

Dave cringed at the sight of Barton. He looked away momentarily and then back to the body.

Adams adjusted a light that hung from the ceiling over the body and turned to Dave, his hand holding the magnifying glass extended. "At first I thought that it was just a bruise," he said after Dave took the glass, "but I thought it an odd shape and so took a closer look." He pointed to a mark on Barton's neck.

Dave looked first and then handed the glass to his brother. He didn't wait for Don to complete his examination, instead turned and walked toward the door leading to Adam's office, peeling off his gloves and dropping them in the trash can next to the door with several other used pairs of gloves, piled like some creature had been shedding its blue-green skin. He left the examination room, walked through the doctor's office, and into the hall.

Don joined him a few minutes later. "You OK?"

Dave stared off down the hall. "Good guy, nice family, would have retired in a few years."

"Sorry brother." Don had no other words. He knew that Dave had only been in his job for a little over a year; a job he wasn't sure he even wanted, but also knew that didn't matter. You grew close to the people on your team in a hurry. You depended on them and they depended on you, and when you lost one it hurt like losing a family member.

Dave started walking down the hall and Don followed. They exited the building and sat in Dave's truck. "He was executed brother. Somebody stunned him and then shot him. He never had a chance," said Dave as he stared out the windshield at the building in front of him.

"I looked at his face. It's possible he hit something when he was pushed or fell. It wasn't rough and the doc said there was no sign of any gravel or dirt so I'm thinking he may have hit the side of a car, could have been his own. We should have it checked. I'll call." The counties in northeastern Minnesota used the BCA crime lab in Duluth for any analysis as most did not have the facilities.

Don was looking at his brother as he spoke on the phone. Dave had a puzzled, lost look on his face. "You make anything of that abduction a couple of weeks ago?"

Dave looked at Don. "No. It's like she just disappeared."

"OK, so now there has been another one."

"When?"

"Last night. A place called the Passer By Bar over by Big Lake. You know it?"

"No. That would be in St. Louis county, biggest county in the state. Glad I didn't pick that one. What happened?"

"Don't know. The woman lived with the manager of the bar and she never made it home. He called her in missing today when he got up. He was taking care of her two-year-old. She had been closing up. They found her car at the bar but that's about all I know."

"Sounds like the same thing," commented Dave.

"I asked Larry to put together a map of the abductions or abduction attempts on women in this area over the last few years. These two and Carol Algaard aren't the only ones. They don't run much north of here, of course there really isn't anything north of here, but there have been several south and even one in Wisconsin."

"And are all of these women missing?"

Don tilted his head sideways. "Hmm. Sometimes some of my smarts must actually rub off on you. Let me ask Larry to look at it." Don called his assistant who said he would see what he could find and get back to him.

"How's your agent?"

"She's OK. A little shook up I think."

"Any idea who tried to take her out?"

"I got to think it was someone at the school or someone who knows someone at UMD."

"And you think it's related to the Algaard disappearance?"

Don paused. "You know, its got to be but I just can't figure out why. These abductions, or attempts, happened years ago, and long before Carol Algaard disappeared. The only tie I see is Blaine Algaard. He was at the school when these happened and obviously, he was at Chase when Algaard went missing. But I don't know how he knew of what Carlisle was doing and why that would make any difference to him."

"Do you know where he was when your agent was shot at?"

Don looked at Dave. He felt like he had slipped up and he did not like the feeling, especially when Dave was the one pointing it out to him. "Let's go back to your office. I can show you the map of the abductions and we can give Chief Fowles a call on the way to see if he would happen to know what Algaard has been up to."

Dave drove while Don called Fowles. He caught a few words but found he had to keep his attention on the road. Seeing Barton again had left him feeling isolated and disconnected.

Don clicked off and turned to Dave. "Your boy Algaard has disappeared."

"When?"

"Fowles isn't sure. He had someone watching him. No lights came on at Algaard's house Sunday night and he never opened the liquor store Monday. They went to check his house. Nobody there and his car is gone. Didn't appear that he had taken anything with him."

~~~

Carlisle and two other agents spent the better part of the rest of the day looking at the suspects she had identified. Five had criminal records, ranging from felonies to misdemeanor drug violations. They found one man without a record who had an aunt that was a professor at the college but it turned out that he was in Utah on vacation and had been for the last week. There were no other suspects that had current ties to the college as far as they knew after a day of phone calls. It was entirely likely that someone on this list still had a tie to the school that they had not found.

It was nearing seven and the two agents helping Carlisle had left over an hour earlier. She stood and stretched, several empty sunflower seed shells falling from her onto the floor like she was shedding scales. She looked at the worn carpet around her chair and realized it looked like a squirrel had just finished its Thanksgiving dinner. She walked to the closet and pulled out the stiff-bristled broom with the dustpan attached and swept up what she could, dumping the empty husks into her garbage can. She returned the broom to the closet and then went back to her desk, putting her hands on the back of the chair and leaning forward, looking at the suspect list on her desk.

As the day had gone on she became more convinced that her attacker had not been someone on her list just as Trask suggested. At the same time it occurred to her that she had forgotten her original assignment, namely to see if there was any tie-in to what had happened to Hollister and to Algaard. What they needed to do was to go back through the suspect list to look for any suspects that may have known Hollister and Algaard, especially any way they may have known

Algaard when she was in Chase. They'd have to go back through the list.

Carlisle wanted to keep going, keep looking, but the last two days had finally caught up to her. She called to see if her balcony door had been repaired, found it was, and decided to head home. She was leaving the BCA building, looking forward to sleeping in her own bed, with no crying kids to wake her, but at the same time found she felt anxious, and a bit nervous. She tried to put it off to being tired but she knew her attacker was still out there, and he or she knew were she lived. She had been lucky. She got in her car and sat staring out the windshield. Out of the corner of her eye she caught sight of a man in tan slacks and a dark blue polo approaching her car from the left. She turned and stared, thinking she may have seen him somewhere recently, maybe at the school. He looked at her as he passed in front of her car. Carlisle felt herself tense up, feeling for her pistol, relaxing only when he had entered the building and passed from her sight. She released a breath and thought about going back to Hillary's for the night, or maybe a bit longer, so that she could look for a new place to live. She turned on the ignition and shook her head back and forth. Nobody is running me from my place. She headed home.

Chapter 40

Carlisle went through the drive-through at Dominos and picked up a medium Hawaiian with extra pineapple. She had called ahead and told them who she was and asked for her regular. The kid at the drive-through window was a pimply faced blonde named Tommy who was a senior in high school and knew her by name. He asked her how it was going and she said fine and she asked him the same and he said he just got a new video game about drug warlords and asked her if she wanted to come over to his house and play. Carlisle politely refused and drove off after tipping him. She felt a momentary lift in her spirits thinking that a seventeen-year-old had attempted to hit on her; at least she thought it was, but after more consideration she wasn't sure.

What she was sure of was that for the briefest of moments, she had actually considered his invitation. Danny wasn't what you would call an addicted gamer, but she did like to play, and spent a fair amount of her off time on-line. There was no way she would have ever accepted the kid's invitation but as she thought about it more she realized that the only reason his invitation had any appeal was that she didn't want to be alone. Not tonight.

She felt her trepidation building as she climbed the stairs to her floor. She opened the door to the hallway and looked both ways before entering and moving toward her door. She tried the door, found it was locked, and put her key in the lock. She heard the bolt click back, took a deep breath, and turned the knob. Normally Carlisle would have flicked on the light, turned immediately to the right, put the pizza box on the counter, and tossed her keys there too. Now she stood in her dark entryway and listened, her senses on high alert. She could see looking straight ahead that her sliding door had been repaired but that the curtains were open. She moved quickly across her apartment and pulled the cord shutting the curtain.

Danny stood to the side of the balcony door, behind the wall, and felt her heart race. She took two deep breaths to calm herself down and then realized her left hand was warm from the pizza box she still held. She moved to the kitchen table and put the box down and then walked through the rest of her apartment, turning on lights as she went. Certain she was the only one there, she returned to the kitchen, putting her purse, gun, and keys on the counter, and pouring herself a glass of chardonnay from the box in her refrigerator. She sat at the table and opened the box, lifting a piece of pizza to her mouth.

Carlisle surveyed her apartment as she chewed. She stood and walked to the center of her living room where she could see that they had patched the holes in her wall, now white splatters on her pastel wall. White dust coated the mopboards below with pieces of her vase still lying there. Her eyes moved across the carpet and picked up glitters in the tan Berber like someone had dropped diamonds there. She bent and picked up a piece of glass and held it between her fingers. Carlisle had interviewed victims of home robberies and heard them talk of their feelings, feelings of being on edge, insecure, untrusting of others, of being violated. As she held the shard of glass in her fingers, she now knew what they meant, but Danny Carlisle felt something more, she felt angry.

She went back to the table and quickly downed the glass of wine as she chewed, staring at the piece of glass she had placed on the table. Carlisle had never been one to scream and shout when she was upset. Instead she tended to internalize her emotions, going quiet as they simmered inside, thinking about what it was that had set her off. It was what she was doing now, thinking about who had taken a shot at her. She had tried to keep her focus on the assignment at work today but in the back of her mind she couldn't help but mull over what had happened the night before. The more she thought about it the more she was convinced that Trask was right, that it was someone at the school who felt threatened because she had looked into the old abductions. But as she worked during the day she also became convinced that it wasn't because she was getting too close to who may have done the crimes, it was because of the incidents themselves. She thought about her conversation with Hillary Thomas after she had first looked at the files on the abductions. The school had covered them up. And Lane was the responding officer.

Carlisle thought about Lane when he had tried to see what she was looking at in his office and how he had shown up when she was in the Records Room. It had to be him. But was he on his own or taking instructions from someone? Carlisle no longer felt tired. She had to find out whom Lane was working for when the abductions took place and she believed she had that information in the files she had at the office. She took one more look at her apartment, decided she'd clean it later, took one more bite of pizza, and picked up her keys, purse, and gun.

~~~

Twenty-one women had been reported as abducted in northeast Minnesota in the last four years, the majority in the Duluth area. Four had been murdered and raped, in each case a husband or male acquaintance had been found guilty of the crime and all were serving time. Three more women had been abducted and then later released or escaped. Two of the abductions had taken place in Duluth and they had arrested a suspect. They had not captured the abductor of the other woman in Superior. Someone she described as older, with greasy black hair, and unshaven had abducted that woman at gunpoint. She managed to take off running when they pulled into a park east of town and made it to a house nearby. Stoxon attached a sketch.

"That leaves fourteen women who have disappeared in the last four years, including Carol Algaard," said Don as he looked at the map lying on his brother's desk. "Shit Dave, if this was the Twin Cities this would be hard to believe. In this area it's almost unimaginable."

Dave made a mark on the map.

"What's that?" asked his brother.

"Big Lake. That makes fifteen."

The Trasks stood shoulder-to-shoulder, both leaning on the desk, looking down at the map. Don reached over and picked up the sketch of the unidentified abductor and a half dozen other sheets containing information on each of the abductions. He studied the sketch and looked at the witness's description. He passed it to Dave.

"Could be Algaard," said Don.

Dave wasn't sure. The woman had said that the man was older but he had seen too many eye witness descriptions to put much faith in them. "Yeah, maybe."

Don walked back to the front of Dave's desk and sat, shuffling through the other sheets, finally putting them down in his lap. There was something there that he should be seeing but he didn't want to pass the sheets to Dave, afraid he would see whatever it was before him. He bowed his head as he rubbed his forehead, letting out a protracted yawn as he did. He was feeling tired, worn. It was happening more often lately. It seemed like he could go for days without sleep when he was young, the adrenaline pushing him on, but now his body and his mind seemed to slow down after a twelve-hour day.

Dave looked up to see his brother yawn. He had barely slept since the shooting of his deputy and now could not hold back a reactionary yawn of his own. He sat and picked up the daily incident reports on his desk. He found it nearly impossible to retain any of what he read, his thoughts bouncing around in his mind like a pinball, too much there. "Come on brother," Dave said as he pushed himself up. "BCA is buying dinner."

They returned to Don's car. As Don drove Dave scrolled through the call reports for the day on his phone. The calls were divided into those from other law enforcement agencies and those from the public. Many of the calls from the public were to report things of a suspicious nature that often turned out to be nothing. But a call to the Two Harbors office by a woman named Melissa Hanes caught his attention. "Pull over."

"What?"

"I said pull over," answered Dave.

Don looked over at his brother engrossed in something on his phone and then slowed and pulled to the curb. "What? You got to pee?"

Dave shoved his phone in his brother's face. "Read this."

Don read through the report of Melissa Hanes' call. He handed Dave's phone back to him. "You're thinking the lighted stick is a stun stick, that the guy that has been abducting these women is using the stick, and that Barton ran into him."

"It fits. We need to talk to Melissa Hanes."

Chapter 41

The driver heard the man running around upstairs shouting for him until he clumped down the wooden stairs, stopping when he reached the concrete floor at the bottom. The basement was partitioned into two sections, most it a utility and storage area. Three steps from the bottom of the stairs on the partition wall was a door to the other room, a room bearing little resemblance to the one next to it. The walls had all been studded and sheet rocked, insulation between the studs, although the sheet rock had not been taped or painted. The floor had a pad of carpet under a couch but the rest was unfinished like the rest of the basement. Thick one-foot by one-foot asbestos tiles hung from a metal grid on the ceiling. Four recessed lights lit the room. Because of the dropped ceiling the distance from floor to ceiling was less than six and a half feet, giving the room a cramped, subterranean feeling. The head of the bed frame was pushed up against the wall to the right, hooks and metal loops screwed into the studs at varying heights on the wall, some on the ceiling above the bed. There were shelves along the wall to the left of the bed littered with duct tape, chains, padlocks, the knife, rags, an open box of industrial size plastic trash bags and paper towels. A baseball bat leaned against the shelf.

The driver came out of the door of the room with the bed and stopped. He faced the man and could see the seething anger in his face.

When the driver had first moved in the man had taken care of him, making sure he had enough to eat, enough beer, even buying him clothes occasionally. He purchased a big screen television and a video game console, getting new games when the driver wanted them. In return, the driver secured the women they shared, and for the most part, only ventured out at night, and even then, avoiding the area around Chase.

But increasingly the driver came to feel like a prisoner, the man getting paranoid that someone would catch the driver. The man had GPS tracking installed on the driver's phone and called him daily to check up on him. He stopped asking what the driver wanted to eat, telling him he could eat whatever the man bought. And then Carol Algaard happened.

The driver was out of beer and texted the man to bring some home. The man said he was too busy and that the driver would have to wait. The driver was fuming. It was now after seven and he had been working outside all day, splitting and stacking wood, and he wanted a beer. The liquor stores in Minnesota close at eight so the driver had no choice but to go to the Save Big in Chase.

The driver circled around town, coming in on the south side where the liquor store stood just off the highway. He parked in the lot next to the side of the building where he hoped the man wouldn't see him if he cruised by. The driver entered the store and made his way past the wine aisle to the beer cooler that lined the wall to his right. He picked out a case of Miller, regular Miller, not Miller Lite. He detested the taste, or rather the lack of taste, of light beer. The driver walked down the aisle with whiskey and vodka, to the counter on the other side, and set the case on the counter. The woman behind the counter scanned the case, looked at the readout on her till, and then looked at the driver, telling him he owed $18.24.

The driver had watched the woman as she rang up his purchase, thinking she was cute and he would like to have some fun with her, when she turned to face him and he froze. It was her. She was older and a little tired looking but it was definitely her. He remembered. She had been at UMD when he had taken the other woman in front of the library. The driver immediately lowered his head, looking down at his wallet, and removing a twenty. He slapped the bill on the counter, mumbled "keep the change", grabbed the case, and nearly sprinted from the store. The woman yelled something after him that he did not hear. He jumped in his truck and sped out of the lot, his tires screeching when he hit the highway, not worrying that he may attract the attention of the man or anyone else. He just wanted to get away.

The driver had finished a six-pack by the time the man made it home a little over an hour later. He had debated about telling the man what had happened but decided to let him know. The man swore at him, called him every name he knew, and then told the driver to stay put for at least the next week, that he would take care of things. And he had done just that. Two nights later he had come home with the woman. She was out cold with a gash across her forehead that was bleeding heavily. The driver heard the man drive up and had opened the door for him, but the man had said nothing as he passed, carrying the woman across his shoulder and taking her directly to the basement. The driver listened upstairs but there were few noises, and no sound at all from the woman. Roughly half an hour later the man came up the stairs, told the driver to go down to the basement and clean up the mess, and went to bed.

The driver listened to the man slam his bedroom door before he walked down the stairs, holding the handrail to steady himself. By the time he reached the bottom stair the smell of death was strong. He walked to the nearly closed door of the other room and pushed it open. Carol Algaard lay naked on her back on the bed. Blood was still on her forehead but now he could see that it had also run down the front of her face and he noticed that her eyes were missing. He would find them later on the floor. The nipples on her breasts had also been removed and the driver guessed the man had used the long-bladed hunting knife that was driven into Algaard's chest to do the cutting. There would be no sharing of this woman.

~~~

Following the Algaard abduction, it seemed to the driver that the man had become increasingly worried about getting caught. Paranoid. And now the man's face was so red that the driver thought the man would have a heart attack. There was a revolver in a holster on the man's hip and the driver was sure that only one of them would come out of the basement alive. He realized he had no weapon and thought about the knife in the other room. As the man stared at him, the driver had images of driving the knife into the man's fat stomach, pulling the blade up, and seeing the man's eyes go wide and hear the oxygen escape from his gut.

The man could not believe that the driver had been so stupid as to kill a cop. When you killed a cop, other cops took it personally. You went to the top of every cop's priority list. Your chances of getting caught were much higher as well as your chances of not surviving to make it to court.

On the drive to the house he had decided to shoot the boy but now, as he faced him, he could feel some of his anger dissipate. The odor coming from the other room was strong and the man, breathing through his nose, coughed, and was forced to breathe through his mouth. Still the stench made his stomach uneasy, and he could feel the odor-laden air permeating his clothes and skin. It would not be easy to wash off. The man could see fear in the bloodshot eyes of the kid, as well as hatred, and something more.

The driver tried to explain that he had no choice, and that he had been careful, but the man wouldn't listen. "It's your fucking fault. If you had the driveway graded my tire wouldn't have gone flat!"

The man's eyes narrowed. The kid may have a point, but that didn't change the fact that the cops would be coming hard, doing all they could to find the cop killer in front of him. Lots of heat coming. "Aw, fuck. Get her out back and I'll help you bury her after I change." The man turned and went up the stairs.

The driver watched the man disappear up the stairs but he remained tense. That had been too easy. The man was up to something. The driver walked back into the other room, found the knife on the counter, and stuffed it in the back of his pants.

Chapter 42

The BCA office was quiet. Carlisle nodded to the man on the phone at the front desk as she entered. He was fifty-five, stocky, with crewcut blonde hair that was coarse like bristles on a scrub brush. A retired Duluth policeman, he had taken the night desk job as a way of keeping busy and making some additional cash on top of his pension. He waved at Carlisle and then went back to taking notes.

She turned on the lamp affixed to the shelving above her desk and sat down, picking a couple of sunflower seed shells from her chair as she did, and tossing them in the wastebasket. She faced the file of Blaine Algaard as well as the other suspects she had identified thinking about how Trask had told her to focus on her assigned task, not to go off on her own. She pushed the files aside and pulled her notebook and another file close.

The sheets she was looking for were on the bottom of the file. They listed the members of the administration for the year of the abductions as well as a year before and a year after. She spread them out, side-by-side, so she could compare. Dr. Lee Severson had been the Chancellor of UMD in each of those years. A Vice Chancellor in the first two years, a Stephen Reems, had been joined by another Vice Chancellor in the third year, Barbara Davis. As Carlisle looked back and forth between the years, she could see that some positions had changed, people had moved to new positions, people had apparently left, and new people were added. She ended up making a list of all of the administrators who had been on the lists all three years and noted their titles. Blake Lane wasn't listed on any of the sheets, apparently he wasn't high enough up, but she found a Dave Walls who was head of the campus security for all of the years, and whom she assumed was the same guy who was now VP of Administration. Mr. Walls had done well.

She realized she needed a list of the current administration at UMD to compare to who had been there during those years. Carlisle pulled up the UMD website and discovered the structure of the administration had changed considerably in the last few years as had the administrators themselves. Carlisle decided her best option would be to do a search on the eighteen people on her three-year list on the current UMD website. Only seven of the names returned hits. They have involved all of those people, including Walls in the cover-up as well as the attack on her. Her trouble was that she did not understand the structure of the administration. She knew who reported to the current chancellor, but did not know where the individual department heads reported, both in the current administration and in the three years she was targeting. Walls seemed the likely connection to Lane, but it was possible someone had given Walls an order. She looked at Walls picture on the UMD site. Could this guy have taken a shot at her?

Carlisle could feel herself slowing again. She needed rest. She pushed the papers she had been viewing back into folders and placed her notebook on top. She said goodnight to the guy at the front desk and walked outside to her car. It wasn't until she had turned the key that she realized she would have to go back to her apartment. She was suddenly awake.

~~~

As Walls pondered what to do about Lane, he realized that the only thing tying him to any of this mess, including Lane, was Lane himself. It had probably been a mistake telling him to go after the woman. Any reports on the abductions only had Lane's name on it, he had made sure of that. And what were the odds that she would even look into the investigation, or lack of investigation, of each? Lane was stupid but he was also sneaky. Walls figured he had something on him somewhere that tied him to the cover-up. No, he should have left it alone, he could see that now, but it was too late for that. Lane had to be taken care of but how to do it?

Walls sat at the desk in his home office and removed his glasses, squeezing the bridge of his nose. This whole thing was giving him a headache. He pushed back his chair and stood, picking up the tumbler of scotch from the desktop, and walking his six-foot two frame to the window of his study. The window looked out on the front yard of his home on London Road, roughly half-a-mile north of the infamous Glensheen mansion. Wall's red brick colonial was on the Superior side of the road, but he did not own any lakeshore; there was another home between his and the lake accessed by a short service road on the south side of his property. He told others he had the best of both worlds – a lake view without the taxes – but inwardly he hated the fact that he had no control over his lake view, one that was blocked entirely by his neighbor's trees in the summer.

A row of tall arborvitae lined his property next to the road, but the deer had eaten them bare to a height of nearly five feet, negating much of their intended purpose as a privacy buffer between his property and the road. He watched the headlights travel back and forth down London Road until one slowed and turned into his drive. As it passed under the lamp by the road, it was easy for him to see the car. Lane.

Walls moved to the front door and watched Lane get out of his car. Lane wore a maroon windbreaker to cover the pistol in the back of his pants and Walls thought it a little strange that Lane was wearing a jacket. Lane slammed his door shut and turned to the house. Walls stood on the steps, his drink in hand. He wore jeans and a red polo, tan loafers with no socks. The overhead light shined off his slicked-back brown hair like he was wearing some kind of skullcap with lights. Lane walked up the steps and Walls held the screen door open for him, neither man saying a word as they passed.

The house was small considering the homes nearby, but it dwarfed the rambler Lane called home, and he felt uncomfortable standing in the two-story entryway with its crystal chandelier hanging above.

"You want a drink?" asked Walls as he finished what remained of his.

Lane's tongue went to the roof of his mouth immediately. He liked to drink and he especially liked the expensive scotch that Walls drank. "Yeah, I'll have the same as you."

Walls disappeared down the hall to his left. Lane looked around the entryway at the abstract paintings Walls ex-wife had selected that hung there, thinking they looked like some kindergarten kid had painted them, absentmindedly feeling for his gun through his jacket. Walls returned with two glasses, handing one to Lane.

"Let's go in the den," he said as he motioned with his free hand and then walked through the doorway to the right.

Walls liked this room, and he felt the term 'den' fit it well. It was his place to relax, feel at home. The parquet floor was covered with a large hand-knotted Persian rug in warm earthy colors. A sandblasted flesh colored brick fireplace was across the room, surrounded by over-stuffed tan leather chairs and a couch. Walls had picked out the art in this room, mostly outdoor prints of fish and waterfowl, but also prints by Monet and Renoir. He sat on the couch to the right of the fireplace, picked up the remote lying on the end table next to him, and clicked on the gas for the fireplace. Blue, orange, and yellow flames quickly appeared between faux logs on a grate. Lane sat opposite Walls.

"You want to take your jacket off?"

"No," answered Lane a little too quickly, "I'm fine."

Walls cocked his head and looked at Lane. He was up to something.

Both men stared at the fire and sipped. Walls had decided that it was no longer of any use to get rid of the BCA woman. That would only bring more scrutiny and by now she had likely filed some kind of report of her findings. What he decided he did need to do was get rid of Lane in a manner that would look like suicide, leading the police to the gun Lane had used to try to kill the agent, as well as somehow explaining it by the fact that Lane was afraid of losing his job because of what the agent had discovered. Tricky, but it would work.

"I think we need to cool it," said Walls.

Lane leaned forward, the gun digging in his back, his scotch cradled in both hands as his elbows rested on his knees. "What are you talking about? I thought you said we had to get rid of the woman."

"Well, you fucking botched that didn't you?"

Lane opened his mouth to protest but Walls held up his hand.

"Listen, you got the cops all stirred up by taking a shot at her but the reality of it is that they have nothing. She's had the information for a week now and no one has said boo. They're not interested in you and me and what we may have done or not done seven years ago, they're looking for a killer, someone who may have taken a shot at the agent because he found out she was after him."

Lane stared hard at Walls. He had absolutely no trust for him but what he said made sense. The Carlisle woman hadn't come looking for a cover-up, she was looking for a killer. Maybe he was right. Lane took another sip of his scotch and felt it warm his throat as it traveled to his stomach. He liked that feeling. He peered down at his glass and could see it was nearly empty. He held it out to Walls.

"Got a refill for me?"

Walls hated wasting his twelve-year-old scotch on a cretin like Lane but he could see he was winning him over. He stood and retrieved Lane's glass from his hand and walked to the other room to refill the glasses. Lane was still leaning forward, staring at the fire lost in thought, when Walls returned. Lane's jacket had pulled up in back when Lane leaned forward and Walls could see the pistol there as he handed Lane his refill.

"Thanks," said Lane as he accepted the drink.

Walls words and the scotch had mellowed Lane. He decided he still wasn't sure about not killing the woman but thought maybe Walls was right that they should just cool it for a while. They talked some more about keeping tabs on the agent if she continued to poke around at the school, agreeing that any surveillance would be passive, and that Lane would be cordial should they interact. They finished their drinks and Walls offered to get another refill. Lane thought he was feeling it a little bit, but it was a good feeling, and he guessed Walls would let him pass out here if he didn't want to drive.

"Sure," replied Lane, "But then I need to get going."

Walls took Lane's glass again but made a quick detour to his ex-wife's bathroom where he found her sleeping pills on the counter. He dropped four in Lane's glass and went back to his study to refill the glass, making sure they dissolved before returning and handing the glass to Lane.

Lane looked up at Walls suspiciously as he accepted the scotch. "I thought you might have got lost."

"Sorry. Had to pee. It happens."

Walls watched Lane consume his drink. Walls kept talking, trying to make sure that Lane stayed and finished his drink, going over the details of how he had hooked a near-record pike on the fly-in. Lane hated fishing and Walls' long story about the pike was putting him to sleep. He decided to go home. He threw back the rest of his drink and tried to push himself up. Lane liked the chairs at Walls' place. He had been here before, and found the chairs felt like they were giving him a gentle hug, but getting out was a challenge. He slid his butt forward on the chair because it was a lot easier to get up from that position, but when he tried to rise he found he had no strength in his legs. Walls watched him with an amused look on his face, sure Lane thought he would like to slap it off of him, right before Lane passed out.

~~~

Carlisle decided to drive by Lane's place on her way home. Somehow she thought she would feel better going to her place if she knew Lane was in his house. As she approached the address she had for Lane a red Durango pulled out and turned in the opposite direction. She recognized Lane's vehicle. Where was he going?

Lane wound through his neighborhood until he reached London Road, turning north. He drove past Glensheen, making a right turn into an unmarked driveway a short distance north. Carlisle kept going, taking the first left on 43rd, left in the alley, and then right on 42nd where she could park facing the driveway Lane had entered. She could just see his truck under a lamp along the drive. She pulled out her phone and punched in the address. David Walls.

All Carlisle could see was a portion of the garage. She tried to tell herself there had to be a number of reasons that Lane was visiting Walls. They had worked together for years. They could just be friends. But she knew. It was Walls and Lane who were protecting themselves by coming after her. She hadn't met Walls, but she surmised that because he was a VP at the school, he was likely the smarter and more ambitious of the two. But that didn't mean he hadn't been the one to shoot at her. She remembered that Walls assistant had said he was out-of-town so she made a mental note to check and see if he had been back at the time of the shooting.

She thought about the reports on the abductions at the college. There was no doubt they had been hushed up, but she really had no proof. So would these guys try to kill her if they felt she could prove something and their jobs might be in jeopardy? Certainly there needed to be an investigation as to why the abductions were not reported to the Duluth Police Department, but right now that was about it. These guys must feel really threatened if they were the ones to shoot at her. Was that enough? Were they somehow tied into the killer of Hollister and had alerted the killer to her investigation?

Carlisle was mulling over the possibilities, feeling exhausted again and about to head home, when she heard the sirens. Two squads turned into the drive behind Lane's vehicle and another parked on the road in front. Carlisle jumped from her car and dodged a truck as she rushed across the street. A cop at the end of the driveway grabbed her arm.

"Sorry, you can't go in there."

Carlisle pulled out her ID. "What's going on?"

"We got a 911 call about someone being shot."

Chapter 43

Melissa Hanes lived about six miles west of Knife River off a gravel road. It took the Trasks roughly twenty-five minutes to reach her home after two wrong turns and missing her driveway, the darkness and thick forest making it difficult. Her driveway looked to be an old logging road, not much more than path cut through the trees and brush, and a large doe shuffled through their headlights as they crept over the rutted ground. Don was sure they had made another wrong turn until they exited the driveway and were greeted by a dramatic change from the wilderness that surrounded them.

A large galvanized outdoor light high on a treated wooden pole illuminated the area as they parked on a crushed limestone driveway in front of a two-stall detached garage. The garage was a rust-colored cedar with chocolate brown trim matching the single-story rambler next to it. A boulder-lined pathway of the same crushed limestone in the driveway led to the front door with arteries of more paths lined with solar lights that ran off in varying directions. They meandered through a garden of shrubs, trees, flowers, and plants in a multitude of sizes and shapes and colors that merged into something that seemed planned to the last detail. It was impossible to see the entire yard as it faded off into the darkness, but just what the Trasks could see in the fading light was like some fairytale land.

"Wow," said Dave as he stood staring.

"Nice garden," responded Don as he made his way toward the front door.

"What do you mean 'nice garden'? Do you have any idea what it would take to grow something like this? This is amazing!"

"If you say so," replied Don, his tone saying he was unimpressed.

Dave was about to belittle him for being totally clueless about the enormity of what went into creating what they were seeing when the front door opened. A stout woman just over five and a half feet tall with close-cropped black hair and matching dark eyebrows over green eyes stood behind the screen door. She was wearing a short-sleeved faded green canvas shirt and blue jeans and leaning on a cane.

"Agent Trask?" Hanes was momentarily confused as she looked past Don to see Dave turn toward her. "OK, I'm guessing there is some kind of relation between you two."

Don glanced back at his brother and then to Hanes. "Yes mam. I am Agent Don Trask of the BCA," he said as he held out his identification, "and this is Dave Trask, sheriff of Lake County."

"My, I'm going to have to make my first call to the sheriff's office from now on if I'm going to get this kind of attention. Come in please."

The front door opened into her living room, a dining area to the right, and a small kitchen that you could enter through the dining area or by going straight through the living room. The feather gray fabric sofa and matching burnt orange side chairs were not new but well-kept as was the teak coffee table that sat in front of the sofa. A smaller teak table was placed under the window that looked out on the yard, a ceramic rose-colored lamp with a stone shade sitting at its center. A leather lounge chair sat to the left of the sofa facing the front window, an open paperback face down on its seat. It secured photos of landscapes and towns in identical size frames in neat groupings on the walls.

"Sorry if it's a bit messy in here. Had to work today. Please be seated."

The Trasks could see no mess, and they could also see no television, which seemed a little odd. Maybe there was one in the kitchen or her bedroom?

Dave stopped to look at photos of sand dunes on the wall just inside the door. "These are very nice. Did you shoot these?"

Hanes eased herself down in the lounge chair, leaning her cane on the armrest, and putting the book on a small table by her left elbow after putting a bookmark between two pages. "Yes, thank you. Iraq."

"You were in the service?"

"Army, sixteen years, two tours in Iraq. Very hot there."

"Beautiful yard too," added Don, his brother shaking his head in disbelief. "Did you plant it?"

"Most of it. My aunt used to own this place and she got it started. Now, I suppose you want to hear about the attack at Cliffside?"

Dave sat. "As we said on the phone, we'd like you to take us through the attack you reported, if you don't mind, and then have you look at some photos."

Hanes described what happened, almost verbatim to what she had reported on the phone to the deputy.

"The other woman, Julie Powers, you wouldn't happen to have her contact information would you?"

"No, sorry. You might want to check with the resort. She quit right after the attack. Too shook up to go back."

Don stood and walked over to Hanes. He opened a folder and handed her a photo. "Could this be the man who attacked you?"

She said no to the first three images and then stopped when he handed her the fourth. "I believe that is the man. He is older than the man in this picture, and had a rough beard, but I am almost sure that is him."

He handed her a picture of Blaine Algaard. "Not this man?"

She studied the picture, and then asked to see the last picture again, holding them side-by-side. "My, these men do look alike. But I still think it was this man," she said handing Don the picture she had identified before looking at Algaard.

Don took the picture back from her and flashed it at Dave. "You live alone out here?"

"Oh no. Sam is here somewhere."

Don didn't see a ring. "And Sam is...?"

Just then a large orange tabby wandered in and rubbed up against Don's leg.

"That would be Sam," he said looking down.

They chatted for a moment more before the brothers showed themselves out and sat in the car. Don pulled out the photo and turned it over. "Marcus Dexter."

"You think he's the one?" asked Dave.

"I'd bet on it. The detail that woman reported, she doesn't miss much."

Dave stared at the house. "Let's see if Julie Powers will confirm. In the meantime, we need to track down Dexter, in a hurry."

"What about Blaine Algaard?"

Don turned as he backed up. "I believe Hanes but we should probably contact Fowles to see if he has a lead on Algaard. We're half way to Duluth. Let's head to the BCA office there. That work for you?"

Dave was looking at the photo of Dexter, thinking about Gary Barton, his anger building. "Yeah, that works."

~~~

The man sat on the edge of his bed, staring out his window, thinking about it. He had calmed down now. Bad decisions were made too many times in the heat of the moment. He'd seen it happen. You needed to be rational.

He had changed out of his work clothes and was now dressed in jeans and a t-shirt. There were heavy stains on the pants and shirt but he didn't care, he was going to get them dirty anyway. And then he would burn them.

For some reason it had taken the driver a long time to drag the body out. The man had sat in his bedroom and listened as the driver struggled to drag the body up the stairs, listening as he backed up the stairs one at a time, the head or feet of the girl, he couldn't tell which, making a thump on each step as he climbed. He heard the scrunch of the plastic as the driver altered his grip and then heavy, slow footsteps and a soft hissing as he dragged her through the house to the back door. The screen door creaked open and then slammed behind the driver. He came back in, and the man, still in his bedroom, could hear the driver pop open a beer in the kitchen. He got thirsty thinking about it, thinking about how good a beer would taste, his mouth getting dry, but he stayed in his room.

Eventually the driver finished his beer and yelled down the hall. "You coming? I'm not doing this all the fuck by myself!"

The man wanted to walk down the hall and kill the kid right then. He'd been nice to the kid. Given him a place to live, food to eat, bought beer for him. Hell, he'd even brought him coke now and then, but not enough that he thought the kid was getting hooked. But the kid never showed any appreciation. He never did a damn thing around the place unless he yelled at him at least three times, and it was only getting worse. And now he'd killed a cop, a county deputy. And he acted like it was no big fucking deal. The man wanted to go into the kitchen and put his hands around the kid's neck and choke the life right out of him. But he didn't. "Get the mattress out to the burn pile. I needed a nap. I'll be there in a minute." He heard the driver mutter something about him being a lazy bastard and then open another beer. Eventually the man heard the kid go down the stairs. It wasn't long after that he heard him trudging back up, dragging the mattress behind him.

"Get out here! I got the fucking mattress!"

The man could see the sun setting out his bedroom window. He got up and walked down the hall, bending to pick up the back of the mattress as the kid was dragging it out the back door.

"About fucking time," said the driver.

They carried the mattress to a spot about thirty yards to the southeast of the house in back. The yard here was mostly weeds and clover, stumps here and there, but it had been mowed. In the middle of the yard stood a spot of bare earth, about ten yards in diameter, most of it covered in a pile of charred remains except for the last foot or so on the outside that was simply dirt. The burn pile was slightly over a foot high in the center, charred cans and springs and other metal items sticking out at odd angles all around. The driver dropped his side of the mattress as soon as they got to the pile. The man held on to his side, walking around the edge of the pile until it was mostly on top of the burned portion before setting it down. Then they flipped it over so that it was in the center of the pile. Both men stood looking at it, swatting mosquitoes.

"You going to burn it now?" asked the driver.

The man looked back at the house where a gas can sat by the back door. "No, we need to get her buried before the animals get her."

The driver slapped a mosquito on the back of his neck. "Bugs going to get really bad soon."

"We need to do it now!" yelled the man.

The driver looked at him in defiance and then shook his head slowly back and forth. "Shit."

The man followed the driver down the trail to the clearing. It was nearing dark now and the man shined a flashlight on the trail as they walked. Soon a reflection off something shiny appeared. The girl wrapped in plastic. The man's light traveled the length of the plastic. She was lying on her back and when the light hit her dead eyes staring out at him through the opaque plastic, his head went back in fright. He was glad the driver hadn't seen.

The driver slapped his cheek. "Should have fucking done this earlier if you would have got your fat ass out here to help." He slapped his arm.

The man glared at him in anger before he produced a can of spray from his pocket. He shined his light on the can as he held it out to the driver. "Here, use this. But don't use it all. I need some too."

The driver grabbed the can and shook it before he closed his eyes and sprayed his head and face. He kept his chin up as he sprayed his shirt in front and then got his arms before giving each leg of his jeans a shot. The man was shining his light on the driver as he sprayed, slapping himself periodically. Finished with his pants the driver tossed the can underhand at the man who missed it, the can hitting him in the chest. The driver laughed and the man cursed him, bending at the waist to pick up the can. He shook it. Nearly empty.

"Get started," he ordered. He used the flashlight to point to a spot about ten feet to the east, just north of the last fresh grave. "There."

There were two spades leaning on the woodpile. The driver grabbed one and started digging while the man used what was left of the bug spray.

"Shine the light over here! I can't see what the hell I'm doing!" shouted the driver.

The man illuminated the area in front of the driver and he began to dig. The two men took turns digging. The ground was soft, a thin layer of decomposed material on top of peat. They ran into the occasional rock and a few roots, but were soon to where the grave was large enough. The men leaned on the shovels as they stood next to the hole; the flashlight on a stump behind them, casting their shadows over the inky blackness of what seemed a bottomless pit. They were sweating, their shirts damp and sticking to their backs, and breathing hard, especially the man who had just climbed out of the hole, his mouth open trying to suck in more air. The black flies were on them and the mosquitoes were after them again, too.

"Let's get her in and covered and get out of here," ordered the man.

The kid drove his spade into the pile of peat to his left while the man walked his shovel over to the woodpile and leaned it there. The man went to the feet of the woman and bent to get hold the plastic, waiting for the driver to come and grab the other end. The driver took his time, making the man wait.

"Can't you do it yourself, old man?"

The driver's back was to the light, and the man couldn't see his face, but he knew the kid had that shitty smartass grin on his face that he hated. But he said nothing, waiting for the driver to grab the other end. The driver had tied off each end of the heavy plastic with twine. He felt for the twine in the dark as he bent and then lifted, taking a step backwards. The man's hands were sweaty, and not prepared for the body to move away from him. He lost his grip on the plastic and his end dropped to the ground.

"Jesus! Do I have to do this all by my fucking self?" said the driver.

"Shut the fuck up!" The man stepped forward, found the tied-off end again, and lifted. "OK, go."

They were both bent over, holding the body only a foot or so off the ground as they shuffled over to the hole. The man was going to tell the driver that they should toss her in on the count of three but the driver didn't wait, swinging his end over the hole and releasing it. The move caught the man by surprise and he almost stumbled forward and into the hole at the sudden movement and extra weight, letting go at the last moment before he lost his balance.

"You stupid shit!"

The driver was standing sideways to the hole, facing the man, and his face and body lit from the side, almost appearing as if he had been split in half. The man could see the grin and wanted to strangle the kid with his bare hands, feel the life go out of him. He wanted to see the look of terror in the boy's face as he realized that he wasn't going to be taking another breath. He would do it soon. Walking to the stump, he bent and picked up the flashlight. He walked back to the hole and shined it down. Because he had held on after the driver released his end, the body had not fallen in the center, now leaning on the wall of the hole closest to the man.

"God damn it! Now look what you've done!" shouted the man as he stared into the hole, the flashlight panning over the body. "Get in there and lay her flat!"

"Why don't you?" came the driver's reply from the dark.

The man had had all he could take now. He was going to kill the skinny bastard right now. He turned toward the driver, swinging the flashlight that way as he did, the ghastly full-toothed smile and wide eyes of the driver fully in the light. On the edge of the light he caught the fact that the driver's left arm was pulled across his chest, his left shoulder close to his face, and then the left arm moved back across the driver's body. The man sensed what was happening, but processed the information too slowly. He started to raise his left hand to protect himself but he was far too late and the back of the blade of the shovel struck him solidly across the side of his head. Instantly the man's right hand opened and he released the flashlight. It tumbled into the hole and the man followed. The area was plunged into darkness.

"Shit!" shouted the driver. He looked behind him in the direction of the house. He knew the light by the back door was on but the woods may as well have been a wall of brick. He could make out no light in that direction. He turned slowly, thinking he may be looking in the wrong direction, but there was no light to be seen. He had been out to the burial site enough that he thought he could feel his way down the trail and back to the house to get another flashlight, but it wouldn't be easy. And there was poison ivy along the trail, the driver was highly allergic. "Fuck!"

The driver bent at the waist, reaching out with the blade of the shovel, moving it over the ground in the direction of where he thought the hole should be located. The blade dropped over the edge of the hole and the driver pulled it back slightly, laying it down, keeping one hand on the handle. He went down on his knees, following the handle of the shovel as his guide, sliding his other hand through the loose peat as he crawled. He soon found the edge, running his hands from side to side over the rough ground to get oriented, and then stopping. He listened. He thought he could hear the man breathing and edged his way along the hole until the sound was louder. The man was still alive. The driver was pretty sure the man was unconscious but he didn't want to give himself away so backed slowly away from the breathing, keeping one hand on the edge of the hole, until he felt the corner of the hole farthest from the man. He turned his head away from the hole and then backed up until his knees went over the edge and he was flat on his stomach. He took a breath and then pushed himself backwards, sliding over the edge as he did, his stomach just reaching the edge as he touched bottom.

The driver's right foot touched first, hitting dirt, but his left foot landed on the skull of the woman, his foot sliding on the plastic causing him to lose his balance and fall forward, his face hitting the side of the hole. He screamed as he felt the sharp edge of a rock move up his cheek, ripping his skin open. The driver's hands reached out to grab the edge of the hole as he slid down. He steadied himself and then pushed himself up, spitting out peat as he did. He slid his feet until they were on either side of the head and stood, wiping the dirt from his face. There was a warm flow of blood on his cheek, and he moved his hand to the front of his jeans to rub it off. His breathing was loud, his heart pounding, and he tried to calm himself so he could listen. Mosquitoes buzzed his right ear and he waved them away.

He turned his head slightly so he thought his right ear would face the end of the hole and then he heard it again, the steady breathing of the man.

Certain the man was unconscious the driver bent forward at the waist, feeling down the plastic over the girl's chest with his right hand until he touched the heel of the boot of the man. He quickly pulled his hand away but could detect no change in the man's breathing. He found the boot again and ran his hand up to the back of the ankle and determined that the man must have landed on his stomach. He grabbed the man's ankle in both hands and pulled with his arms.

The man didn't budge. The driver took a deep breath, adjusted his grip and leaned back this time, pulling hard. Suddenly the man's body moved, sliding over the plastic that wrapped the woman, the driver losing his balance and his grip, his back hitting the end of the hole hard. The driver's head hit the side of the hole next and then fell to his chest as he dropped to a sitting position, his legs splayed in front of him, the girl's plastic-wrapped head between them. He slowly raised his head and opened his eyes. There was a sliver of light at the other end of the hole.

The driver knew he had connected solidly when his shovel hit the man's head, but he had no idea how long the man would be out, and was getting concerned. He pushed himself off the wall and shuffled along the side, his hands clutching the upper edge as he moved, eyeing the light. He contacted the woman's body almost immediately as she was wedged along the side. The driver stopped and looked at the light. He bent and stretched out his left arm toward it, but it was a good two feet out of his grasp. In addition, he could only see a bit of light, the flashlight itself was still under the man. He had to move the man.

The driver went down on his knees, kneeling on the body of the woman as he did, feeling it's rigidity through the plastic, the plastic crunching. Sweat stung his eyes and built on his brow and he wiped it away with his hand before he ran his grimy fingers straight back over his head, trying to delay the sweat from building again. His hands found the back of the man's legs and he followed them to the man's hip. He pushed, the man sliding slightly to the side. "Fuck!" He moved a leg over the man's leg, and then as he leaned on the man's butt, he brought his knees up under him and slowly stood on the body of the woman. He felt for the waist of the man's jeans and slid his fingers under it. Something cracked and seemed to give way under his left foot, the woman's chest collapsing, but he kept his hold on the jeans and didn't fall. The driver leaned back and pulled. The man moaned.

Chapter 44

Carlisle showed the officer at the front door of Walls' house her identification and walked down the hall to where another officer stood next to an open door. She showed her identification again as she said," Carlisle, BCA, what have you got?"

"One man dead, shot. There's another man in the kitchen who called it in. Looks like suicide. You should have boots and gloves if you're going in. There should be some in the squad."

She walked back to the front door and told the officer there that she needed gloves and boots and told him she'd wait for him at the door. The officer went to his squad, found two boxes with what she wanted and walked back to the door, holding them out to her. She pulled on two disposable boots from one box and two gloves from another and was about to go back inside when an unmarked car with its lights flashing pulled into the driveway.

Detective Les Berger was the front seat passenger in the maroon Dodge and got out first. Berger was in his mid-forties with thick blonde hair that he kept cut short because he didn't like the fact that it got wavy when it was long. He had ocean-blue eyes that drew the women in; something his wife did not appreciate when they were out. He was six feet tall and fit, wearing jeans and a blue polo.

Darin Olson was the detective driving. Darin was three inches shorter than his partner, probably thirty pounds heavier and five years his senior. His dark gray hair was parted on the right, bushy gray eyebrows over his brown eyes. His nose was short and pushed up a bit, not quite your classic pug nose, but close. Olson wore khaki slacks and a button-down blue and red checked cotton shirt.

"Carlisle," said Olson as he walked up to the front steps. "What are you doing here? Getting shot at isn't enough excitement for you?"

"You know me Darin. I hear gunshots from ten miles away and I just got to see if I can get in on the action." She looked over to Berger. "Les." Carlisle knew both detectives from her time at the Duluth PD. Berger had been a little upset when Carlisle had been accepted by the BCA and he had not.

"You been inside?" asked Berger.

"Just got here. I was waiting for you fellas."

"Yeah right," said Olson as he slipped on boots and gloves. "Let's go see what we got. And Carlisle, please stay back and let us do our job," he added as he looked at her.

"What are you doing here anyway?" asked Berger as he passed her going down the hall.

Carlisle had been thinking about this before they arrived. She did not want to get in trouble with Trask for going after Lane on her own. "I'm looking into some abductions that happened a few years back at UMD. I was driving by and the address seemed familiar. I pulled over, looked at my case notes, and saw it was the address I had for one of the administrators at the time of the abductions, Dave Walls."

They had both stopped outside of the den as Carlisle spoke. Berger looked hard at her; not buying her story before turning and going in. Carlisle followed, her view of the body blocked by Berger and Olson. She walked around behind them until she could see the man half on a chair, half on the floor, head turned to the side, the back of it matted in blood. Lane.

~~~

The manager at Cliffside had been hesitant to give out Julie Powers' contact information, but when Don mentioned the attack and Hanes, he told them what they wanted to know.

"Shit, she lives in Two Harbors. I really don't want to drive back up there again."

Dave looked up from the file that Carlisle had given Don and shrugged. Don called.

"Miss Powers?"

"Yeah, who is this?"

"Miss Powers I am Special Agent Don Trask of the Minnesota Bureau of Criminal Apprehension. We have a couple of possible suspects in your attack at Cliffside and was wondering if we could get a few minutes of your time to look at a couple of pictures? We could be at your place in Two Harbors in about an hour."

"Um, OK, but I'm not home. I'm in Duluth."

Don had been sitting on the edge of a desk but now stood. "OK, where are you?"

"I'm at the Boulder Brewery in Canal Park."

"We can be there in ten minutes."

"Alright I guess. I'm out on the patio by the fire with two other girls. But I never really got a good look at him."

"Thanks. We'd like you to look anyway. See you in a few minutes."

Dave was sitting at the desk. He looked up at his brother as he disconnected his call to Fowles. "Fowles was out of the office."

"How about a quick interview and then a beer and a burger?"

Trask parked his Lexus and they walked around the outside of the brewery towards the lake. They had both been here before, Dave liking the porter they brewed and Don one of their IPAs. The building had floor-to-ceiling windows giving the patrons a view of Superior. It also gave the Trasks a look at the customers around the fire pit on the patio as they approached. There were six people, two men and four women, all appearing to be college age, the men standing, the women in Adirondacks around the fire in the raised pit. They were talking loud, like they had had a few beers, but quieted as the Trasks approached.

"Julie Powers?" said Don.

A blonde on the opposite side of the fire pit rose and walked up to them. Don and Dave both showed her their IDs and asked her if she wouldn't mind stepping inside for a minute. It was dark out and the faces around the fire were in the shadows, especially the men. One of them called out asking if Julie wanted him to come with but she replied that she would be fine and the three walked around the side of the building and entered the brewery. It was noisy inside, not too crowded, an empty waiting area to the right of the host station. Powers and Don sat while Dave stood in front of them.

Powers looked at the photos but would not commit to any as the attacker. "Sorry."

Don and Dave were both disappointed but tried not to show it.

"Thanks anyway," said Dave as he put the photos back in his folder. "You can go back and join your friends now."

Powers looked a little confused. "Aren't you going to ask me about the truck?"

Dave looked down at her. "What truck?"

"The truck the guy drove. I saw it parked there for a couple of nights."

"Um, OK, how would you describe the truck?"

"It was an older Chevy with a crew cab, I'd say late nineties. It was black with a dent down the driver's side like it had scraped a railing or something. There was some rust around the back wheel-well on top. It had a slightly jacked suspension and a muffler that was going."

Dave was writing as she talked. "OK, anything else?"

"I think one of the fog lights in front was broken."

Dave looked at Don. "You got any other questions?"

"You seem to know your trucks."

"My dad and both of my brothers are into restoring old trucks. I guess I just picked up some of it."

"Well, thanks Miss Powers. We appreciate your time."

They watched her return to her friends. "I need to eat and then I need to sleep," said Don.

Dave was excited about the new information on the truck but he felt the same fatigue. "Yeah."

The brewery had a restaurant so they grabbed a table. They said little while they ate. Both wanted to get after the new leads but both knew their minds and bodies, especially after a meal and two beers apiece, were not up to it.

"I can't keep my eyes open. Let's go back to my place and get a little rest."

Don was leaning back in his chair. All of the information of the last day was now banging around in his head, nothing seeming to stick. He needed rest. "Sounds good. I'm going to leave a message on Carlisle's phone to have her look at Marcus Dexter and give her a description of the vehicle that Powers provided."

As they drove north on 61, they passed Walls' house, they looked at the squads on the street and in the driveway.

"Wonder what's happening there?" asked Dave.

Chapter 45

The moan startled the driver, and he released his grip on the man's pants and stumbled backwards, tripping on the woman and hitting his head on the side of the hole. His heart was trying to pound its way out of his chest as he scrambled to his feet, his back sliding up the wall of the hole, turning to grab the edge of the hole and pull himself out. But there was no other sound. He turned and found the light in the bottom of the hole. The light illuminated the neck and face of the man, the man's face that of a ghoul, and his eye sockets black holes between the light on his cheeks and protruding forehead. The driver needed the light.

The driver thought he should be able to free the light now. He listened a bit longer. Sweat ran through his brow and into his right eye, stinging. He shut his eyes tight, reached down and pulled up his shirt, wiping his brows and forehead. A mosquito bit him in the back of the neck and another on his exposed stomach. He dropped the shirt and slapped at both simultaneously. He thought he could hear the man breathing, ragged breaths, like he was working hard to suck in the air.

When he had fallen backwards, he had ended up kitty-corner from the light. He turned now to face the edge of the hole, his hands on the edge for balance, working his way slowly to the left. He made it to the corner and turned, his foot bumping into the woman as he had done before. Lifting his foot, he stepped lightly on her, the heavy plastic crunching again, holding himself in position on one leg until he felt steady, and then putting his other foot on her. He continued toward the light, stopping when his foot came up against the man lying on the woman.

The driver did not want to do anything that would wake the man but there was no other way to get to the light than to crawl over the man. He went to his knees on the back of the man's thigh, slowly lowering his hands, feeling with them as he began to move them forward. He found the top of the man's pants and moved his left knee forward so it rested on the man's butt. The man made a loud raspy gurgling sound like some prehistoric creature, and the driver arched backwards, but he held his position. The man didn't move. He brought his right knee forward so it was even with the left and then moved his right arm forward, his hand resting on the man's back just below his shoulder. He felt the man take a breath and almost backed away, but the man was still again so he moved his left hand next to his right.

The light was close now. He could see the lens of it poking out under the man's neck. He wiped more sweat from his brow with the back of his hand and then moved his knees up close to his hands again. The driver reached forward and grabbed the lens of the flashlight in his right hand and pulled. It wouldn't move, wedged under the man.

"Fuck!"

The weight of the driver on top of the man was making it impossible to get the light free. The driver slid his left knee to the left until it slid off the man's back, hit plastic, then slid further, his toe touching the earth. He pushed himself off the man, sliding off, his right leg now in front of the left, wedged between the wall and the woman. It was getting suffocating in the hole, his breathing labored, the bugs attacking. He pushed himself off the man, finding the man's shoulder as he did. He followed the shoulder, down the man's arm to his elbow. He grabbed it with both hands and pulled. The man's body shifted, the light nearly out from under him. The man scrambled back over the man, grabbed the light, and pulled it free. He held it in his right hand, his left hand on the man's back between his shoulder blades, the light now pointed at the man's face. The driver looked at the face in the beam, covered in bloody dirt, just as the man's eyes opened.

The man's head was pushed up against the wall, almost at a right angle to his back. The man moaned again and the driver scrambled off, gripping the top of the wall, and pulling himself out. He rolled once and then was up on his feet. He paused, thought about what to do next for a minute, decided he needed better light to finish the job, and went back to the house.

~~~

Carlisle stepped back as she saw Lane, his head lying back on the seat of the chair, his eyes wide like he had seen a ghost.

"You know him?" asked Olson as he viewed her reaction.

"Yeah. Blake Lane. Director of the UMD police."

Olson watched her as she stared at the body, seemingly in a trance. "And you know him how?"

Carlisle looked at him. "The abduction investigation. I talked to him a few days ago."

They both watched as Berger went through Lane's pockets. He stood next to Olson.

"Looks to me like he must have slid down off the chair after he shot himself," said Berger.

There was blood and other matter on the back of the chair, and although the leather on the chair was a dark maroon and the room softly lit, a trail of blood running down the seat behind the head to the back of the chair was visible. His right hand was in his lap, the gun on the floor between his legs.

"Does that seem odd to you?" asked Carlisle. "These chairs look way too soft for him to just slide off." She didn't wait for an answer but sat down in the chair opposite, pretending to put a gun in her mouth and pulling the trigger. "I don't know."

The detectives watched her and then turned back to the body.

"Maybe the young lady has a point," said Berger.

"Maybe," replied Olson. "But she is just a girl, and a BCA girl at that."

"Fuck you," said Carlisle as she stood next to the chuckling detectives. "No, he was sitting in that position when he shot himself, but why was he sitting on the floor like that?"

The three of them stood shoulder-to-shoulder, looked at Lane for a few minutes more without saying anything, and then began to look around the room. Carlisle walked over to where Walls had been sitting, his glass of scotch still on the table in front of him. She looked over at Lane and then walked back to where he was. She found what she was looking for on the carpet next to the back leg of the chair.

"Look at this," she said as she stood pointing to the glass tumbler on its side.

The two men walked over and stood by her.

"I got two problems with this. Why was he holding a glass when he shot himself?" She paused as she looked at the glass. "And why is his glass way back there when he shot himself up here," she said pointing to the man resting against the chair. "We need to talk to Walls."

She started toward the doorway but was halted by a hand on her shoulder.

"Hold it there agent," said Berger. "While we greatly appreciate the fact that the great BCA has seen fit to bestow its wisdom on us poor Duluth Police officers, you will not be talking to Walls. In fact, you will be leaving. Now."

Carlisle felt her face growing warm, not trusting that Berger and Olson would handle this as she liked, but also knowing that she had no real jurisdiction. She also knew she could get the details from Hillary later. She looked from Berger to Olson, and then left, stripping off her booties and gloves as she reached the front door. As she was about to step out she looked down the hall behind her, and seeing it was empty, tiptoed back down the hall, past the den, and peeked in the kitchen. Walls was sitting at the kitchen table with a cup of coffee in front of him. She remembered his picture from the UMD website. The officer sitting across from him looked over at Carlisle. She smiled, waved, and hurried back out the front door.

She walked across the street to her car and got in. She started the engine and sat staring at the flashing lights across the road. Why had Walls shot Lane? She wanted to go to Lane's house and see what she could find but knew she would only get trouble for it. But his house wasn't far.

Chapter 46

The driver ran into the kitchen, pulled open the junk drawer to the right of the sink, and grabbed the flashlight there. He tested it to see that it was working and ran back outside, a flashlight in each hand. He ran back across the yard to the woods, down the path to the burial plot, to the new grave. He shined both lights in the hole.

The man was still where he left him, his eyes closed again, but the driver knew he was still alive because he was making gurgling noises. He moved to the side of the hole and set a flashlight on top of the dirt pile there, angling it down toward the hole. The light barely crept over the edge of the hole, most of it still in black. He picked up the flashlight and walked to the foot of the hole opposite the man's head. He used his heel to make an indentation in the edge of the hole and then set the flashlight in it, lifting his hand slowly, not trusting that the flashlight wouldn't slide off into the hole. It stayed in place. He looked ahead to see the man's head was in the light and then used the flashlight in his other hand to locate the shovel where he had left it. He pulled it from the peat with his free hand and followed the light on the ground to the head of the hole. He peered over the edge at the man whose eyes suddenly popped open again as he let out a loud groan.

The driver took a step back in fright but then just as quickly dropped the flashlight and grasped the shovel handle in both hands. He stepped back to the edge to see the man looking up at him, raised the shovel over his head, and swung it down as hard as he could. The back of the blade hit the man square in the head. His body shivered a bit and his eyes closed, his mouth falling open. The driver watched for a minute and then hit him again and again, six times until he was too tired to continue. He stood above the man and looked down, holding the shovel at his side, breathing hard. Blood was running down the neck of the man and over the top of his head, the skull in back a pulpy mess. He wanted to be sure the man was really dead, that he wouldn't somehow make his way out of the hole and come after him, but decided he didn't want to go back in the hole to be sure. He stuck the shovel in the pile of peat and filled the hole, stopping periodically to shine the flashlight over it, to see how full the hole was getting and where it needed more fill.

The driver had been shoveling furiously and now was sweating profusely, his heart racing, thinking he was having a heart attack. He dropped the shovel and bent at the waist, hands on his knees, both hands nearly black from the peat. After he picked up the flashlights, and surveyed the hole one more time, before heading to the house just after midnight. He walked into the house, into the kitchen, and pulled a beer from the refrigerator. Leaning on the sink, he downed the beer in two long gulps, black drops dripping from the sweaty can. Leaving the empty can on the counter, he went to the bathroom where he turned on the shower. He used the toe of the opposite foot to hold the back of his tennis shoes as he stepped out of them before stripping off his clothes and dropping them on the floor. He stuck his hand in the spray to feel if it was warm, the water running black on the floor of the shower, noticing the trail of dirt on the floor as he did. He stopped the water three times thinking he heard something, heard the man, sticking his head outside the shower curtain each time. He toweled off and then peered down the hall as he leaned out the doorway of the bathroom. After padding naked down the hall to his room, and flipping on the light before he entered to be sure no one was inside, he threw the towel on his bed and pulled a pair of boxers from his drawer. He went back down the hall slowly, looking down the steps to the dark basement as he went past, listening hard. In the kitchen he pulled out another beer, flipped the top and walked to the back door.

In the light he could see the burn pile with the mattress, but it was far too dark to see into the woods to the burial plot. He stood looking in that direction anyway, sipping his beer, and wondering if the man would be coming.

The driver had seen those horror movies where the zombies push their way out of the grave, and he was afraid that the man might do that, that maybe he should have shot him just to be sure. But he needn't have worried. His blows to the head of the man with the shovel had killed him, but the man wouldn't have been going anywhere anyway. When he fell into the hole, he had hit the edge with his chin, instantly breaking his neck and paralyzing him. He was aware of the driver in the hole as he lay there, but there had been nothing he could do about it.

The driver did not sleep well; every sound in the house amplified each time he woke, hearing noises that were never there. He had finished a six-pack before passing out on his bed, thinking the beer would calm him, but it didn't. He knew that eventually people would come looking for the man. He'd have to leave.

~~~

Carlisle did not sleep well either. She decided not to go to Lane's house and had returned to her apartment. She lay in bed waiting for her bedroom window to explode, or her balcony door to slide slowly open, finally drifting off, only to awake as the sun made its way into her bedroom. She had slept in her clothes on top of her covers, rationalizing that she needed to be ready should someone try to break in, feeling sore and stiff as she sat on the edge of the bed. Her running clothes were in the corner on her clothes hamper, her running shoes on the floor next to the hamper, and she looked at them like they were her mother telling her she had to get up and go to school. "Not today." She stripped off her clothes, let them fall to the floor, and headed to the shower.

She pulled on tan slacks and a short-sleeved navy blue blouse, made her way to the kitchen for a yogurt and two cups of coffee. Feeling slightly better she drove to the office. She stopped in the break room for more coffee on the way to her desk, easing herself into her chair and leaning back, holding the coffee in front of her, her eyes slowly closing.

"That coffee may not go well with your slacks," said Farmer.

Carlisle's eyes popped open and she looked at the cup tipping in her lap, sitting up, and placing it on her desk. "I didn't know you were such a fashion plate, Bob."

Farmer did a quick assessment of his agent. "You get any sleep?"

Carlisle knew that there was no use trying to lie, her baggy eyes easily gave her away. "Not much, but I'm OK."

"You make any progress yesterday?"

Farmer had been Carlisle's supervisor since she joined the BCA. He was matter-of-fact, clean-cut, no-nonsense, and straight-laced. His uniform of every day – khakis and some kind of shirt with a sports coat, always crisp and clean. He was happily married with two kids and mowed his lawn every week. He kept tabs on his agents but gave them enough rope; cutting in when he felt it was needed.

"It's slow. Nothing has jumped out at us yet."

Farmer studied her. "There was a shooting at a UMD administrator's house last night. The head of the campus police was shot. Probable suicide. But you already knew that didn't you?"

"Bob, I was just driving by when the cops pulled in. I recognized the address from my investigation and stopped. That was it."

Farmer shook his head. "Yeah, just driving by. Geez Carlisle, don't you remember what Trask said? You had somebody take a shot at you. You can't be doing this."

She wanted to argue but was just too tired. Besides, her boss was right. She held the cup between her hands looking straight ahead and released a heavy sigh. "OK, I'll keep to the assignment." Then she looked up at Farmer. "So, if you don't mind, what else did you hear?"

He laughed. "Good grief. You are not one to let go are you? Nothing much more than that. Possible suicide. Now forget it. Please."

Carlisle lifted her hand in surrender and Farmer walked away. She needed to call Hillary. Reaching for her phone, she noticed she had a message. She listened to what Trask had to say and then put down her phone. "Aw crap." She pulled a bag of sunflower seeds out of her drawer, poured a small pile on her desk, popped a few in her mouth, and looked for her file on Marcus Dexter.

Marcus Dexter had been an engineering student at the time of the Hollister abduction. He had not registered a vehicle with the school but that didn't mean he didn't have one. By registering a vehicle with the school they could get a parking pass for the semester, but many students just thought it was too much of a hassle, paying daily rates for the lot or finding spots close to campus. Dexter had graduated from Denfield High in Duluth. He listed a home address that was north and west of Duluth, and only one parent, Marina Dexter. His father was listed as deceased.

Carlisle looked for Marina Dexter, found no one by that name in Duluth, and then looked up the address Dexter had listed in the reverse directory. They listed no phone number for that address. She punched in the address on Google Maps on her phone. "Road trip."

Carlisle knew she should probably go to the courthouse and look up records on the address and Marina Dexter, but the address wasn't that far out of town, and she was having a tough time sitting still. She was 'antsy', that's what her mother would say. She made a mental note to call her mother, finding it took six or seven mental notes before she finally caved in and called. Not that she didn't love her mother; she just couldn't handle the phone calls. Her mother would go through, in detail, every ailment being suffered by her friends, anyone at her church, and any relative, and then go on to say how she was experiencing symptoms that indicated she had most, if not all, of these ailments.

The one-story rambler at the address Dexter had listed with the college was tucked away on a three-acre lot crowded with aspen and poplar and pine. It sat on the crest of a hill, the asphalt driveway leading to a single-car attached garage. The home was sided in cedar that had been stained a redwood color. There was a small roofed redwood deck in front, two large hanging baskets overflowing with pansies and geraniums hung from hooks in the front of the deck. A yellow plastic watering can was on the deck below. Carlisle walked up the two steps to the deck and rang the bell next to the door.

A woman with white hair pulled back in a tight bun and turquoise-framed glasses came to the screen door, the door to the house being open. Carlisle guessed the woman to be in her mid-to-late sixties, and not quite five and a half feet tall. She wore a lime-green t-shirt that said 'GRANDMA KNOWS BEST' across the front over jean shorts.

"Yes?"

Carlisle showed her ID and identified herself. "I'm looking for someone who lived here a few years ago, a Marina Dexter. You wouldn't happen to know her would you?"

"My, you're up rather early. Do you get going this early every day?"

Carlisle was momentarily thrown off track. "Um, no, I guess not. Anyway, the question still stands. Do you know Marina Dexter?"

"I'm afraid not," the woman replied, "but I've only lived here a little over a year."

"I see Mrs…?"

"Rand, Cecelia Rand."

"So you don't know anyone named Dexter who used to live here?"

"Well, I didn't say that, young lady."

"Um, so you do know Marina Dexter?" Carlisle was thinking that the lady might be a little confused.

"No, I told you I don't know her. But I do know a Robert Dexter. Well, by name anyway. I never actually met him but he is who I bought the house from."

"Robert Dexter. And would you happen to have any contact information for him?"

Rand pushed open the door. "You may as well come in and sit down, this may take a minute for me to find."

The front door faced a closet, with a living room immediately to the left. The woman turned and looked at Carlisle.

"Would you like some coffee, dear? You look a little tired."

Carlisle smiled as she looked down at the woman. "That would be great, thanks."

"Well, I guess if you are a Bureau Of Criminal Apprehension agent, you must be somewhat intelligent, so I'll let you go in the kitchen and pour your own while I look for the papers." She pointed to the door on the interior wall at the far side of the room. "There are cups hanging just above it and some cookies on a plate next to the pot. Help yourself."

Carlisle watched her disappear through another doorway just in front of her and then made her way to the kitchen. She took down a cup that hung from a small bronze hook attached to the underside of the cabinet above the coffee pot and poured. The cookies were arranged on a flowered porcelain plate and covered in plastic wrap like Rand had been expecting company. The cookies were chocolate chip, Carlisle's favorite, but something she approached with trepidation after being forced to eat her mother's horrible baking for so many years. Still, she couldn't resist. She lifted an edge of the wrap, snuck her fingers under it like she was afraid the cookie would move away if it knew she was coming for it, and grabbed one by the edge. She took a bite.

The cookie was delicious, almost melting in her mouth. She took a sip of coffee and found it to be some of the best coffee she had ever tasted. She took another bite of the cookie, pressing it to the roof of her mouth, savoring its chocolaty goodness, not hearing Rand come up behind her.

"How is the cookie?" Carlisle jumped a little, almost spilling her coffee. "My, you're tired and a little on edge too. Why don't you come and sit down? I think I have what you want."

Carlisle followed her back into the living room and they both sat on the couch, the woman setting a coaster in front of Carlisle for her coffee as she held a stapled group of papers in her hand. She flipped about three pages over and found what she was looking for.

"Yes, it says right here. Robert Dexter, 816 Carmel Way, Mantoch, Wisconsin 57822. Would you like me to write that down for you?"

"That would be great Mrs. Rand, and would you mind if I had one more cookie? They are the best chocolate chip cookies I have ever had."

Rand smiled, patted her on the knee, said that would not be a problem and went to the kitchen with her papers. She returned with a single sheet of paper and a plastic sandwich bag with several cookies. "Here you go dear, and here are some cookies for you," she said holding out the paper with the address and the bag.

Carlisle stood and said, "I have to ask you one more question, mam."

"Yes?"

"How do you make your coffee? It's wonderful."

The woman reached out and grasped Carlisle by the left elbow. "Come with me, dear."

Rand had Carlisle sit at the small Formica-topped table in her kitchen and showed Carlisle her secret mix and how she made it. Carlisle had another cup while she listened as well as another cookie.

"Can I ask you just one more question Mrs. Rand," said Carlisle as she stood to go.

"It's Cecelia dear, and yes, you can ask me another question."

"Can I give you a hug?"

Rand showed a full smile and the two women hugged. She walked Carlisle to the front door, telling her to be careful chasing criminals, and inviting her back to visit.

Carlisle promised she would do both. She got in her car, set the cookies on her passenger seat in easy reach, and backed out of the driveway. Once she had driven a block she pulled over, looked up Robert Dexter in Mantoch, and called.

"Yes? Who is this?" was the brusque reply.

Carlisle explained who she was and asked if he knew the whereabouts of his wife, Marina.

"Marina wasn't my wife, she was my sister-in-law. She just disappeared five or six years ago."

"But wasn't she living in the house you sold to Mrs. Rand?"

"Yeah, she was, but like I said she just disappeared. I tried to find her but gave up. The house was my parents', and I owned it, but I let Marina live there after my brother passed. After she disappeared, I sold it to Rand."

"She disappeared?"

"Yeah. I guess she didn't show at her sister's house and so her sister's husband went looking for her. Her car was at the house but no sign of her. Talked to the police a few times but nobody ever heard from her again."

Carlisle was trying to process what he had said. "Did Marina have a son?"

"Yeah. I visited them a few times but honestly, my sister-in-law was so weird, well it was creepy. Anyway, I stopped going. I'd call the kid now and then but once he got to be a teenager that was about it."

"And you have no idea where he may be?"

"Not really. I think he may have gone to live with his mother's ex after she went missing."

"Her ex? You mean Marina had another husband?"

"Yeah, her sister told me she had remarried when she called looking for Marina. A Policeman. Fowles was his name I think. Not sure of his first name."

Carlisle thanked him and hung up. She opened the plastic bag and put another cookie in her mouth. Fowles. The name rang a bell. She held the cookie in her mouth as she put the car in gear. Fowles. She knew she had something at her office about a Fowles.

Chapter 47

Don could smell the coffee and something else cooking in the kitchen as he rolled out of bed. Nice. He made his way to the shower. He was back in the kitchen, shaved and dressed in jeans and a white polo a short time later as Dave was sliding scrambled eggs and sausages on a plate across the counter of the bar. Don walked around the bar, helped himself to coffee, and then sat back at the bar in front of his plate. "Will you marry me?"

"I would but I talked to your two ex-wives. They warned me to stay as far away from you as possible," replied his brother in a serious tone.

Don smiled, not so much at the smart-ass remark, but the fact that it showed his brother was doing better. Both men had slept in, unusual for them, but the long day past and a late meal and beer had taken its toll.

Don felt rested. He felt himself start to think about what had happened with the case, putting things together unlike what he was able to do yesterday. They talked as they finished their meal, walking the plates over to the sink when they were done, Dave rinsing them and putting them in the dishwasher. He put a dishrag under the tap, wrung it out, and wiped down the counter. Unlike his brother he could not afford a cleaning lady and he liked things neat.

Don watched him clean up for a minute, putting his cup in the dishwasher, and then turned away and dialed Carlisle. She did not answer her office phone so he dialed her cell.

"Sir," answered Carlisle.

"I think you can call me Don when we're talking like this, Danny."

"OK."

Carlisle was silent and Don thought he detected a frosty tone to her voice. "Did you get my message from yesterday?"

"Yes sir," she replied. She related what she had discovered, finally revealing the information about Fowles. "I know I have something about him in my notes at work. I'm headed there now."

"No need," replied Trask. "If it's who I think it is, he is the Chief of police in Chase. I am on my way to see him."

"OK, I remember."

"You find anything on the truck?"

"No sir, haven't had time to look yet."

Trask was going to say something about her addressing him as sir but decided to let it pass. "Great work, Danny. Let me know if you find anything on the truck."

"Yes sir."

Trask's tone softened. "How are you doing?"

"I'm fine."

"No you're not. You want to get the asshole that shot at you and so do I but we need to wrap this thing up first. Thanks to you I think we're close. Call me on the truck." Trask disconnected. He pictured Danny Carlisle. She was very fit, very attractive, and very young. She was also a BCA employee, ultimately reporting to him. He had felt something between them but had held off. It had not been easy at the time but now, with Mel, well; he pocketed his phone and walked back in the kitchen. "We need to go see Fowles."

~~~

Carlisle sat in her car and stuck her tongue out at the phone in her hand after Trask had disconnected. She was the one to do the digging to find out about Fowles and now Trask was going to swoop in and take over. Probably make an arrest and get a big news story and a commendation. And now she was supposed to find an old truck.

She had just pulled into the BCA lot when Trask had called. The day was going to be sunny but cool, a northeast breeze pushing across the lake. She thought she should probably start the search for the truck. She also needed to update Farmer so he could pull the agents helping her on the background information now that Trask was going to crack the case. Carlisle extracted another cookie from the bag, held it between her lips, and pushed the button for Hillary Thomas.

"Hey stranger. How was the first night back in your apartment?"

"OK. Sorry, I should have called and let you know I wasn't coming back."

"Hey, no problem. I didn't need John looking at you in your PJ's thinking about what I used to look like before kids anyway."

"You're looking pretty good."

"I know I got to lose a few pounds but it's tough. Maybe I should start running with you?"

One of the things Carlisle liked about running was listening to her music as she ran at her own pace and not really thinking about anything.

"You could try, but then you'd have to work nights. Don't worry, if you really want to drop a few pounds I'm sure you'll be able to do it."

"Thanks. So, why did you call anyway?"

Carlisle explained how she had 'happened' on the shooting the night before.

"So you want to know what's going on with the investigation?"

"Yeah, and I'd like to know what Walls said."

"Obviously, there hasn't been anything formal put in the system yet, but I can ask."

"That would be great."

"But Danny, I think you should just talk to them. They'll know it's me asking for you. Besides, if Lane is a suspect in your shooting, you have every right to follow up."

Carlisle listened to what Thomas said as she finished her cookie and decided she was right.

"What are you eating?" asked Thomas.

"OK, so I went out to follow up on this lead in the abduction case and I interviewed this little old lady at her house and she had the most incredible chocolate chip cookies I have ever had in my life. Anyway, she gave me the recipe so I'm going to cook up a batch."

Thomas laughed out loud. As far as she knew about the only thing Carlisle had baked was frozen pizza. "Uh, OK. So, you're going to bake?"

Carlisle hadn't really thought about it when she was saying it but now she was a little steamed at her friend. "Well, yeah. I mean, I can bake."

Thomas laughed again. "I don't doubt it. You may just want to call the fire department before you do just to give them a heads-up."

"Stick it, Thomas!" she replied in mock anger. "I will bring one over to you after I'm done and you'll be begging for more – and I will not share the recipe!"

"OK Betty Crocker. Maybe we should grab a beer this weekend?"

"Sounds good. Talk to you later."

Carlisle had completely forgotten about going into the office now. She dialed Les Berger.

"Berger."

"Danny Carlisle."

Berger looked out the front window of Lane's house and smiled. "My goodness. And to what do I owe the honor of speaking to Danny Carlisle two days in a row?"

"I'm just looking for an update on the shooting. You guys still think it was suicide?"

"Well, we did, but then this super-agent from the BCA stopped by and pointed out all this stuff that we lowly police detectives would never have seen in a million years, so now we're just not so sure."

Carlisle raised her eyebrows and shook her head. "Listen Les, I'm sorry if I stepped on your toes last night but this is personal. Lane or Walls took a shot at me and I don't really like that."

"I get it, but you got to let us do our jobs."

"OK, I'm sorry, again. So have you been to Lane's place?"

Berger looked around the living room where he was standing and then moved out on the front steps. In a quiet voice, "Yeah, I'm there now. Listen. We're not done processing his place yet but we found a rifle and it had been fired recently. We think he's the guy that tried to kill you."

Carlisle put head back and let out a big breath. "The bastard!"

"Hey! What kind of language is that for a lady?"

"So what did Walls say happened?"

"He said that Lane came in all upset, saying he had shot at you because he was afraid what you had found would cause him to lose his job and then he pulled a gun out from behind him and shot himself."

"And you believe him?"

"I don't know. He seemed shook up, but like you noticed, some things just don't look right. So what did you find?"

Carlisle wasn't sure she wanted to let Berger in on what she knew but returned his favor of sharing with her. "There were three abductions at UMD, one of them the Hollister murder. Lane was the investigating cop. He essentially buried the reports, never reported them to you guys. You done at Walls' place?"

"Yeah."

"You book him?"

"Got nothing that says we should. He's free."

"He shot him, Les."

"Listen Danny, that might be true or it might not be true, but right now we don't have anything that says he did and the chief has reminded us that the chancellor of the college is very concerned about this."

"And that means?"

"That means we make sure we got what we need for a solid case if we make an arrest." Berger had been pacing in the yard as he talked. He stopped and looked at the house. "Listen Carlisle, I'd like to chat longer, but unlike the BCA, we're kind of short-staffed so I need to get back to work. Have a nice day."

Carlisle was sure Walls was behind Lane shooting at her and was covering up. She dropped her phone in her purse and reached for the cookie bag noticing there were only two cookies left. A quick glance back at her passenger seat confirmed that none had fallen out. She held the bag up and looked at the two remaining cookies, trying to figure out how many she had eaten. As she was looking at the bag, she noticed the cup in the cup holder between the seats, overflowing with sunflower seed shells. She moved her right leg to the side to see that they had spilled onto the floor on her side and could easily see that there were shells decorating the console, a scattering on the passenger seat, and the empty bag she had purchased just a day or two ago on the floor in front of the passenger seat. Carlisle wondered if she didn't have some kind of compulsive eating disorder. There was a clip about it on the news not too long ago and it sure seemed to her that once she started eating, she had a hard time stopping. She looked back at the cookie bag. "Geez girl, get a grip. An extra mile for you tomorrow."

She thought about having another cookie but dropped them in her purse too. A shadow passed in front of her car and she looked up to see Agent Charles Bird walk past. He was wearing an ocean blue oxford and shale gray chinos. Carlisle watched him walk up the steps to the building and go in. Charles Bird was new to the office. He had come from Fargo a month ago and Carlisle knew little about him except that he seemed to fit in his chinos very well. She wondered if he was married, or engaged, or gay.

She released a sigh. Her mind seemed to be jumping between thoughts like a pinball that wouldn't stop. The wonderful coffee she had shared with Mrs. Rand was losing its effect and now she felt tired, almost hung over tired, without the headache and dry mouth. She mentally went through her list – find the truck, update her boss, check out Walls, check out Charles Bird, and..... There was something else, something that had zipped through her mind like a flash of lightening, but it would not come back. Get coffee? No, that wasn't it, but that seemed like a good idea. Another sigh and she was out of her car and on her way into the building.

Carlisle allowed herself a half a cup of coffee at her desk, resisting one of her last two cookies, before she walked to Farmer's office. She knocked on his open door and he waved her in as he finished a conversation on the phone.

"What's up?"

She settled into a chair in front of Farmer's desk and updated him on what she had discovered as she had with Trask, adding the fact that Trask would now see Fowles, neglecting to mention that Trask had ordered her to look for the truck.

Farmer leaned back in his chair, twirling a pencil between his thumbs and forefingers. Carlisle was expecting some praise for what she had done but she had seen the pencil thing before and knew something else was coming.

"I suppose I should tell you that you did a good job tracking down Dexter as far as you went, but did you ever stop to think for one minute what you might have been walking into?" said Farmer, his voice rising. "From what you have told me you had no idea whether Dexter may have been at the Rand house before you went out there. Did it even occur to you to have someone go with you – like your partner?"

Carlisle hadn't thought about it, but now that Farmer had pointed it out it seemed pretty obvious. "Sorry Bob. I just, I just screwed up."

"Yeah, you did. Now I know you're tired and under a good deal of extra stress, but I can't have you doing things that are going to endanger yourself. I want you to take the rest of the week off. Go home, take naps, whatever. Just no BCA work. You got that?"

"But Trask wants me to find the truck."

"Dave can handle it. I'll let Trask know. Now go home Carlisle."

Carlisle was pissed. So pissed she didn't notice Charles Bird smile at her as she stamped by his cube. Grabbing her purse and a bag of seeds from her desk, she strode out the door, slamming her car door as hard as she could after she got in. She slammed the heel of her hands on the steering wheel. "DAMN!" She folded her arms across her chest. Farmer was right; she had screwed up and she probably did need some rest. But there was no way she could sleep now. Carlisle thought about her father, how when he was upset with her mother he would go down in the basement, turn on the little television that was down there as loud as it would go, and drink beer until he'd pass out in his worn rocker.

But Danny was never a drinker, it was much more like her to try to run her anger out of her, but she didn't feel like running. She thought about what Farmer had said about no BCA work and suddenly she sat forward with an evil grin. Walls. Walls technically wasn't BCA work. She started her car and then found her phone in her bag.

Chapter 48

Don pushed the Lexus south on 61 and then cut west on County 14 south of Knife River. Dave found out that it was Fowles' day off when he called but had got the dispatcher to give him Fowles' address and cell number. He dialed but there was no answer.

As they closed in on Chase, Don suggested that they stop at the police department to see if there were any new developments in locating Algaard. They came in on the south side of town, drove past the liquor store that was dark inside, and then continued to the police station.

Randy Palmer was standing by the front desk, chatting to the woman there, when they walked in. "Can I help you?"

Don looked at Palmer's nametag. "Deputy Palmer, I'm Don Trask of the BCA and this is my brother Dave, sheriff of Lake County.

"Oh, I remember you," said the woman at the desk.

Don looked at her nametag and then remembered. "Oh yeah, Officer Little. You helped us before when we were here."

The woman smiled and replied, "I talked to one of you just a little while ago. Sorry, but as I told you on the phone, the chief isn't in today."

Dave had moved to his brother's shoulder. "That's OK. We really just wanted to talk to whoever happened to be looking into the Blaine Algaard disappearance."

"That would be me," said Palmer.

"So what do you know?" asked Dave.

"Not much I'm afraid. We did recover his vehicle a couple of miles from here yesterday. Nothing in it. He's disappeared."

"No sign of a struggle? No keys or wallet or phone."

"Nope. His wife goes missing a few years back and now he's gone. Just weird."

"Any activity on his bank account or credit cards?"

"Um, well the chief never said anything about checking those."

"OK, don't bother. I'll have someone do it. Thanks for your time," said Don as he turned to leave.

The brothers got back in Don's vehicle, both men staring at the police station ahead of them.

"I don't know," said Don. "I don't think Algaard would dump his vehicle and take off without anything unless it was arranged. Unless someone picked him up." He called his assistant.

"Are you having fun in the great north woods sir?"

"Not really. Anything going on I need to be concerned with?"

Stoxon took him through what he knew. "Um, two other things. The Superintendent would like to see you when you return. I believe it's about the Benning shooting."

"Aw geez. OK, what's the other thing?"

"Well sir, the tax return thing for Blaine Algaard kind of bothered me so I took the liberty of looking at some of the other liquor stores in the area. It seems that the people in that part of Minnesota are very thirsty, or else they like to use liquor for medicinal purposes or to start fires."

"Hmm. So you're telling me their books look funny too."

"Exactly!"

"Any connection between all these stores?"

"My, great minds do think alike! The only tie I can find is that they all used the same distributor which probably makes sense because I'm guessing it would be that distributor's territory. Would you like me to check him out?"

"I'm pretty sure you were going to do it anyway, so yeah, go ahead. Also, please check for any activity on Blaine Algaard's bank account or credit cards."

"Goody! I will let you know what I find out. Bye!"

Don turned to his brother with a contemplative look. "Remember I told you that Larry thought that Blaine Algaard was cooking his books?"

"Yeah?"

"Well, he found a bunch of other liquor stores in the area that seem to be doing the same thing. The only thing tying them together is that they have the same distributor."

"Probably just his territory."

"Yeah, maybe. Larry is going to look at him." Don pushed the button to start his Lexus. "Let's go visit Fowles."

~~~

The driver looked out the screen door leading to the back yard. He was nervous, spooked. He'd had three cups of coffee and four ibuprofen so that didn't help but it was more than that. He kept hearing sounds all night, imagining the man coming for him. Had to look, had to go see. He pushed the door open and stepped into the yard. He paused again, looking toward the burial area and then at the woods surrounding it. There were lots of places to hide, to wait for him to come by. But he saw no movement. He listened for a moment more; the only sound that of a woodpecker on a rotten birch. He moved toward the trail leading to the burial plot.

The sun was well up now, and although it wasn't particularly warm, the yard was shielded from the northeast breeze and he could feel himself start to sweat beneath his arms. He walked down the trail far enough to see the woodpile. His shovel was still leaning there, but where was the shovel used by the man? The brush was too dense to see into the cleared area of graves; he'd have to go further. The driver moved cautiously, watching where he was stepping so he wouldn't trip or make a noise that would give away his position. He unconsciously bent forward, looking from side to side as he moved down the trail. At last the grave came into sight.

He could see the second shovel lying on top of what remained of the pile of peat. He moved closer and stood over the hole. An animal had walked across it during the night, a wolf perhaps, but he could detect no other disturbance. The hole had only been filled to ground level, not enough according to the man because the fill would settle, but he didn't care about that any more. The man was dead and he was leaving. He glanced at the other grave markers and then turned and walked back down the path towards the house.

There was a five-gallon red plastic container half filled with gas by the back door. He walked over, picked it up, and carried it to the burn pile. He poured the gas over the mattress, walking around it as he did, can held high, making sure it was well soaked. After returning the can to where he found it, he went in the house for a book of matches and returned to the pile. He tore a match from the book, slid it across the abrasive strip on the back of the cover, and watched it come to life in his hand. Stepping closer to the mattress, he looked for a spot where he had soaked it, and then tossed the match. He backed up quickly but stopped as the match just lay burning on the mattress. He was about to step forward to throw another match when the flame met the gas. There was a mighty whoosh, the flames shooting up, the mattress jumping. The driver raised his arm over his face as he nearly stumbled backing further away, the heat from the flame suddenly intense. The flames shoot up, the driver watching, the black smoke from the fire being pushed skyward, above the trees.

The driver went back in the house. He returned in a minute with his clothes from the night before and threw them on the mattress. They flared up instantly and almost seemed to melt. He briefly watched them disappear, blackened springs from the mattress now easily visible where his clothes had been, and then walked back toward the house. Time to clean up and move on.

Chapter 49

Carlisle called Walls' office as she drove. Lisa Klang answered and initially refused to provide any information on her boss's location. When Carlisle threatened her with an obstruction of justice charge, Klang revealed that Walls was not in, and wasn't expected in for the remainder of the week, before hanging up. She was on 35W, about to exit for the university, but now continued north.

She turned into Walls' driveway and parked beside a small silver Mercedes. She stepped from her car and could see that the crime scene tape was gone from the front door, the front door open behind the screen door. It felt to Carlisle like it had been a week since she was here, not the night before.

She walked up the steps to the front door and pushed the button for the doorbell. Chimes that reminded her of the alien communication musical notes in Close Encounters of the Third Kind sounded in the hall. She peered through the window in the screen door, the hallway lit by light coming through the back. The kitchen was at the end of the hall and she watched as Walls walked toward the door from there. He wore jeans that had a crease down each leg and a patterned cotton shirt with similarly creased arms.

"Yes?"

Carlisle saw no sign of recognition in his eyes thinking he was a very good actor or he really did not know who she was. She showed her identification through the screen. "Agent Carlisle, Minnesota Bureau of Criminal Apprehension. Are you Mr. Walls?"

Walls smiled as if he knew a secret that no one else did. Lane hadn't told him how attractive the agent was. She wasn't as tall as he was, but he thought she had to be approaching six feet; he liked tall women. She was obviously fit, but not so thin that her figure wasn't evident. He thought he detected some fire in her eyes, but they looked tired. He stood on the other side of the door.

"How can I help you agent?"

"I'd like to ask you a few questions about your relationship with Blake Lane."

Walls thought about shooting Lane. It had been messy, and he didn't like things to be messy. It had ruined his chair and he'd have to replace his carpeting too. If Lane had just been able to keep his mouth shut things would have been fine, but he couldn't trust Lane to do that, so now he had to deal with the mess and the inconvenience. "I've already answered questions for the police for hours. I can't imagine what else I could possibly tell you."

She caught Walls' Cheshire-cat smile turning to a frown before he answered. "I know sir, but the BCA is a separate agency, and I just need a few minutes of your time."

Walls shook his head back and forth before pushing open the screen door. "Fine, but just a few minutes."

Carlisle grabbed the edge of the door and stepped in, following Walls down the hall. She glanced in the den as she passed, trying to think of some way that she could get in there again, but couldn't come up with anything and followed Walls into the kitchen.

The kitchen area was something that Carlisle could only dream about. An eating area was directly in front of her as she entered, French doors leading to a redwood deck on the other side of a three-foot round walnut and maple planked table stained a dark blonde with four matching chairs. Floor to ceiling cherry cabinets lined the walls directly to her left and right. The floor was a gray-blue slate. Brass lights hung over a long center island topped with granite to her right, a stove-top in the center nearest the sink and matching counter top of a molten mix of taupe, white, and robin's egg blue along the far wall. Stainless steel appliances with cherry-panel insets were almost hidden among the cabinets. There was an open laptop on the table with some papers lying near it that Walls quickly gathered together. He made a quick note on the top sheet and placed them in a briefcase that was on the floor next to the chair facing the laptop.

"Can I get you something to drink? Water or a pop?"

"No thanks."

"Why don't you sit?" said Walls as he pulled out the chair closest to the entry.

Carlisle sat and Walls took the chair to her right, reaching to pull over a glass of water that had been next to his laptop.

Carlisle studied Walls. He had thinning blonde hair that was combed straight back, some kind of mousse holding it in place. His blue eyes seemed to protrude slightly, never blinking, and looking at her like she was on the menu for dinner. He had a professional, confident air about him, like he could fit easily into a boardroom somewhere.

"I understand you're taking some time off from your job?"

"Yes. I just need a break after what happened here," he replied as he looked past her down the hall, like he was afraid someone was coming.

"I understand. It must have been quite a shock."

Walls stared at her for a moment before he abruptly stood. "It has just come to me now that you are the one who Lane mentioned was looking into the abductions on campus aren't you?"

Walls was agitated, upset, at least he appeared to be. "Yes. I was investigating their link to another series of abductions."

"I understand you had your reasons for looking, but if it wasn't for you, Blake Lane would still be alive and I would never have had to go through any of this!" he exclaimed, his arms extending from his sides.

Carlisle stood and faced Walls. "Lane covered up those abductions, not me."

Walls seemed to think about what she said before answering. "No, you brought it on a good man, a good friend. You need to leave."

Carlisle stared at Walls. He had thought of something, some reason he did not want her here or want to talk to her. He was putting on a show; that much she was certain. She turned and started down the hall toward the front door, but upon reaching the entry to the den, quickly stepped in.

Walls was still in the kitchen entry, watching her walk down the hall, when she did her detour into the den. He ran after her. "Where are you going?"

Carlisle didn't know what she was looking for in Walls' den, only that she felt that there must be something there she had missed before. She was standing in front of the chair where they had found Lane when Walls shot into the room, hanging onto the doorframe with his left hand to keep his balance.

"What the hell are you doing in here? You need to leave now!"

Walls' face was flush with anger but Carlisle didn't notice, she was trying to picture the scene she saw the night before, her eyes surveying the room. She rotated her head slowly from where Walls was sitting to the chair in front of her.

"Did you hear me? Get out!" shouted Walls now inches from Carlisle.

"Sorry, I thought I might have left something here last night."

This comment seemed to blindside Walls.

"You were here last night?"

"Yeah. Sorry we didn't get to talk then."

Carlisle reached into her purse and extracted her phone. While a seemingly stunned Walls looked on, she looked down at the screen, hit the camera icon, and held it up so the chair was framed. She took two quick shots and then dropped the phone back in her purse. Carlisle looked to where his chair was last night, his unfinished scotch still on the small table next to the chair. She looked at it for a minute, thinking she should be seeing something, but nothing came to her. She looked back down at her bag to see that it was closed.

On a table next to Walls was a foot-high metal cross standing on a mahogany base. Walls had declared the den his sanctum when he was married, and had decorated it himself, but his wife had insisted on adding her touch, the cross. She found it at an antique store in one of her many trips to Minneapolis, the cross supposedly from the eighteenth century. Walls was now happy he had never bothered to get rid of it. He picked up the cross and swung it at Carlisle's head.

Carlisle caught the movement out of the corner of her eye, bowed down to move out of the way, but wasn't quick enough to avoid the blow altogether, the base of the cross catching her on the top of the skull. Pain shot down her spine and a lightening bolt flashed behind her eyes as she collapsed to the floor.

"Why were you in here agent?" growled Walls in a low, menacing tone as he stood over her, the upside down cross held high.

Walls' words seemed to echo in Carlisle's head. They were far away, like when she was a child sleeping and her mother sat on her bed, calling her name to wake her from a dream.

"Tell me now agent or you are dead!"

Carlisle's eyes were out of focus, and she felt herself drifting off. She tried to push herself off the floor, but with no strength in her arms, she only managed to roll on her side. Walls' pants leg was in front of her and she followed it up to his chest and then finally his furious face came into fuzzy focus. Walls raised the cross above his shoulder.

~~~

Trask's car scraped bottom three times as he maneuvered back and forth down Fowles' driveway barely above idle, cursing each time a wheel hit a hole. Don's patience was at an end when they finally pulled into the yard.

"Fucking unbelievable! How is anyone supposed to drive on that?" Don yelled as he got out.

"Pretty sure he must drive a truck," replied Dave as he closed the passenger door. He put his nose in the air and sniffed. "He's been burning."

The house sat at an angle facing the opening where the drive came out of the woods. A two-stall garage was to the north of the house, ten yards off, and facing the drive. Its siding was the same army green as the house, but there was a slight sway in the roof, like the garage was older and had been there before the house. There were ruts leading from the drive to the garage stall closest to the house, but only grass and weeds in front of the other. There were no windows in the garage doors, only small single windows on each end of the building. The yard sloped away in front of the house, two large Norway pines side-by-side along with a few clumped birches and the odd stump, the ground covered with a thin mixture of grass and weeds. There had been an attempt at landscaping in front of the house at one time, river rock visible among the weeds, three unkempt shrubs on either side of the steps leading to the front door. They both surveyed the property for a minute and then Dave followed Don to the door and stood at the bottom of the steps as Don knocked.

~~~

After burning his clothes the driver started the cleaning, wiping down everything upstairs he could think of that he may have touched, but gave up after a short time, realizing that he had touched so many things in the house that it would nearly be impossible to get them all without missing something. And then there was the basement. He'd have to power wash that to even have a chance of getting rid of any trace he had been there. No, he decided, better to just burn it down. He'd ventured into the man's room, emptied the cash box he knew he kept there in the bottom drawer of his dresser, finding $400. He stuffed the bills in his pocket and went to his room to pack. The driver was in his room putting the last of his clothes in a heavy green denier duffle when the Trasks drove in the yard.

He could tell they were cops when they got out of the car, a nice car by the looks. He knew that the cops would come eventually looking for the man; he just didn't think it would be this soon. After he closed the bag , he carried it quickly to the back door, quietly pushing it open, and then setting his bag down to hold it open. He reached down and grabbed the gas can, running back to the entry to the basement.

He poured gas down the stairs and then around the kitchen and hall as he backed out. The fumes were strong as he put the gas can down inside the back door and stepped outside the house, reaching in his pocket for the matches. He tossed his bag out in the yard while he held the back door open with his foot. A match head dragged across the strike plate and it caught immediately. He used that match to light the rest of the matches in the book and then tossed them into the house. There was a whoosh from the flame as he turned to run.

Chapter 50

Don had turned to say something to Dave about Fowles when Dave pointed at the front window and shouted, "Fire!"

Don pounded on the front door, shouting Fowles' name, trying the lock. He stepped back and kicked it with his heel. The frame splintered and the door swung in hitting the stop against the wall and bouncing back. He turned to Dave and said, "Try the back!" before he disappeared inside.

Dave ran to his right, in the direction of the garage, and hustled around the corner, down the side of the house, and around the corner to the back. As he turned the second corner, he thought he caught movement to his right but he didn't look, hurrying to the back door. He stopped short. Flames were already coming out the back door, climbing up the side of the house. He ran to the garage and cupped his hands as he looked in a side window. He could make out a pickup inside that he assumed was Fowles. Fowles had to be here. Dave ran back to the front door; smoke pouring out of it now, and no sign of Don. He lifted his shirt to his face and leaned inside calling for his brother. There was no answer.

His eyes started to water and he dropped to the floor. It appeared the entire right side of the house seemed in flames but there was only smoke moving across the ceiling going down the hall to his left. He was about to call for Don again when Don came charging from a doorway and down the hallway toward him, his shirt pulled over his face.

"Get out!"

Dave popped to his feet and shot out the door, Don close behind, both men leaping off the steps like they had been fired out of a cannon. Dave stumbled when he hit the ground, catching himself with his left hand, and pushed himself back up. Before he could fully rise, he felt Don grab him under the arm and pull him along.

"Keep running!"

They'd taken only half a dozen more steps when the house seemed to explode, the men diving for the ground. Both lay on their stomachs, hands clasped over the backs of their heads, pieces of glass and wood raining down on them. Their ears were ringing, and they could feel the heat of the fire on their backs, as they rolled to their sides, looking back at the house. The structure of the entire half of the house to their right was gone, flames reaching high, the heat blowing the leaves on the birch closest to the house. The other side of the house was still intact but smoldering, smoke pouring from the broken windows like gray waterfalls turned upside down, flames visible behind the swirling smoke.

Dave pushed himself to a knee, Don standing. The heat bore down on them, both men raising hands to protect their faces.

"We need to get out of here! It could blow again!" shouted Don, knowing that his hearing was impaired and not sure how much his brother could hear.

He started to run towards his car, Dave slowly standing, still stunned, hands on his knees. Don came back and grabbed Dave by the arm and led him to the car. Dave walked around to the passenger side and got in while Don slammed his door and hit the start button. The engine roared to life and he spun the wheels in the gravel as he backed in a semi-circle before putting the car in drive.

As they reached the point where the drive left the yard Dave looked back and noticed that the door on the far stall of the garage was up. "Wait!"

Don hit the brakes. "What?"

"The garage. Someone was in there."

Don had to turn sideways in his seat to look back at the garage to see what his brother was talking about then looked down the driveway ahead of them. "He didn't get far," he said as he pointed to the black truck sitting at an angle only a hundred yards ahead of them.

~~~

Fowles had called Denton Contracting the prior week to see if they could come out and grade his driveway. They said that they couldn't get to it for a couple of weeks. Fowles thought about calling someone else but decided he'd just wait and told them to get it scheduled. Unfortunately for Marcus Dexter, this would put a severe crimp in his plan to escape.

Dexter had watched the second cop run back to the front of the house and go inside from the corner of the garage. He quickly lifted the garage door and threw his bag inside his vehicle. He started the truck and put it in gear, launching himself out of the garage just as the house blew. Dexter took a quick glance back at the fireball shooting skyward, thought it was pretty cool, and then continued toward the drive. He was focused on leaving, as fast as he could, not on the large pothole that was the driveway's welcome to anyone leaving the yard. It was one of those potholes that let you drive in down an easy slope that abruptly stopped at a wall of several small boulders. Dexter knew it was there, knew he could swing to the left and into the weeds a bit to avoid it, but that didn't register with him until he hit it hard with his front right tire.

Dexter nearly lost control of the truck as it bucked like a bronco in a rodeo, sliding forward in his seat and hitting the steering wheel with his chest, his foot coming off the gas and clutch at the same time. The truck had veered to the left; its nose now in the brush, the engine dead. Dexter groaned and pushed himself back in his seat, his head down as he tried to recapture the breath that had been knocked out of him. He put the truck in neutral, stepped on the clutch, and turned the key. The motor started. He jammed it into gear and pressed on the accelerator but the engine only raced. He could feel the back tires spinning but he wasn't moving. Dexter jumped from the cab and ran to the front of the truck. The bumper was nearly on the ground and it looked to him like his axle was broken, which didn't really matter because he'd blown a tire too. The truck wasn't going anywhere.

Dexter had been a slightly above-average student, with an ACT score and grades just high enough to get him into UMD. In the sports he'd tried growing up, football and hockey, he had an uncanny ability to anticipate what his opponents were going to do, but frustrated his coaches because he was unwilling to put in the work at practice. As he pulled his bag from his truck, he figured he had three options. He could go back to the house. He assumed the fire department would soon be coming and they'd have to move his truck out of the way. He knew where the man kept the keys to his truck and he could wait in the woods, or maybe the garage, for the right time to get in the truck and drive off. There would be plenty of confusion at the house, possibly enough to sneak off, but he also assumed that members of the Chase police would show, and they would know the man's truck. It could be several days before he could grab the truck.

The second option was to head into the woods. He'd probably have to leave his bag, but he didn't think anyone would follow, at least until they brought in dogs. That could be awhile. Eventually he could make his way to a road, and another house, where he could steal a vehicle, but it could mean a day or more in the swampy, bug-infested woods, and he'd barely made it through the night before behind the house.

The third option he considered was hustling down the driveway to the road. He'd have to ditch his bag in the brush, but it may be possible to come back and get it in a few days. There was no way the cops at the house could follow by car; the driveway was blocked. The fire trucks wouldn't stop for him but, if he could flag down a cop or, better yet, a first responder once he got to the road, he was sure he could convince them to give him a ride to the hospital. No one in town knew who he was. He could explain that he was a nephew of the man, visiting and staying at his house when it exploded. Then it was just a matter of getting rid of whoever picked him up and taking off.

The driver grabbed his bag and ran toward the road. As soon as he was past the bend where he could no longer see his truck he hurried off the drive and into the brush. Almost immediately his progress was reduced to a slow walk as the thick quack grass and low thistles grabbed at him like a thousand tiny hands, the branches of the saplings whipping him as he pushed through. He didn't have to go far. A large leaning poplar had come nearly all the way down in a storm in the spring, pulling up its roots, leaving a natural cubby for him to store his bag. He pulled it open, found his revolver inside, and then closed the bag back up before stuffing it under the root ball. And then he was off.

~~~

Dave's door flew open and his gun was in his hand as he hit the ground. He yelled at his brother to call the fire department and the police but Don was already on the phone. He ran toward the truck, his gun at his side, until he had closed to about thirty yards, when he bent low and held his weapon in front of him. Dave reached the back of the truck, taking a peek over the tailgate into the cab. He couldn't see any movement but with the sun now high it was hard to tell. He looked back to see Don slip his phone in his pocket and signaled to him to go around the passenger side. Dave waited until Don reached the truck and then they both duck-walked to the cab doors, reaching up and pulling them open simultaneously, their guns leading the way inside.

They both stood, Dave walking up and opening the driver door, while Don made his way to the front of the truck. Dave checked the floor and flipped open the armrest, but found nothing of interest. Don came back to the passenger door and opened it, checking the floor there and then the glove compartment. There was an old manual for the truck and a small flashlight, but nothing more. He turned on the flashlight and bent to look under the front of the truck. "Looks like he busted an axel," said Don.

Dave was at the front of the truck, looking at the ditch and the woods beyond. "Someone walked around the front of the truck but I can't tell which way they went. Could have headed into the woods but I don't see anything."

Don looked into the woods for a moment and then up the drive. "I need to get an APB out on Dexter and Fowles."

Chapter 51

"Walls! Walls, open up! Police!"

Walls moved to the doorway into the den. He peered around the corner to see the same two detectives who had been at his house yesterday on his front step. He thought it was possible they just had some more questions but he deemed it much more likely they were here for him. He looked at Carlisle trying to push herself off the carpet, bent at the knees to quietly put the cross on the floor, and then made a dash down the hall to the kitchen.

Berger and Olson had parked on the road. They now stood together on the front step and looked at the Mercedes and the Carlisle's Subaru beside it. They didn't see Walls run down the hall to the kitchen.

Berger turned back to the door and banged on it again. "Mr. Walls, we have a warrant and we are coming in."

Both detectives drew their weapons and slowly entered the home. Most of the house was to their left, the dining room, living room, and a hallway that led to a bathroom and two bedrooms. The den was to their right, the kitchen straight ahead. Olson went left; moving quickly around the large oak table in the dining room while Berger took two steps down the hall and peered into the den. He caught movement and turned, training his gun on Carlisle who had struggled to her knees. He rushed to her side and helped her stand.

"You OK?"

"Yeah," she replied as she felt for the bump on the top of her head.

"What the hell are you doing her and where is Walls?"

"He killed Lane and he tried to kill me."

"Where is he?"

Carlisle tried to clear the fog from her eyes by shaking her head. "I don't know."

Berger was about to tell her to stay put until they searched the house when he heard the car start. He ran to the front door to see Walls' Mercedes turning out of the driveway. "Shit! Olson! Walls is running! Let's go!"

Olson came tearing out of the dining area, gave a surprised look at seeing Carlisle, and then was out the door on Berger's heels running for their car. Carlisle was right behind. She hopped in her car and threw it in reverse, missing most of the tarred turnaround and running over some mums and hostas, before putting it in drive. Carlisle slowed only slightly as she reached London Road, leaning as far forward as she could, hoping that no one was coming. Berger had parked facing north and did a u-turn; just starting south as she reached the road. She fishtailed across the road, narrowly missing a Suburban that had slowed for Berger, and was right on Berger's tail as his lights and siren came on and he began to pull away.

Walls was less than a mile from 35W, flying down London Road. He figured that if he could make the freeway, he could exit south of Duluth and then get lost, work his way south and west, or maybe circle back north. He knew a donor that had a cabin in Ely that he said he never used after mid-August. Walls could stay there until he figured out a more permanent solution to his problem. He slowed slightly as he came up to the light for the exit to 35W where two cars ahead of him had been waiting at the light. The light turned green and he stepped on the accelerator, quickly moving to their right, then cutting back in front of the lead car before it could block him from getting on the ramp. There was no one ahead of him as he floored it.

~~~

Travis Colby is an independent trucker. He lives on ten acres just outside of Ames, Iowa. His home had been part of a five hundred acre farm that the owner had sold ten years prior. The owner had retained the homestead that included a barn, a large metal-roofed Quonset hut, a two-stall garage, and the two-story home, thinking that he would retire there. Three years later his daughter and son-in-law, who lived in Minneapolis, announced they were having their second child. The owner's wife decided they needed to be closer to their grandchildren and so he sold the home to Travis.

The set-up was perfect for Colby. A large circular turnaround made it easy for him to get in and out with his semi, with plenty of parking space for it in the Quonset hut, and ample space next to the barn for the times that he stopped at home pulling a trailer. There was a big yard for his two young kids to play in, and the house was only five miles from town where his wife worked as a teacher's aide. He also had easy access to 35W, a ramp only a little over two miles away, with interstate 80 only a few miles to the south. Colby mainly worked the 35W corridor from Texas to Minnesota, with the occasional jobs running to Illinois and Michigan or west to Omaha and Denver. He was busy.

Colby was making his first trip to Duluth, dropping off equipment for a new brewery being built just north of the end of 35W. About a mile before 35W turned into 61 it passes through the Leif Erikson Tunnel, a 1500-foot, four-lane tunnel that passes under the Duluth Rose Garden, part of the Leif Erikson Park. Visitors to the garden can feel the vibrations of the vehicles as they pass underneath, a somewhat eerie experience, but the roses have flourished and don't seem to mind. The tunnel has a fourteen-foot posted clearance, something that made Colby a bit nervous as he pulled his thirteen foot ten inch high trailer up the freeway. As he approached the tunnel from the south he slowed, allowing two cars to pass, before moving to the center of the tunnel, straddling the centerline between the two lanes. He guessed the height of the tunnel would be at its highest in the middle. He made it through without incident and made his delivery.

Colby had entered the freeway going south only a minute before Walls. He had planned to spend the night at a truck stop somewhere south of the Twin Cities, but the delivery had gone quicker than he expected and he figured if he pushed it he could make it home and surprise his family. He shifted and gave the truck gas as he entered the tunnel. Colby moved to the center of the tunnel again as he had coming north. He had checked to see there was no traffic behind him, but as he passed nearly a quarter of the way into the tunnel he picked up headlights behind him coming up fast. He moved the rig to his right.

Colby did not want to run into the underside of the tunnel with his rig, especially at his speed of just over forty. He considered remaining where he was, making the car behind him follow him until he was out of the tunnel, but he did not want to be reported by an irate driver. He down-shifted and slowly began to move further into the right lane.

~~~

Walls drove a Mercedes SLC Roadster. He liked how it looked; he liked how he looked in it. It was quick and fun to drive, except in Minnesota winters when the rear-wheel drive could be an issue. He had an older four-wheel-drive Jeep for the snowy days, but it never saw daylight in the summer. As he made the first turn onto 35W, he could see the tunnel ahead, both lanes were clear. He felt the car jump as he gave the turbo-charged V6 more gas. He was doing eighty and gaining speed by the time he hit the tunnel. It was a mostly sunny day and he found he was nearly blind in the sudden darkness of the tunnel. He opened his eyes as wide as he could trying to adjust to the relative darkness of the tunnel, his headlights automatically coming on, picking up the center wall now only inches to his left. Walls corrected, pulling his foot off the gas and trying to hold the car in its lane, when he looked up to see the brake lights directly ahead of him.

The hood of the Roadster is barely over two feet above the ground. This lends to its striking style and aerodynamics. Unfortunately for Walls, this also meant that the vehicle would not impact the high tailgate of the semi until it had reached the passenger cabin. The windshield, passenger compartment, and Walls' head were all removed as the car disappeared under the semi.

~~~

Dave decided Dexter was headed to the road. He had seen the keys in the ignition when he looked in, now he jumped in, pushed down the clutch, and turned the key. The truck roared to life.

Don jumped back. "What the hell are you doing?" he yelled.

"We need to get to the road. Get out of the way!"

Dave slammed the truck into reverse and hit the gas as he cranked the wheel as far to the left as it would go. At first the wheels just spun in the gravel, but then they caught, dragging the truck backwards. It didn't get far, but the truck turned slightly, just enough. Dave shut it off and jumped out, running for Don's car. "Let's go!"

Dexter had reached the road. He was bent over, rubbing dirt on his face and arms and shirt, trying to alter his appearance, when he heard his truck start up. He looked back down the drive, almost expecting to see it coming, but knowing it wasn't going anywhere. They're trying to move it. He looked to his right. That direction would take him away from town, away from the direction that any fire and rescue vehicles would likely travel, with nothing for at least five miles as far as he could remember. His plan had been to go left, toward town, flagging down someone who was responding, but now he was concerned that maybe the cops at the house might be able to move his truck and get around it. He was thinking about what he should do when he heard the siren and started to run along the road toward town.

Don moved as fast as he dared up the driveway. He cursed as he hit the potholes and scraped the bottom of his car on a deep rut. "Where the hell was that when we drove in?"

Dave was looking straight ahead for any sign of Dexter. The slow progress was painful and he was sure Dexter was getting away. He held the door handle, wanting to jump out and run. Suddenly a siren and flashing lights were bearing down on them as they nosed out of the driveway onto the road. Don cranked the wheel hard to the right and gave the car gas leaving it precariously close to diving into the ditch where the drive met the road. The approaching fire truck came within a foot of his car as it turned down the driveway.

Dave was looking down the road, in the opposite direction from which the fire truck had come, assuming that that was how Dexter would go, if he had even come this way, when Don yelled.

"There!"

A red Ford Escape was stopped on the side of the road not two-tenths of a mile from them, a man in jeans and a faded yellow t-shirt with black hair leaning on the roof above the driver's window. He glanced over at the Trasks, stared hard at them for just a second, and then got a shitty grin on his face. His right hand came off the roof and swung in front of him. Don yelled, "gun!" just as Dexter fired. Dexter pulled open the driver door and yanked the driver out of the car and onto the road. He glanced back down the road at the sound of more sirens coming his way and then jumped in.

Don cranked his steering wheel to the left and stepped on the gas. The car's wheels were off the asphalt and it barely inched forward as the tires spun in the gravel and soft soil on the side of the ditch.

"Fuck!" screamed Don.

Without a word Dave jumped from the car and leaned on the doorframe. "Go!"

Dexter chuckled at the sight of the cops stuck ahead. He looked out his side mirror to see flashing lights getting close. He stepped on the accelerator and pulled ahead.

Don straightened his wheels until they were almost parallel to the road and slowly applied the gas as Dave pushed. It was enough. The car moved slowly at first and then Don could feel his left front wheel hit the pavement. He looked to see Dexter barreling down the road in their direction and screamed at Dave. "Get back!"

The Lexus grabbed the roadbed as the Ford neared, the small red SUV running down the center of the road, its speed increasing. Just as it was reaching their position, Don stepped hard on the gas. The big engine in the Lexus responded immediately, shooting the car forward.

Don thought he could see the smile on the face of Dexter as he passed and then Don gritted his teeth. The Lexus caught the Escape just in front of the rear bumper on the passenger side. The rear of the Ford swung to the side and then physics took over, the momentum of the vehicle causing it to roll. Dave had his gun out and in front of him, sprinting after the Ford.

Dexter's vehicle ended up in the opposite ditch on its side. Dave raced to the front of the vehicle and peered through the splintered windshield. Dexter was gone. Dave looked up the road and then ran around the front of the SUV. There was no Dexter.

"Here!" called Don.

Don was standing in the ditch fifteen yards behind where the Ford had come to rest. Dexter had been thrown from the vehicle when it rolled. Dave hurried to where Don was standing awkwardly in the ditch, leaning into the side of it, his arm stretched to feel for a pulse on Dexter.

"Is he alive?"

"Yeah. Call for an ambulance."

Chapter 52

September is a wonderful time to be in Minnesota. The days sunny and warm, the nights cool enough that you'll want the windows open but a blanket at the foot of the bed. The leaves have begun to turn, making their progression from north to south, the whole thing tracked on a Department of Natural Resources website so you can see where the peak colors are in the state on any particular day. Fall leaf tours by car and bike and boat can be found across the state, bed and breakfasts in the small towns along the St. Croix River and North Shore, not to mention the cabins on the state's eleven thousand plus lakes, booked well in advance this time of year. Hunters are putting up deer stands and checking trail cameras for big bucks while duck hunters prepare for the migration.

September is also the time when the bass in Minnesota put on their feedbags before winter, especially the big fish. The Trask brothers were in Dave's boat as he maneuvered it slowly around a three-acre boulder-lined island on his lake. They started fishing by throwing jigs tipped with three-inch plastic grubs towards shore, but had only caught a few small smallmouth bass. Dave noticed a couple of arcs on his depthfinder below the boat and let his jig drop towards the bottom in the deeper water. Instantly he was rewarded with a sixteen-inch fish with another soon to follow.

"The big ones are deep!" yelled Dave to Don who was still casting toward the shore.

Don watched his brother release another fish. A smoldering Swisher Sweet protruded from his mouth.

"Hmm." Don changed his grub for a plastic minnow bait and dropped it over the side. Two jigs and his rod was bent. An eighteen-inch smallmouth shot to the surface and then dived for the bottom. Don played it expertly and was soon reaching over the side of the boat to lift the fish in by its lower lip. "The biggest ones seem to like my bait best."

Dave watched his brother release his fish. It had been nearly a week since the fire at Fowles and the capture of Dexter. Dave had returned to his sheriff duties while Don and the BCA had worked the site.

"How many bodies at Fowles' place?"

"Seventeen. We're still trying to identify them all. May take a bit."

"Seventeen including Fowles?"

"Yeah."

"You believe what Dexter said about him?"

"Yeah. From what we found in the remains of the house and the autopsies on the recent kills, yeah, not much question." Don dropped his bait over the side. "He would stun the girls with the shock stick we found in his truck, tape them up, and then bring them back to Fowles' house. They both would rape them before they killed them."

Dave dropped his jig straight down but just let it sit. "Dexter killed Barton, didn't he?"

"Most likely, but Dexter won't admit to it. Things fit though."

A breeze from the south came up and moved the boat into deeper water. Dave increased the power on his trolling motor and pulled them back closer to shore. He watched his depthfinder for fish.

"You'll be at the Algaard funeral next Thursday?"

"I'm planning on it but the superintendent may have something to say about it. Lot of heat still coming down on the Benning deal," replied Don.

"And what about Blaine Algaard and his distributor?"

"Geez brother! Can't we just fish?" Don jigged his bait. "I think Chase PD is a little too busy right now to put much time into looking for Blaine but I expect they will get back to it. Larry says the distributor is dirty and I have someone on him."

Dave noticed a mark on his screen and lifted his bait twice in quick succession. He looked back at his brother. "And how's your agent doing?"

"Carlisle? She's been suspended. She disobeyed a direct order. Almost got herself killed."

"Bother you at all?"

"What? Her suspension?"

"Yeah."

Don was quiet. "I guess. I put her on the assignment. But it's her boss's call."

"She's a good agent, isn't she?"

"Damn good. Duluth PD found evidence that Lane was following orders from Walls on the cover-up, and on the shooting, but she sniffed it out first. She'll be OK."

"And what about you?"

Don set the hook on another fish, this one coming in the boat at close to twenty inches. He held it up for Dave to see. "I'd say I'm a lot better than you."

About the Author

Thanks for reading Bring Her Home. You can find links to my other books and a little about me at www.cenelsonbooks.com. If you'd like to join my mailing list, just go to the Contact tab and put "Mailing List" in the subject line. (I will never share your email with anyone.) And if you enjoyed this book, please leave a brief review on Amazon. Thanks!

C.E. Nelson

Made in the USA
Las Vegas, NV
31 January 2024

85162227R00187